Mrs W

The Arlington Affair

By

Jilly Fry

Copyright © 2024 Jilly Fry

ISBN: 9798872575634

All rights reserved, including the right to reproduce this book, or portions thereof in any form. No part of this text may be reproduced, transmitted, downloaded, decompiled, reverse engineered, or stored, in any form or introduced into any information storage and retrieval system, in any form or by any means, whether electronic or mechanical without the express written permission of the author.

This is a work of fiction. Names and characters are the product of the author's imagination and any resemblance to actual persons, living or dead, is entirely coincidental.

The views expressed in this work are solely those of the author and do not necessarily reflect the views of the publisher, and the publisher hereby disclaims any responsibility for them.

By the same Author:

Mrs Wynter Investigates

Chapter 1

A savage crack of thunder reverberated throughout the house. Startled, Mallory put down her embroidery and moved to look out of the window. 'Good grief!'

She watched the swirling, purple-black bruise in the sky, its malevolent intentions clear; it was going to show no mercy when it released its rage. The London summer of 1890 had proved to be a wet one until the last couple of days, when they had enjoyed hot weather; now once again the weather was proving to be capricious.

Another boom of thunder rendered the air. She returned to her seat. A brilliant flash of lightning illuminated the room just as her maid Gertrude entered the room.

'Shall I draw the curtains, ma'am,' she queried, 'and shut out the storm?' She shivered. 'Aren't you afraid of thunder and lightning?'

'Not if I am safe inside,' Mallory replied. 'Are you scared?'

Gertrude nodded. 'I'm scared of the damage it can do, I once saw a house struck by lightning, since then I've been terrified of its power. Every time I hear thunder, I think the house is going to collapse.'

'Then draw the curtains if it makes you feel better and light the lamps.'

Although it was only late afternoon the impending storm had darkened the room, the cosy glow of the lamps was comforting, and would provide enough light to continue with her embroidery.

'How are Ruby and Archie coping with this storm?'

'Storm?' Gertrude turned her worried face toward her.

'I rather think this is a prelude to a storm.' As if to verify her words the first raindrops splattered against the windows.

'You see? Hopefully it will be over soon.'

It was a false hope. Within minutes the storm unleashed its fury, the rain hurling itself against the window, battering the glass as though it was desperate to get in and seek shelter.

Gertrude looked anxiously at Mallory.

'Why don't you make some tea and bring a cup for yourself. You can help me untangle some threads in my sewing basket. Let me know if the staff need further reassurance.'

Gertrude nodded and scuttled out. Mallory smiled; she knew her maid would find tea making soothing.

'Did I hear you ask for tea?' her brother Ambrose enquired as he strode into the room.

'Yes, I thought it would take her mind off the storm.'

'Ah!' He smiled at her. 'I was going to do the same for you.' He held out a book. 'I have a present for you. I hope you haven't read this particular novel.'

She took the book from him. 'Jane Austen! My favourite author.' She held the blue book reverently in her hand and opened it joyfully.

'No, I haven't read Emma.' She looked up at him gratefully. 'Thank you, Ambrose, I shall dip into this after my tea.'

He sat in a chair, facing her. 'We've had an invitation from Mrs Fortescue for a picnic.'

She pulled a face.

'Don't you want to go?'

'It's not that, I was just thinking about the weather, if the ground is soaking it won't be much fun.'

He shook his head. 'It's not for tomorrow, it's the day after so plenty of time for the ground to dry out.'

'How do you know that?'

'Because the weather is going to turn hot. A heatwave is predicted. There was talk of it in my club.'

'I hope so, I shall be glad to see the sun again. The hems of my clothes have suffered in the wet weather, poor Getrude has to deal with it.'

Ambrose rolled his eyes at the mention of servants.

'I shall confirm our attendance then.' He stretched out his legs. 'I suggest that after dinner we settle down and read our books here. I bought myself a Stevenson novel, The Strange Case of Dr Jekyll and Mr Hyde, just the right choice for this weather. I think it will go rather well with a glass of cognac.'

She laughed. 'Don't get nightmares.'

'My version of a nightmare would be reading your Austen novel.'

'That's because you have no appreciation of a good novel.' She smiled. 'So that's tonight taken care of, it's unlikely we'll have visitors.'

'Ah. Yes ... hmm.' Ambrose frowned.

Mallory looked at him curiously. 'Are you seriously expecting visitors in this weather?'

'I am expecting a new client. The letter said he would call today.'

'Who is it?'

'I have no idea; I couldn't read the signature.'

'Did it mention a time?'

He shook his head. 'No. I don't think —'

The front doorbell clanged. 'Perhaps it's your appointment.' They both turned towards the door.

Finch entered bearing a letter. 'The postman apologises for its lateness; he only found the letter once he finished his round. I've taken the liberty of giving him a cup of tea whilst he dries out, the poor man was soaked.'

Ambrose peeled open the envelope due to its dampness. He quickly scanned the contents.

'Ah. The appointment will be rearranged.' He looked up at her, 'and no I still can't decipher the signature.'

'How very mysterious.'

Gertrude knocked and entered bearing the tea tray.

'I'll just fetch yours, sir,' Finch commented. 'Would you prefer it in the study?'

'Yes please, Finch. I'll see you later, Lory, at dinner.'

He left the room and Gertrude poured two cups of tea.

'I know Mr Finch would be grateful, ma'am, for you to speak to Ruby to reassure her about the storm. She is behaving rather oddly today, and neither Mr Finch or myself can work out why.'

She placed Mallory's cup of tea on a side table. 'I should let it cool first.'

'Did Ruby not say what was wrong?'

Gertrude shook her head. 'She just pulls a face when asked.'

'Let's hope it resolves itself then, but please do let me know if it's something we can help with.' She picked up her cup and blew gently on the tea.

'I'll come to the basement and speak to Ruby once we've drunk our tea, in the meantime there is some thread to unravel.'

Gertrude fetched the basket and between them they sorted the threads to Mallory's satisfaction and then drank their tea.

Mallory descended the basement stairs. Ruby was busy in the kitchen wiping down the table.

'Isn't this storm awful?' began Mallory pleasantly, 'but it won't last. I've come to see how you are all bearing up.'

Ruby pulled a face. 'I 'ate storms, I do. They can do nasty fings. Wouldn't surprise me if I found a puddle of water in me bedroom.'

Mallory frowned. 'Is there a problem with the ceiling in your room?'

Ruby shook her head. 'Not yet, but I bet there will be an 'ole in the roof and the water will soak me bed, then I'll get a chill and die.'

Mallory sighed. 'It will be fine, Ruby. There's no cause for concern.'

'Ain't there? Wot about that lightning, it kills people, it does.'

'Very rarely, Ruby.'

Ruby harrumphed. 'Well, it's bound to 'it our roof and blooming well burn the 'ouse down. We'll all die in our beds, burned to a cinder, everyfink I own will be burnt to ashes.'

'It will do no such thing, Ruby.' Mallory firmly replied. 'The storm won't last, and I've been assured that we're in for a heatwave.'

Ruby bit her lip, she daren't contradict her further.

Mallory continued in a calming voice. 'The storm will wear itself out very quickly. There is nothing to worry about. I shall ask Archie to check the attic rooms for any damage, will that reassure you that nothing awful will happen?'

Ruby didn't reply, she kept her head down and concentrated on her task of cleaning the table for their supper.
'Where is Archie?'
Ruby pointed to the scullery without raising her head.
Mallory sent Archie off to assess the attic floor. Delighted that the rain had started to ease and that there was no damage, Mallory gave the good news to Ruby and then returned to the drawing room. Ruby could be her own worst enemy at times, Mallory reflected as she picked up her new book. She sighed and opened her book and settled back in her chair ready for the charms of Emma.

Chapter 2

Mallory awoke to the sun streaming into her room as Gertrude drew back the heavy brocade curtains.

'Morning, ma'am,' Gertrude cheerfully announced, 'it's going to be a beautiful day for the picnic.'

Mallory yawned and stretched, pleased that Ambrose had been correct in his assessment of the weather. It really did seem to be a glorious day by the way the sun's rays flooded the room. Such a difference from the storm two days ago.

'I've brought you some toast and coffee as Mr Weston requested breakfast in the study.'

'How odd.'

Gertrude shook her head. 'There were a lot of letters this morning, so he decided to tackle them straight away.'

'Ah, yes that makes sense.' Gertrude placed the tray on the bed.

'Do you need anything else, ma'am?'

'No thank you. I shall read for a bit before getting dressed. If it's going to be hot, I think a cotton dress would be better.'

Getrude nodded. 'I'll come back in a while, ma'am.'

The sun was shining fiercely. Heat radiated from the pavements, even the trees seemed to be seeking shade as Mallory and Ambrose made their way to Kensington Gardens. After meeting Mrs Fortescue, the party found a suitable spot for their picnic. Wispy, white clouds drifted lazily across the blue horizon; Mallory could see the lake shimmering in the sunshine. As she shielded her eyes from the sun with a lace-gloved hand, the distant hum of conversation reached her ears; smiling she glanced towards a gathering of people, amused at the children's antics. Kensington Gardens were busy, but they were lucky enough to find a tranquil spot, well away from the crowded lake.

'Do sit down, Mallory,' Mrs Fortescue urged, 'the blankets have been unfurled, but there are a couple of chairs if you would prefer it.'

10

'Rosy, you must have a story to tell, there must be one from our father's repertoire.'

'Actually, there is one, now I think about it,' replied Ambrose. 'Did you know, Sanderson, that our father was a lawyer?'

'Yes,' confirmed Edward, 'a rather esteemed and powerful one at that.'

'Indeed. Well, here is a story for you. When my father was younger, and newly qualified as a lawyer, he came across a curious case – of a man killed by a mouse.'

'A mouse!' There was an explosion of laughter.

'Oh, please do share it with us!' Lady Marsham begged, her hand over her mouth trying to stop the laughter.

'Very well. He was asked to defend a factory owner. The story goes that a mouse dashed on to a worktable in the factory making the women scream. A gallant young man picked up the mouse by its tail and held it aloft, savouring the grateful praises of the women. Unfortunately for him the mouse escaped down his sleeve and up his shirt straight into his open mouth and the young man swallowed it in shock and consequently died.'

'No!' Lady Marsham was amazed.

'Yes, indeed. The family of the young man made a fuss and took the factory owner to court.' They all burst out laughing.

'I do beg your pardon for laughing at the poor man's demise, but really! Killed by a mouse! Why did they go to court, surely it was an accident?' Mrs Fortescue smiled, her eyes wide with disbelief.

'For having a dangerous animal on the premises?' There was more laughter.

'Please tell me you are joking, Ambrose?' Mallory's blue eyes sparkled, her smile lighting up her lovely face. Edward glanced across at her and caught his breath.

'No, I'm not Lory. That was exactly how our father described it.'

Edward quickly looked away and laughed. 'That must have been an easy win for your father?'

'Yes,' smiled Ambrose, 'one of his funniest cases.' They finished their wine, and Edward moved to refill Ambrose's glass,

'Why was that disturbing?' Mallory queried. 'It's a perfectly acceptable present. He was clearly enamoured with her to give her jewellery.'

'My dear, it was a mourning brooch, need I say more?'

'Hmm ...' agreed Edward. 'I concur. It certainly wouldn't be the gift I would choose to give the love of my life.' He glanced sideways at Mallory, but she hadn't noticed. She was busy trying to fend off a bee that was trying to settle on her skirt.

'Ah, I see your point, Mrs Fortescue. It's not the best way to win a girl's heart,' Mallory replied, finally shooing away the bee. Smiling she added, 'although if it was a treasured item of his, perhaps he was showing his love by giving her something he treasured. So quite a sweet thought, if that was the case.'

'That's a very charitable viewpoint, Mallory,' Mrs Fortescue smiled.

'It was a delightful tale, thank you.' Lady Marsham smiled. 'Did the romance end well?'

'Sadly, I don't know. I returned to London shortly after that. Let us hope she saw the wisdom of ending the friendship, because I dread to think what the next present would be.'

Lady Marsham put down her plate and brushed off some crumbs that had fallen onto her skirt.

'It's very hard to stop your servants from falling in love,' she continued. 'I try not to get involved in household disputes, I leave that to the butler and housekeeper.'

'Very wise,' Ambrose agreed, 'that's something you should learn, Mallory, especially when you get your own house.' She gave him a withering look.

'Oh yes, you're a woman of substance now, aren't you!' Lady Marsham smiled. 'I'd forgotten about your inheritance windfall. How is the house hunting going?'

'Not very well. I haven't seen anything that is suitable so far.'

'You will find it, my dear, when you least expect it.' Mrs Fortescue advised. Mallory changed the conversation back to stories.

'What we need now,' said Edward, 'is a few tales to entertain us. I'm afraid my tales would all be court related, very boring I fear.' He gave a rueful smile. 'Any suggestions?'

Mallory turned to Ambrose. 'Rosy? You usually have an anecdote or two.'

'That honour should belong to Mrs Fortescue, our host.'

'Indeed,' Lady Marsham agreed, before taking a delicate bite from a slice of pigeon pie.

Mrs Fortescue laughed. 'Well, I do happen to have some anecdotes from when I stayed with my sister in Hampshire.'

'Please do share!' Mallory bit into her scotched egg, her napkin held beneath it to catch the crumbs.

Mrs Fortescue took a sip of her wine before clearing her throat. 'Dear me, where shall I start?'

'Whereabouts in Hampshire does your sister live, Mrs Fortescue?' Edward politely enquired.

'Oh, near Winchester. She has a town house in London but prefers to be in the country.'

'Sounds idyllic.'

Mrs Fortescue nodded her head. 'Yes, it is. I thoroughly enjoyed my stay there.'

'So, what tales do you have to share?' Mallory asked.

'Oh, it's regarding her maid.'

Edward and Ambrose smiled politely but their eyes glazed over, but Mallory was keen to hear the tale.

'It's a tale of unrequited love.' She smiled, a twinkle in her eye. 'Her maid had just started seeing a young man. We knew nothing about him, except that he liked to give her presents, very odd presents too; I believe one of them was a stuffed squirrel, then there was an empty box.'

'Where did he get the squirrel from?' Ambrose was intrigued.

'I really don't know, and I'd prefer not to. Understandably she wasn't thrilled. The butler managed to accidently throw away the squirrel, as for the box she still uses it apparently, but it was the most recent present that was rather disturbing. He gave her a brooch.'

8

7

Mallory turned and smiled at her. 'The blanket will be fine.' Mallory sat on the nearest one and noted with irritation that Edward Sanderson also chose to sit there. It didn't leave her very much room to eat given the length of Edward's legs. Ambrose had a blanket to himself. Lady Marsham claimed one of the chairs and Mrs Fortescue the other.

'Shall I open the hamper?' Edward offered. He lazily extended his arm and flipped open the lid of the wicker basket.

'Why don't you start with the wine, Mr Sanderson,' Mrs Fortescue advised.

'You've done us proud, Mrs Fortescue,' Ambrose said as Edward produced from the hamper two bottles of white wine, a pigeon pie, ham sandwiches, scotched eggs and a bowl of strawberries. Ambrose poured glasses of wine. Mallory eyed the strawberries with misgiving, heavens, how was she going to eat them without staining her cream gloves? Lady Marsham came to her rescue.

'I think if you gentlemen don't mind, we ladies will take off our gloves to eat, fortunately we are far away from prying eyes to be noticed. Do take off your jackets, it's far too hot to worry about etiquette.'

Ambrose and Edward nodded and gratefully took off their jackets, relieved not to have to swelter in the name of politeness. They had chosen a spot far away from the crowds who preferred the more scenic views. Mallory set up her parasol to provide some shade, Edward and Ambrose gallantly set up parasols by the chairs.

'Isn't this delightful?' Lady Marsham smiled as she took a sip of white wine, a plate of food on her lap.

'It's very kind of you to provide a picnic, Mrs Fortescue,' Mallory held up her glass in acknowledgement.

'Oh nonsense, it's so much nicer when you are with friends, a picnic is no fun at all when you are by yourself. Anyway, my housekeeper did all the work, and the butler carried all the equipment. So the thanks go to them.'

but Ambrose declined with a wave of his hand. He took out his hunter's watch and checked the time.

'Well, I must thank you for the delightful picnic, Mrs Fortescue,' Ambrose told her. 'Unfortunately, I have to leave. I'm sorry I can't explore the Italian Garden with you, only I have a visitor this afternoon, a possible new case.' He stood up brushing his trousers before putting on his jacket.

'Oh, is this the mysterious client from the other night? I'll come with you.' Mallory turned towards her brother.

'No need, Lory, you stay here and enjoy the gardens. Mr Sanderson can escort you ladies.'

'No, Rosy, if it's a possible investigation I insist on going with you, I'm eager to see our mystery client.' She got up and closed her parasol.

Edward glanced at her. 'Perhaps I can show you the garden another time, Mallory.'

'That would be nice, Edward, thank you.'

She picked up her plate and glass and took them to the hamper.

'Oh, please don't worry about that,' Mrs Fortescue assured her, 'the butler will be here soon to pack everything away, leaving us to enjoy the gardens, however ...' she smiled sadly at Mallory, 'I ... I'm hoping you will do me a favour; my cook's niece is in need of help ... I wonder if you would mind ... I do so hate to ask—'

'Please send her to us, Mrs Fortescue, we shall be glad to help – won't we Ambrose?' Mallory turned towards him. He hesitated then nodded and smiled.

'Oh, thank you, it will be such a relief.'

Mallory smiled at them, straightening her hat before putting on her gloves. 'I hope you all have a lovely time.'

'Goodbye, Mallory,' Edward bowed to her. 'I hope to see you soon.'

She smiled but didn't reply, she wasn't sure of her feelings. She was comfortable with her widowhood, despite being young. Instead, she picked up her parasol, nodded at them and followed

Ambrose across the grass. The floral perfume of roses drifted in the air and mingled with the smell of cut grass. She breathed in the delightful scent, to her it was the smell of summer. It was a shame, she thought, that she would miss the Italian Garden – it would have been delightful, but the prospect of a new case outweighed any regret. Truth be told, life was a little flat after experiencing her first investigation, she welcomed the chance to be involved in another.

'What have you dragged me into, Mallory?' he whispered as she took his arm. 'You know I don't get involved with servants.'

'It isn't a servant, it's a young lady who happens to have an aunt who is a cook. We shouldn't treat her any differently.'

He sighed. 'As long as it isn't a servant's dispute. I draw the line at that.'

She changed the subject quickly. 'So, was the signature still undecipherable?'

He smiled. 'Yes, we'll just have to see who turns up, in the meantime we need to hail a cab.'

'A cab?' she queried. 'But we live in Kensington! It's not that far to walk, Rosy, it seems an unnecessary expense.'

'Two reasons, Lory. The heat is one; time is the other. We don't want to be late for our mysterious visitor, if we walk in this heat, we are likely to be dishevelled by the time we return home as well as tardy. It won't be a good first impression.'

'There's another reason for the cab,' Ambrose added as he flagged down a Hansom. 'I think there's another storm coming, I can feel it in the air.'

Chapter 3

Finch announced the visitor with a gentle knock on the door.

'Lord Arlington, sir.'

Ambrose and Mallory rose as a middle-aged man with neatly trimmed sideburns and moustache, a few silver threads running through his dark hair, entered the room. He stood looking at them as if summing them up, one gloved hand resting on his hip, before walking across and shaking hands with Ambrose and nodding towards Mallory.

'How can we be of service, Lord Arlington?' He motioned him to a chair. Lord Arlington brushed his striped trousers with a hand as though to expel any dust before sitting stiffly on the chair.

'I want you to right a wrong.'

'I beg your pardon?'

He glared at Ambrose. 'I thought I had made myself clear. I am employing you to find something for me.'

Ambrose chose his words with care. 'I certainly take commissions.'

Lord Arlington waved his hand airily. 'Whatever you want to call it, you'll still be my employee. Let us speak man to man,' he glanced towards Mallory.

'My sister, Mrs Wynter, aids me in my investigations. You may speak freely in front of her.'

His Lordship stared at her for a few seconds before nodding his head.

'Very well. I do not believe in beating about the bush. My wife, Lady Arlington, wishes to reclaim a valuable family heirloom. Please understand this is a delicate matter.'

Ambrose nodded. 'Perhaps it would be better if we took notes? Mallory, could you oblige please?'

Mallory picked up a notebook and pencil. His Lordship paused to gather his thoughts before explaining.

'My wife, Honoria, inherited a ruby necklace from her grandmother Augusta Arlington, it was originally owned by a Russian Grand Duchess. Yes, my wife and I are distant cousins, but how we are related is not the point. The point is that it is an Arlington heirloom.' He stopped to allow Mallory to catch up.

'May I ask how it has gone missing?'

'It's not missing exactly.' Ambrose arched an eyebrow but remained silent. Lord Arlington got up from his chair and wandered to the window and looked out.

Mallory cleared her throat. 'May we offer you some tea, Lord Arlington?'

'No thank you,' he replied brusquely, 'your ... butler ... has already offered and I declined.' She widened her eyes and looked at her brother who shrugged his shoulders.

'You were saying, your Lordship?' Lord Arlington turned back towards them and frowned.

'It pains me to say this,' he replied, 'but my wife gave it to our son, foolishly believing he was going to get married and give it to his wife.' He paced the room for a few moments and then gave a deep sigh. 'We only had one child, Oscar. We thought ... hoped ...' he bit his lip, 'we were led to believe an engagement would soon be announced – but it didn't happen.'

Mallory said quietly, 'What happened to your son?'

Lord Arlington returned to his seat and closed his eyes before replying.

'He died.'

Ambrose spoke softly. 'Is that when the necklace disappeared?'

His Lordship shook his head. 'No, before that. You see, he gave it to his ... mistress.'

Mallory paused in her note taking, she wasn't expecting that statement. Ambrose waited for a few moments to see if his Lordship would explain, but he remained silent.

'I see,' Ambrose said.

'Do you? Do you really?' He glared at him. 'How could you possibly understand?'

14

'Perhaps then you would care to explain. We cannot act without the full details.'

'Can't or won't act?'

Ambrose looked calmly at him. 'Neither. Unless we are in full possession of the facts it is going to be very difficult to fulfil your request to reclaim the heirloom.'

'I understood you to be a successful investigator – have I been misled?'

Ambrose shook his head. 'No, but success can only be achieved with knowledge, and the only information you have supplied is that the necklace was given to a mistress. I'm not exactly sure what you wish us to achieve given that the piece is now legally owned by someone else.'

Lord Arlington twisted his mouth into a moue of annoyance.

'All you need to know is that the necklace needs to be returned to us. That is what I am paying you for. I am not paying you to ask further questions. Anything else is none of your business.'

'Then we cannot help you.'

'I suggest you try the police.' Mallory added, slamming her notebook shut.

'I can recommend an Inspector, if you wish.' Ambrose got up to pull the bell.

'Wait!'

Ambrose turned towards him.

'Perhaps, I have been a little hasty. My wife tells me it's one of my faults.'

Ambrose sat back in his chair and looked at him keenly.

'So far, your Lordship, you have failed to give me any reason as to why I should accept your commission.'

'I suggest you speak with my wife. Lady Honoria will give you full details, I am not a man for emotions but the whole business with my son has left me … empty.'

'Be so kind then to furnish us with your address and we will visit her.'

Lord Arlington looked shocked. 'Visit her? I thought I would bring her here.'

'No.' Ambrose spoke firmly. 'It would be best if we went to see her.'

Lord Arlington blew out his cheeks. 'I'm not … it really is not—'

'I'm afraid I must insist. I always interview my clients in their homes, it is part of my fact finding in a case.'

'Well really!' Lord Arlington got up and walked to the window. Frowning he looked out at the street, his hands in his waistcoat pockets.

Mallory stared at him noting his irritated demeanour, clearly he disliked being overruled. She held her breath wondering who was going to win this battle.

'Very well.' Lord Arlington turned towards them. 'But I must insist you make an appointment. I cannot have all and sundry turning up at my door.'

Ambrose arched an eyebrow. 'All and sundry? It will just be myself and my sister.'

'Perhaps it would be best if my wife wrote to you instead.' He frowned. 'Yes, I think that would be best.'

'No, that would not be best, I need to ask questions. Perhaps a police detective would suit you better, after all.'

'No!' Lord Arlington was adamant. 'I told you, it's a delicate matter.'

Mallory cleared her throat discreetly.

'If you are worried about Lady Arlington being interviewed by a man, I could talk to your wife, naturally my brother will accompany me.'

Lord Arlington remained silent for a few moments, whilst he thought the matter through.

'Very well, but I insist you make an appointment here and now.'

Ambrose smiled at him. 'Would tomorrow be convenient?'

'Certainly not. I need to make arrangements, but I suppose if you must come then 2 o'clock the day after tomorrow.'

'Very well, but I will need your address.'

Lord Arlington nodded; his brow creased with a frown.

'Pinnerton Hall, Norwood. I shall let my wife know. Good day to you.'

Finch showed Lord Arlington out.

'Well! What do you make of him, Ambrose? I don't think I like him very much.'

'Nor I, but we don't have to like our clients to act for them.'

'It helps though, I would have thought. It's hard to be objective otherwise.' Mallory flicked through her notebook. 'There was no information given, all I have written down is his address. He hasn't given us the name of the mistress.'

'Lady Arlington will give us that.'

'I hope she will be more forthcoming than her husband.'

Ambrose nodded. 'One thing I am sure of – he was nervous.' He stroked his chin with his fingers, deep in thought.

'Yes, I watched him, but what is he nervous of? Why is he worried about his wife being interviewed?'

Ambrose shook his head. 'No point speculating, let's wait and see what she has to say.'

Mallory voiced her concern. 'Rosy, he didn't ask us about our fees. Why? Do you think he will pay us? I suspect he will have something to say about the price.'

'Until we have all the necessary facts to start the investigation I cannot estimate our fee, but yes, you are right to be concerned over collection of the fee. I rather think on this occasion I will request part payment in advance.'

Mallory nodded. 'I don't know about you but I'm in need of a cooling drink, I'm hoping there is some fresh lemonade.' She rang for Gertrude. 'Your prediction of a storm was wrong.'

He smiled. 'I'm pleased about that, it proves I'm human after all.'

Chapter 4

'It's a nice change to have sunshine instead of rain,' remarked Gertrude as she entered the kitchen with a pile of linen in her arms.

'I wouldn't know, I never get to see it,' moaned Ruby. 'I never get a chance to get out of this blooming basement.'

'Ruby!' Finch frowned. 'What has got into you today? Since this morning I've heard nothing but complaints from you.'

'I ain't complaining, just stating facts. If you want to call 'em complaints that's up to you.'

'Something is clearly the matter so out with it.'

'It don't matter, nobody would understand anyway.'

Finch sighed. 'Why don't you tell us what is wrong, you have been in a strange mood for several days.'

She shook her head obstinately and bit her lip.

He gave her a searching look.

'All I'm saying, Mr Finch, is I never get to leave the 'ouse, so I don't get to see the blooming sunshine.'

'You've had plenty of chances to leave the house on errands, Ruby, but you've never taken them.'

Ruby huffed. 'Too busy in 'ere to run errands, that's why. Everybody else gets to spend time upstairs, I don't and it ain't fair! I wanna be a lady's maid, I do, and I don't get the chance – it ain't fair, that's all I'm saying.'

Gertrude put the linen on the table. 'Do you think you are ready to be a lady's maid, Ruby?'

'Course I am, I just need to learn the routine as I ain't 'ad much practice. I'd make a good lady's maid.'

'Well, you can have some practice. Come with me upstairs and I'll start you on some tasks.'

'I ain't cleaning, if that's wot you're finking. I can clean already, I want to do them uvver jobs, those that make you a personal maid.'

Finch gave Ruby a keen glance.

'I'm not so sure. It came across as more of a demand.'

'Yes,' he conceded, 'it did rather, but whether that was a demand for us to take the case or a demand for the mistress to return the heirloom, I don't know.' He frowned. 'I think it will depend on the information we get from Lady Arlington.'

'If she's anything like her husband, I doubt we will.'

The train pulled into Norwood Junction. Ambrose helped Mallory from the train and enquired from an old porter about transport to Pinnerton Hall.

'Pinnerton Hall? I reckon you mean Pinnerton Lodge. Yes, sir, nice lady she is, don't know how she manages to look after that big old house. She don't get many visitors, she'll be right glad to see you. There will be a cart along in a minute or two if you care to wait. Bob Miller usually appears when a train is due. Can't go wrong with him.' He touched his cap in farewell and hurried off to help another passenger.

'Oh dear, he seems to be confused,' Mallory whispered to her brother, 'he's got the house mixed up with another property. Age does that, I'm told.'

Ambrose smiled as they made their way to the station entrance. 'It does seem rather strange, let us hope he hasn't got the carter mixed up otherwise I fear it's a long walk, though I'm surprised Lord Arlington didn't arrange transport for us.'

A cart pulled by a pale horse, trotted towards them. He pulled up in front of them.

'Need transport?' he enquired. 'Where do you want to go?'

'Pinnerton Hall.'

'Hop on. I'll just wait to see if there are any more passengers.'

They settled themselves on a wooden bench as another lady appeared and gave instructions to the carter. She too climbed on board and nodded at them. As no other passenger appeared, the carter shook the reins and the cart trotted away from the station.

Bob Miller turned the cart into the drive of Pinnerton Lodge. He dropped them outside the front door.

'Excuse me,' Mallory informed the driver, 'it's the Hall we needed.'

'There's only the Lodge,' he replied, shaking his head as he pocketed the coins Ambrose gave him. After ascertaining they needed picking up in time for the next train, he drove the cart back down the drive, the horse's feet kicking up dust as it trotted away. Mallory turned to look at the garden and was disappointed to see the lawn overgrown, with the bushes and shrubs rather neglected.

Mallory eyed the grey, ivy-clad house with surprise. The front door was flanked either side by a row of large, mullioned windows. On the right-hand side, a tall, straggly bush blocked the window's view.

'Have we got the right place?'

Ambrose walked to the front door and pulled the bell.

'We'll soon find out.'

A man in an ill-fitting suit answered their summons and showed them into a large room, the one with the blocked view.

'Have a seat,' he said awkwardly, and left the room shutting the door noisily behind him.

'Not much of a welcome, was it?' Mallory frowned as she took a seat. There were just three chairs without coverings, so she chose the nearest one.

Ambrose agreed. 'Didn't even offer to take my hat and gloves.' Ambrose removed his hat, gloves and cane and put them on the arm of a chair and looked around. There were a few paintings on the walls, as expected, but no other furniture except for a few chairs which had been covered up to protect them from dust and damp. Mallory sniffed, a musty smell lingered in the air, or was that her imagination?

'Clearly this isn't the drawing room,' observed Ambrose. The door opened admitting a handsome woman of medium height, her dark hair pulled into a severe bun at the nape of her neck. She smiled at them and waved them back to their seats as they stood to greet her.

'Good afternoon,' she said pleasantly as she sat on the remaining chair. 'I understand my husband has arranged this interview as you require further details.'

'I do apologise if we are late, Lady Arlington, we were looking for Pinnerton Hall.' Ambrose briefly smiled at her.

'Oh, I see.' She gave a rueful smile. 'Ernest can be a little pompous at times.'

Mallory smiled and Ambrose pulled a notebook from his pocket.

'You don't mind if we take notes?' he asked, a pencil poised in his hand.

'Of course not. Where shall I start?'

'Let us start with your son,' Mallory suggested.

'Oh.' She sighed. 'Oscar was our only son. He seemed hesitant to commit to marriage so I gave him my grandmother's necklace in the hope it would encourage him to propose. It's extremely valuable you see; I thought that if he had something precious to offer it might ... well, speed things up. We had an understanding with another family that our children would marry one day.'

'He didn't propose.'

'No,' she replied simply. 'The necklace was a loan, not an outright gift. It was a shock to discover he had given it to a mistress. We kept quiet, hoping he would come to his senses and return the necklace to us, then he died.' She wiped her eyes with a handkerchief. 'We had no idea he was keeping a mistress. He lived here, and now he's gone, there is no-one but us in this house.'

'May I ask when Oscar died?'

'A while ago.' She noted their puzzlement. 'Days, months, years all seem to blur together when you are grieving, so you must excuse me if I am not exact.'

Mallory frowned. 'Forgive me, but why wait until now to claim the necklace?'

Lady Arlington was silent. Mallory waited patiently. Finally, she spoke. 'Grief, I suppose, and now anger has replaced that grief. I want that necklace back.' Mallory glanced at Ambrose to see if he was keeping up – he was. He nodded at her to continue.

'This necklace, could you describe it please, Lady Arlington?'

'Is that really necessary?' she replied, pursing her lips together. 'I would have thought it obvious. I have already explained it's of the finest rubies – valuable, priceless in fact.'

'When did your grandmother acquire the piece?' Mallory asked.

'Why?' Her Ladyship frowned.

'A little bit of background information is always helpful in a case.'

Lady Arlington sighed. 'I'm not really sure, it was never discussed in my family except that my grandmother was given it by a grand duchess for services rendered.'

Mallory tried again to get a description. 'Your ladyship, without a more detailed description, we may end up with the wrong piece of jewellery.'

'Yes, I do see what you mean, but …' she paused, 'I'm loath to give the details because that woman may have had it altered. For all we know the rubies could now be part of a different piece of jewellery.' She curled her lip. 'I wouldn't put it past that strumpet,' she added bitterly.

Mallory allowed a few seconds to pass before breaking the silence.

'If you could describe the original piece, Lady Arlington, it would be very helpful, in case it hasn't been altered.'

'It's a gold chain necklace set with rubies at the sides. You couldn't mistake the necklace, the central pendant stone is a large, crimson, Burmese ruby; it would take your breath away if you saw it. I believe my grandmother said it was called the Crimson Star. Quite rare. It's difficult to describe its beauty.'

'Perhaps we might be permitted to have a little bit of family history, Lady Arlington, it would help us so much.'

'Excuse me?'

'In order for us to recover it, it would be useful to have some knowledge of your family tree. Your husband mentioned you were distantly related.' Mallory smiled sweetly at her.

Lady Arlington nodded. 'Yes, but what does that have to do with my necklace? I fail to see the connection and quite frankly it's intrusive.'

She blew out her cheeks and frowned. 'My Grandmother was Lady Alicia Arlington, who was a relative of my husband. No more questions please on our family name or history, it is not relevant.'

Her demeanour changed, gone was the friendliness, her eyes regarded them warily.

Ambrose posed a question. 'What do you actually want from us, Lady Arlington?'

'Again, I would have thought it obvious. Has my husband not explained things to you?'

'Not really,' he replied. 'You have not supplied the lady's name or address. Equally you have not voiced exactly what you want from us. I know you have stated that you want to reclaim a family heirloom, but what do you require from us? Do you wish us to negotiate its return?'

'Negotiate?' She glared at them, her mouth wide open with offence. 'There is nothing to negotiate, the necklace belongs to me. My husband is paying you to bring it back to us. Steal it, if you must, but we want it back at all costs.'

'I see.' He looked at Mallory, she nodded her head. She knew what he was thinking. He cleared his throat.

'That is a difficult task. Our fee will reflect that. We will not steal anything, Lady Arlington, that would not be legal. Certainly, we can negotiate, but there is no guarantee. I suspect the lady will want compensation if she were to be persuaded to part with the heirloom.'

'Never!' She pressed her lips tightly together.

'Our fees are non-negotiable, and we require part payment in advance.'

He tore a slip of paper from his notebook and wrote two figures before passing it to her. Her eyes widened in surprise when she read it.

'I will have to confer with my husband.'

'The lower figure represents the advance payment, and the higher figure is the balance that will become due upon completion. It does not take into account expenses; they will be billed separately.'

'And if you are not successful?'

'Then nothing further is due except for any expenses incurred.'

She stood up. 'I will be in touch.' She swept out of the room.

Mallory and Ambrose looked at each other in surprise, a servant hadn't appeared to show them out. Ambrose donned his hat and gloves while they waited patiently for the servant. After a few minutes Mallory shrugged her shoulders at her brother.

'It seems we have to make our own way out.'

As they entered the hallway, Mallory peeked into another room as they passed by, the open door was too tempting. Depressingly it resembled the room they had left, except for its smaller size. Outside in the sunshine as they started to walk down the drive, something made Mallory look back at the house. She caught a fleeting glance of a figure of an old lady watching through a grubby, attic window. The figure abruptly vanished. Mallory frowned, had she imagined it? She shook her head, she wasn't given to flights of fancy, so it must have happened. It piqued her interest.

'What's the matter?' her brother asked.

'I'm not sure. Where will the carter meet us?'

'I don't know but let's keep walking and wait on the road.'

'Why call the mistress a harlot or strumpet, if they have never met her? Have they just presumed she was vulgar?' she asked, ducking beneath an overhanging branch, leaving Ambrose to move out of its path altogether as they made their way towards the road. 'Perhaps you know the answer, Rosy, to my next question. If he gave his mistress the necklace, why didn't he marry her?'

'There was clearly a reason, perhaps it was financial,' he replied.

They stepped past the two stone lions guarding the drive and onto the main road.

'When did they know about the mistress? She said they kept quiet hoping he would come to his senses – but she didn't explain what that meant. Did it mean his mistress or not marrying? Did they discover the mistress after or before his death?

'I can't fault your logic, Lory, but until we speak with the lady, we won't know.'

The rumbling of cartwheels announced its return to whisk them back to the station in time for their return journey home. They had learned absolutely nothing, reflected Mallory, as she climbed aboard. There were so many questions, the biggest one was the face in the window. Who was she and did she really exist?

Chapter 6

Ambrose was sitting in his study opening the morning's post. Breakfast was over and as Mallory had nothing urgent to do she decided to have a chat with her twin brother. Mallory watched him from her fireside chair, the fire unlit as there was sufficient warmth from the sun peeping through the small window to heat the room. It was very masculine, Mallory thought, as she turned her glance to the dark bookcase and shelves; it could do with some flowers or a colourful plant to lighten it. Mallory knew better than to ask him, she would simply get Finch to add a small floral decoration and see if he noticed.

'Something on your mind, Lory?' He put the letters back on his desk and gave her his full attention.

'I looked at my notes from the meeting with Lord Arlington,' Mallory said quietly.

'And?'

'It strikes me as odd, Lord Arlington referring to his wife's grandmother as Lady Augusta, yet Lady Arlington stated her name was Lady Alicia.' She stretched out her foot and rubbed the leg of the opposite chair with the tip of her shoe. There was a slight black mark which she was trying, unsuccessfully, to rub off.

'Perhaps they had too many relatives for him to remember their names, it's easy to get confused.' He chuckled quietly to himself as he returned to his correspondence. 'Or perhaps he's just forgetful, like telling us his house was a hall rather than a lodge.'

Mallory shook her head. 'He was just trying to show off, he's rather pompous, his wife is a little more down to earth.'

'Do you think so?' Ambrose murmured as he picked up a letter. 'Anyway, there is a letter from them. Let me read it first before you ask me what it says.'

He was silent for a few moments. 'Hmm. They want us to take the case but object to the terms and conditions.'

'I presume they don't want to pay the advance.'

'Correct, Lory.'

'Oh.' She pulled a face. 'What are we going to do then?'

He put the letter down and met her gaze.

'We have two choices, waive the advancement of fees or turn the case down.'

'Do you think they will pay up at the end of the case?'

Ambrose shook his head. 'No idea. It's an interesting case though.'

'Have you negotiated before, Rosy?'

'I have a little experience at it, yes.'

'What is so intriguing?'

'Why do they want the necklace so badly that they may want me to steal it, yet not negotiate with the lady?'

'Pride?' suggested Mallory.

'Possibly. What say you to waiving the advancement? I'd like to find out about this necklace that's caused so much fuss.'

She cocked her head to one side. 'Why not? What have we got to lose but our time and some expenses. Hopefully there won't be many of those, just a quick trip to see the mistress and another to the Arlingtons.'

'That will be a first then, none of my cases have ever been straightforward.'

'The question is, have they given you the address of the mistress?'

'No. Lord Arlington is coming this afternoon to find out our decision. We can ask him then.'

Mallory took herself off to the drawing room and rang the bell for Getrude, but it was Finch that answered.

'Yes, madam?'

'I really wanted Gertrude. Could you send her to me please.' Nodding his head, he left the room. Gertrude arrived a few minutes later just as the front doorbell jangled.

'You wanted me, ma'am?'

'Yes.' Mallory nodded. 'We have a new case; I might be in need of your help.'

Gertrude's eyes shone, her plump face reflecting the excitement in her smile. However, before she could reply, Finch informed her of a visitor and handed her a note.

'I have asked the young lady to wait in the morning room, madam.'

Mallory nodded and scanned the note.

'Gertrude, we will discuss the new case another time.' She left the room and returned to her brother's study.

'Rosy, we have a visitor and a note.'
She passed the note over to him.

Dear Ambrose and Mallory

I am sending my cook's niece to you, Miss Mary Gage, with this note. Thank you so much for agreeing to see her. My cook is worried about her. It appears Mary's fiancé has disappeared.

It does not do to have one's cook upset – it is reflected in their cooking! I do so hope you can help this young lady so that domestic harmony is restored. Please send your fee note to me, I do not want my cook worrying over the cost.

Sincerely yours
Emmaline Fortescue

'I see.' Ambrose rubbed his chin thoughtfully.

'Shall we interview her together?' she asked him. 'I really would like to help Mrs Fortescue; she has been extremely kind to me.'

He nodded. 'Let's see what the problem is before we decide if and how to proceed.'

Mary Gage was shown into the drawing room and offered a seat.

'I understand from Mrs Fortescue, that your fiancé is missing.' Mallory smiled encouragingly at her.

'Yes, ma'am.' She bit her lip and looked anxiously at them. 'Mrs Fortescue said you might be able to help me. I haven't got long though; the supervisor gave me an hour off to come here. If I'm late, I'll get fined.'

Ambrose nodded. 'Why don't you start from the beginning and tell us all about him.' he advised.

'My fiancé is John Kendle. We are hoping to get married later this year. John's putting a bit aside each week as savings and I've started my bottom drawer, and my parents are saving a bit too.'

Mallory made a note in her book and nodded for her to continue.

Mary swallowed and pulled out a handkerchief from her pocket and twisted it between her fingers.

'I can see you are upset, so take a deep breath,' Mallory told her, 'then when you are ready tell us what has happened.'

Mary nodded and after a few deep breaths she continued.

'John won a prize in a raffle at his local pub. He was hoping for the top prize of a barrel of beer, he promised to save it for our wedding day, but he won a different prize.' She sniffed. 'He was really upset that he didn't win the beer.' She faltered, using the handkerchief to wipe away a tear. 'I'm sorry.'

'No apology necessary, continue when you are ready.'

She nodded and took a few more breaths before continuing. 'He was so sure he'd win that beer that we arranged to meet on Friday night, the night of the raffle, after I finished work to celebrate his winning.' She sniffed back another tear.

'What time did you meet him?' Mallory frowned.

'Well, I finish work at eight o'clock, so it was probably after eight-thirty. I was to meet him at St George's Circus by Borough Road in Southwark, he would have been able to claim his prize before meeting me.'

She shook her head. 'He was waiting for me right enough but was really upset.'

'What was the name of the public house?'

'The Rising Sun, although I've never been there. John said it wasn't safe for women, so I always had to meet him at the Circus.'

'Please carry on.'

'Well, John was upset because his prize wasn't the beer. He wanted to drown his sorrows with his mates back in the pub. He gave me the prize and told me to go home.'

'That must have hurt you.'

She winced; her head bowed. 'It did, but John … well … he can be a bit quick tempered, and once he makes his mind up there's no changing it. He had set his heart on winning that beer, you see, so the disappointment was immense.'

'Was that the last time you saw him?' Mallory made a note.

Mary nodded, biting her lip. 'Yes, we arranged to meet again on Sunday at Lambeth Bridge, on my day off, but he never showed up.' Her tears began to flow freely, she gave up trying to wipe them away. 'I went to his lodgings, but nobody answered. He's never missed a date before, he's always reliable – ask anyone.'

'Have you tried his workplace?'

Mary answered in a quavering voice. 'My brother went there a few days later, but he hadn't shown up and they're going to sack him because of it. It's so unlike him. Something's happened to him, I know it, he would never abandon his job, or me.' She burst into tears, her hands in front of her face, her wedding plans in tatters.

Mallory nodded for Ambrose to ring for Gertrude. She crossed the room and patted Mary's shoulder.

'We will do our best to find John, but we will need some further information from you. Do you think you will be able to continue in a few minutes?'

Mary nodded in between sobs.

'You may feel better after a cup of tea.'

Mary shook her head. 'I don't have time; I can't afford to have my wages docked.'

'Please don't worry,' Mallory sympathised, 'I will make sure you are on time. Go with Gertrude and wash your face, you will feel better and then we can continue our conversation.'

Gertrude on seeing the distress of the girl, put an arm around her shoulders and gently took her away.

'Ambrose, we need to find her fiancé. It does sound like something has happened.'

Ambrose frowned. 'There are two possibilities here. He's either run away perhaps to escape the engagement, or something has happened to him.'

Mallory thought it over. 'The raffle seems to have disturbed his peace, but I can't believe it made him change his mind on marriage.'

'Agreed, but it may turn out that it was just the excuse he needed to distance himself from wedding plans.'

'Surely he wouldn't be that cruel?'

Ambrose sighed. 'We can't rule out anything. The first thing we need to do is speak to his landlady, she may be able to provide information.'

'What about Lord Arlington? He's coming here later.'

'We will see what he has to say. If we take it on, we'll need the mistress's address. It's perfectly possible to run both cases at once.'

Mary returned a few minutes later her eyes red and swollen from crying but she was calmer.

'Thank you for helping.'

Ambrose smiled sympathetically. 'Are you able to answer some questions?'

Mary nodded. 'Please believe me when I say this is not like John. Something has happened.'

Ambrose nodded. 'Yes, we do believe you, that's why we're going to help find your fiancé.' He gave her a keen glance, 'but we need further information.'

Mary raised her chin. 'I'm ready. I'll give you as much information as I can, even if it paints John in a bad light.'

'Good. We're not here to judge, just help, but the more knowledge we have about John will aid us greatly in our search.'

Mallory spoke gently. 'How long has it been since you last saw him.'

Mary thought for a few minutes. 'Erm ... over a week. All my family have been looking for him, we're all worried including Aunt Ada – she's Mrs Fortescue's cook.'

'Has John ever had to cancel a date with you?' Mallory had her pen poised over her notebook.

'Once or twice, but he always sent a message to me. I work in a millinery shop, so he always found a way to let me know. We're not supposed to receive messages, but one of the supervisors always turned a blind eye as it didn't happen very often. I haven't received any note or message this time ...' her voice broke.

Ambrose hastily held up his hand. 'Forgive me, I do not wish to cause you any more distress, but I do need answers.' She nodded and waited for the next question.

'Do you know anything about John's friends?' Mallory asked.

Mary pulled a face. 'I don't know them at all, and I don't like the sound of them. I thought they were leading my John astray.'

'In what way?' Ambrose was intrigued.

She shrugged her shoulders. 'That pub where he won the raffle prize, it was a bit ... rough, if you know what I mean. I don't think John would ever have gone there if it weren't for those mates. He was adamant that he didn't want me going in there, he told me in no uncertain terms that I wasn't to step a foot inside there – that's why I had to meet him elsewhere on Friday.'

'Do you think they were criminals?'

'I've no idea, I didn't really want to hear about them. All I know is that once me and John are hitched, I don't want him seeing them anymore.'

'Can you give me his address please, Mary?' Mallory turned to a new page in her notebook ready to write down the information.

'9 Bell Street, off Horseferry Road, Mrs Strange is the landlady.'

'Thank you, Mary, where should we contact you?'

'Oh, if it's all the same to you, ma'am, leave a message with Aunt Ada at Mrs Fortescue's house.'

Mallory raised an eyebrow.

Mary added hastily, 'I work in Simpsons Millinery on Victoria Street, eight in the morning until eight at night, we're not supposed to have visitors, we either get fined or lose our time off. I've already got to make up the time for today, so it's easier to contact my aunt. Excuse me, but I really need to leave.' She bit her lip in concern.

'Please don't worry. I will give you the fare for a cab.'

Finch answered the summons.

'Please can you hail a cab for Mary and pay the driver, she needs to go to Victoria Street.'

Finch bowed and ushered Mary out of the room.

******

Lord Arlington was late. It was early evening when the doorbell jangled, it was jangled with some force. Lord Arlington marched into the room without letting Finch announce him.

'So, Weston, what is all this nonsense in your fees?'

Ambrose gave him a cold glance. 'What nonsense are you referring to, your Lordship?'

Lord Arlington produced the note from his inside pocket and held it aloft.

'This one, of course! What do your expenses entail? If you are thinking of stinging me for fancy dinners and opera tickets, you can forget it.'

Ambrose motioned his hand towards a seat. 'Do take a seat, Lord Arlington.' He waited until his Lordship sat down before continuing in a calm voice. 'Expenses are for items that I need in order to fulfil the commission. Usually it's cab fares, or tips for information received. However, I try to keep them to a minimum and I keep very detailed records of sums spent. A breakdown of the expenses can be provided if requested.'

Lord Arlington eyed him speculatively. 'I'm not prepared to pay in advance neither am I prepared to pay this extortionate fee.' He waved the paper in the air. 'It's just a simple case of you going to the mistress and bringing the necklace back to us. Nothing that warrants this excessive amount or expenses.'

He glared at Ambrose. 'Here is the fee I am prepared to pay.' He handed a small slip of paper to him. 'Take it or leave it.'

Ambrose, his face impassive, took the paper and glanced at it.

'Not acceptable, I'm afraid.' He handed the paper back. 'I'm perfectly willing to look at our fees again, once we have spoken to the lady involved. Until we have done so, I cannot judge the length of time it will take to bring a satisfactory conclusion to the case.' He calmly met Lord Arlington's gaze. 'If you are not satisfied, please feel free to contact the police.'

Mallory held her breath, her brother seemed to be playing a game of chess – at present it was a stalemate.

A knock on the door broke the tension. Finch entered.

'Excuse me, sir, madam, but it's time for your appointment with the Marquis.'

Mallory tried very hard not to show surprise – Marquis? Did he exist and if so, why didn't she know about the appointment?

'If you will excuse me, Lord Arlington, I must draw this meeting to a close.' Ambrose replied quietly.

'Now look here,' Lord Arlington spluttered, 'if you give me your word you will reduce your fees, I will hire you.'

Ambrose nodded. 'Very well, please provide my sister with the lady's address and then we will be in touch.'

'Not at my house, you won't. We will be away on a visit. I will return here; you have one week only. If it takes longer, I expect a further reduction in your fees.' The muscles in his jaw twitched as he rose from his chair.

'As for that harlot …' he said testily. 'Why would I have her address?' He narrowed his eyes. 'What are you implying?'

'May I remind you,' Ambrose replied, a touch of steel to his voice, 'that we are private investigators, not magicians. Without a name and address we cannot fulfil your request.'

Lord Arlington harrumphed. 'Elowen James. I have no idea of her address – you call yourselves detectives, so you find her.' He glared at Ambrose. 'Do not fail me,' he said through gritted teeth. 'I am not a man to cross.' He strode out of the room ignoring Finch by the door.

Mallory raised her eyebrows and looked at her brother. She heard the front door slam.

'That was … interesting. We appear to have hit a nerve asking for details of the mistress.'

'Yes.' Ambrose was thoughtful, 'didn't we just.'

'So, we have two courses of action,' she continued, 'speak to John Kendle's landlady and seek out Elowen James, wherever she may be.'

'It's too late to do anything this evening,' he replied. 'Lord Arlington's late arrival has put us at a disadvantage.'

'Perhaps that was his intention.' She was puzzled. 'He seems angry at asking us for help.'

'Perhaps he is, perhaps it's his wife who wants us to act and he is merely the messenger.'

Further conversation was brought to a halt by Finch announcing dinner was served.

Chapter 7

'How do we find her address?'

'Archives. I will set Finch on it. We should know by the morning.'

'I know Finch is a miracle worker,' she added drily, 'but what if he is unable to locate her?'

'Hmm. Well, we have a week. Lord Arlington's attitude intrigues me, so I think I will dig into his financial affairs.'

'Which will involve you going to your club,' she smiled as she speared a potato onto her fork. 'I assume a gentleman's club will have gossip, so perhaps you may pick up snippets about Oscar's mistress, Elowen James.'

'I wouldn't call it gossip,' he replied, shifting slightly in his seat.

'What would you call it then?' She knew he was uncomfortable with her question by the way he wriggled.

'Whispers, if you must give it a name, and yes I may pick up … whispers … about her.'

'Good, so if Finch doesn't come up trumps then your club's gossip probably will.' Triumphantly she speared another potato on her fork. Ambrose sighed.

'We will need to visit her as soon as possible.' Mallory popped the fork into her mouth, savouring the potato's minty flavour.

Ambrose pulled a face. 'Now, why didn't I think of that?'

She ignored his sarcasm. 'I think I will visit the landlady.' Mallory swallowed another mouthful as Ambrose shook his head.

'Not alone. You know what happened last time you visited someone alone. You were accused of murder.'

She sighed. 'That's unlikely to happen again. It's just a landlady.'

'Even so.' Ambrose sipped his wine. 'We'll both go to see Miss James, hopefully it will be in the morning, and then I'll visit my club afterwards to see what information I can get on the Arlingtons.'

Mallory had an idea. 'When you do that, I'll visit Edward. If he's free perhaps he will accompany me to the landlady's house.'

'I rather think he would prefer to accompany you to the Italian Garden.'

She ignored him. 'I've made up my mind. Tomorrow, I'm going to speak to the landlady, with or without company.'

Ruby's wailing protestations reached the dining room.

'What now? Can't a man eat his meal in peace?'

'I'll go.' Mallory wiped her mouth on her napkin and left the room.

Ruby was huddled by the wall at the top of the basement stairs, her arms crossed defensively.

'What's the matter, Ruby?'

'I've broken me 'air clip, ma'am,' she wailed. 'It ain't fair, everyfink's going blooming wrong at the moment. It were me grandma's. I loved 'er I did, and now me last link wiv 'er is gone.'

She buried her face in her apron. Finch appeared and spoke calmly to Ruby.

'I'm sure it can be mended, Ruby. Why didn't you tell me instead of creating a fuss. There was no need to burden madam with your plight.'

'It's broken and I'm upset, Mr Finch. It came off when I tugged on me cap. Now me 'air won't stay in me cap and ma'am will scold me and then you'll sack me. I'm right fed up, nothing's blooming right.' She buried her face in her apron again.

'Really, Ruby, you are making a mountain out of a molehill. You won't be chastised or dismissed.' Finch replied firmly. 'Now let me see the clip.' She handed it to him, her bottom lip sticking out and wobbling.

He glanced at it and shook his head. 'I'm sorry Ruby, that's not repairable.'

'No-oo,' she wailed. 'Me poor grandma, I've failed 'er.'

'Ruby,' Mallory said gently, 'the clip can be replaced. When did your grandmother die?'

'Two years ago this week, ma'am. She were the only person in the family that liked me. Now I've got nuffink left of 'er.' She began to snivel. Although Mallory understood Ruby's reactions, she knew sympathy would only fuel her dejection.

'Now listen to me, Ruby,' Mallory waited for Ruby's mournful face to turn in her direction. 'I'm going to ask Mr Finch to give you an hour off, so that you can pull yourself together.'

'And it will only be an hour, Ruby,' Finch warned her.

'That should be enough time to make yourself a cup of tea, wash your face, brush your hair and compose your thoughts.' Mallory added, 'in the meantime I will ask Gertrude to find you a suitable clip from my collection. It won't be the same as having your grandmother's but hopefully it will serve as a reminder of her.'

'Thank you, ma'am.' She gave her a tearful smile. 'I reckon me grandma would be frilled at a fancy new clip.'

'I never said it would be fancy, Ruby.'

'No, ma'am,' she said, a little crestfallen that it wouldn't be jewelled, 'but she would be pleased all the same, I fink.'

Peace restored; Mallory returned to the dining room followed by Finch.

'All sorted?' he asked.

'Yes, sir, it's safe for you to leave the room.' Finch's expression was neutral but there was a twinkle in his eye.

'Thank heavens for that. Could I have coffee in my study, and Finch…' he looked directly at him, 'you and I need to do some research from the archive.'

'Very good, sir, any particular subject?'

'I need you to find Elowen James' address. I need to search for information on Lord and Lady Arlington.'

He nodded and cleared the plates away as brother and sister left the room.

Finch interrupted Ambrose's search of the papers and journals with a folded newspaper and an address.

'I believe this might be helpful to you, sir.' He passed them to him.

Ambrose smiled his thanks.

'Could you ask Mallory to come to my study, I will share your findings with her.'

Mallory took a seat opposite him.

'You have news, I believe?'

'Her address is in Chelsea, and Finch found this in one of the papers.' He passed her the newspaper, carefully folded around the article.

'Read the last few lines of this paragraph.'

'... *Miss Elowen James, who replaced Miss Watkins, exceeded expectations. Her aria was a triumph.*'

Mallory looked up at her brother in surprise. 'So, she is not a woman of ill repute as Lord Arlington inferred.'

'Clearly not, she is an opera singer and actress.'

'That's a surprise, I wonder why they didn't share that information. I wonder what else they are hiding.'

'Indeed. I need to do some digging.' Ambrose restored the newspaper to its original form and sighed as he replaced it on top of the other papers.

'We must tread carefully tomorrow.' He sighed. 'My own search has produced nothing so far.'

'That's annoying.' She glanced at him as he chose another newspaper, he was making a face – not a good sign.

'Ambrose, why don't you put them away.' He looked up at her frowning. 'Wait until you have been to your club. Once you've gained snippets of information, the archives might then help expand it.'

He sighed again and looked at her. 'I agree. It's getting late. Let's see what tomorrow brings.'

Mallory nodded, wished him goodnight and retired to her bedroom.

******

They left mid-morning to interview Miss James. Her small house was in a quiet, pleasant mews. The clang of the bell was answered by a young maid. Mallory smiled at the young girl who only appeared to be about fifteen years old.

'We are here to see Miss James.' Ambrose handed the maid one of his calling cards. It was easier for him to remove it from his waistcoat pocket than for Mallory to rummage through her bag for her card case. She had dressed smartly for the occasion in a blue and white paisley-patterned, high-necked dress; Ambrose's only concession to the summer weather was to wear a lighter coloured suit. The maid curtsied and asked them to wait inside.

'I hope she will see us.' Mallory whispered to Ambrose as they waited awkwardly in the hall. Her wish was granted.

'Madam will see you, if you would like to follow me.'

They followed her up the stairs and were shown into an airy drawing room.

'Your visitors, madam,' she said shyly, as she ushered them into the room.

Elowen James was sitting comfortably on a high-backed chair, her green silk dress draped artistically across the floor and her hands resting lightly on her lap. Small gold earrings dangled from her ears beneath her blonde hair which was neatly arranged into a chignon. Her chair was facing away from the window, so that the sunshine that poured through it framed her like a halo; she knew how to stage a scene. She motioned for them to sit.

'To what do I owe this pleasure?' she smiled.

'We are private investigators,' Ambrose informed her.

'Yes, I saw from your card,' she said in amusement.

Mallory smiled at her candour, Miss James gave the impression that she was not a lady that could easily be intimidated, and she warmed to her immediately.

'It's concerning the ruby necklace, Miss James, Lord and Lady Arlington are seeking the return of it.'

'Are they now.' It was a statement rather than a question.

Mallory smiled at her. 'They have engaged us to oversee its return.'

Miss James smiled back. 'Then I apologise for your wasted trip, but the necklace was Oscar's gift to me. I loved him dearly.'

'Forgive me, Miss James, I understood that Oscar was only given it so he could pass it to his future bride.' Ambrose said.

She laughed. 'Who told you that?'

'Is it not true?'

She shook her head still smiling. 'Not as far as I'm aware. Oscar never mentioned it.'

'You weren't planning to marry then?' Mallory was curious.

'No. Oscar wasn't the marrying kind, he loved me dearly which is why he gave me the necklace. He told me a little of its history but not much else. He certainly didn't mention why he had been given it.' She frowned. 'I would have thought he would have told me, if that was the case, because he was against marriage in principle. We were totally honest with each other.'

'I understand the necklace was very valuable.' Mallory said quietly.

'Yes, so he told me. It is very beautiful, it's the only link I have to him.'

'May we see it?' she asked Elowen.

Elowen took a deep breath. 'No, unfortunately.'

Ambrose raised a quizzical eyebrow.

'Unfortunately?'

Miss James swallowed but held Ambrose's gaze.

'Yes, it was stolen. Somebody broke into my safe and took the necklace.'

Ambrose cleared his throat. 'Stolen? What else was taken?'

'That's the strange thing, I had other jewellery in there but that was left untouched. Some money was taken, but not all of it.'

'Do you think the thief was disturbed before they had a chance to take other valuables?'

Miss James sighed. 'I have no idea. The safe was wide open when I arrived home. Apologies, I should have mentioned that it took place at night. My maid had the evening off, and I was at the theatre that night – as a guest not as a performer. I contacted the police shortly afterwards; they came the next day.

'When was this, Miss James?' Ambrose asked, a frown appearing on his brow.

'A couple of months ago. I think the Inspector's name was Johnson. I haven't heard any more from him, so I am beginning to despair about being reunited with my necklace.'

Mallory hastily scribbled down the information.

'We know Inspector Johnson, we have helped him in the past.' Mallory smiled at her. 'What did the Inspector think at the time?'

She shrugged. 'He didn't say, just took details and said he would be in touch, but he hasn't.'

Ambrose sat back in his chair and thought for a few seconds.

'Miss James —'

'Please call me Elowen.'

'Elowen, who knew about the necklace and where it was kept.'

She thought for a few seconds before replying.

'My staff, I rarely have visitors, Mr Weston. I employ a maid and a part time cook. The cook, though, wouldn't know about the safe. She never comes into the drawing room.'

'Have you recently changed staff, Elowen?' Mallory queried.

'How did you know?'

Mallory shook her head. 'I didn't, but your maid looks very young and inexperienced; I assume she is a new addition.'

'How observant of you,' she replied. 'Yes, she is new, still in training so I'm not sure whether she will make the grade. My last maid received a telegram to say her mother was ill, so she had to leave and return home.'

'How long ago did she leave?' Ambrose was intrigued.

Elowen rested a hand under her chin while she thought. She had no frown, but her eyes were widened in puzzlement.

'Quite soon after the robbery, I'm not exactly sure.' She paused for a few seconds. 'Forgive me but my memory is a little hazy, it's the shock I believe. She was there after the initial police visit, as I recall that she complained about having to stay in the kitchen to keep out of their way. I do remember that she was very apologetic that she had to leave at a time I needed her the most.'

'What was her name?' Mallory asked her, her pencil poised over the notebook.

'Kitty Bunbury. When she was younger, she'd had several tiny acting roles, but it hadn't worked out for her so instead she became a maid. Her references were very good, so I was pleased to be able to employ her. She'd been with me for about three or four months - certainly less than six.' She raised her eyebrows in surprise. 'You're not suggesting she was involved, are you?'

Ambrose held her gaze. 'We're not suggesting anything, just curious.'

Elowen frowned, her voice firm. 'My maid had nothing to do with the robbery, it was just bad timing that she had to leave, the poor woman was beside herself that she had to go. She will return when she feels able to leave her mother.'

She sighed and continued in a softer tone. 'Well, I'm sorry you had a wasted journey. You can inform Lord and Lady Arlington that even if the necklace was still with me, I would not be returning it.'

'Thank you, Elowen. I will report back to them.' He ran his fingers through his copper locks. 'Erm ... may I return if we have further questions?'

She shrugged her elegant shoulders. 'If you like, but I cannot see what else I can tell you.'

'Thank you, Elowen,' Mallory replied, amused by her brother's preening.

They took their leave and headed out to the warm sunshine.

'So, what happens now?' Mallory asked as Ambrose summoned a cab that was trotting along the road. 'I don't think our clients are going to be very pleased with our report.'

'Fortunately, we have a week before we need to deliver it as they are away.'

'Yes, I remember. That gives me an idea, I might go to their house before they return, there is something that I want to check on.'

'What exactly?'

She shook her head. 'You will only laugh if I tell you, so I'm not going to say until I have tested my theory.'

'If it's a minor problem then it can wait for another day. I think I shall still go to my club to gather some inside information for the report, then we can set the case aside so that tomorrow we will concentrate on Mary Gage's missing fiancé. For the moment, let's go home for some luncheon.'

'We won't wait until tomorrow. I'm going to the landlady this afternoon.' She turned towards him. 'It will save time. Tomorrow we can act upon any details that I glean from her.'

'You are not going by yourself to interview her.'

'As I've already mentioned, I shall ask Edward,' she replied as they climbed into the cab. 'If he can't then I shall return home.'

'I will escort you to his chambers on my way to my club.'

'No need, I can find my own way, thank you.'

'There is every need. He may not be there, I'd hate to think of you stranded without a cab.'

She sighed in frustration, when would he accept that she could look after herself?

'Ambrose!' she said sharply as the cab pulled away. 'For goodness sake, I'm quite capable of hailing a cab!' She gave him an indignant glance, exhaling loudly.

'Of course you are,' he soothed, 'but the fact remains that it wasn't that long ago that Edward was attacked outside of his Chambers, so for my peace of mind I shall ensure that Edward is able to accompany you.'

She sighed inwardly, she really needed to make more of an effort in finding her own house. She spent the journey contemplating the best way of finding a suitable home, preferably a suitable distance from her brother.

Chapter 8

Edward was still in his chambers, when they arrived. He looked delighted to see them.

'To what do I owe this unexpected pleasure?' he smiled at Mallory. Ambrose smirked. 'We have a case, two in fact, and Mallory needs to interview a landlady. Would you be able to spare the time to accompany her, Sanderson?'

'I shall be delighted.'

'In that case I shall take my leave and go to my club.'

'Ah, I assume you are after picking up some information?'

Ambrose nodded. 'I'm hoping so.' He doffed his hat and returned to the cab.

'Why don't you sit down and tell me about the case?' He cleared a chair for her by dumping a pile of documents onto the floor.

'My clerk will soon sort those out,' he assured her as he noticed her frown. 'He's far better at storing files than I am. He has his own system.'

He smiled once again. 'Why don't you give me a brief summary? I'd like to know what you're involving me in.'

'It's to do with Mrs Fortescue's cook, or I should say, her cook's niece.' She explained the problem.

He frowned. 'I can see only two solutions – he's vanished on his own account or something untoward has happened.'

'Yes,' agreed Mallory. 'That is why I want to talk to his landlady. She may well be able to provide answers. Mary deserves to know the truth either way.'

'Then let's not put it off any longer.' He stood and took his hat and cane from a stand whilst she gathered her bag.

He opened the door and followed her out. After flagging down a Hansom he opened the doors and helped her into the cab. Closing the padded doors, he settled back on the seat and tapped the roof with his cane for the driver to start.

'Do you know Horseferry Road at all?' he asked Mallory.

'I know where it is, but I haven't actually been there as far as I can recall.'

'Well, it is not the most salubrious of places,' he commented, 'but it's certainly not the worst, that claim belongs to some of the side streets off Great Peter Street.'

'Then I'm pleased we are not going there.'

'I wouldn't dream of taking you, if that was the case,' he replied before adding, 'I once defended someone from there, it is not an experience I wish to repeat; there are a few criminal elements operating in that vicinity.'

Mallory mulled over this nugget of information. 'Do you think his location has something to do with his disappearance?'

Edward turned towards her. 'No point in speculating, let's wait to hear from his landlady. It might be useful to know what kind of tenant this John Kendle is and if it matches his fiancé's view ....' he hesitated, 'there might be another side to him that she doesn't know about.'

She raised her eyebrows. 'Edward, I'm not a fool. I'm aware that could be the case, just as I'm aware he could have cold feet about the wedding.'

'Mallory, I wasn't suggesting—' he left the sentence unfinished as the cab drew to a halt. 'We're here.'

John Kendle's lodging was in a narrow house which was part of a very long row of houses. Beside the front door, with its peeling black paint, there was one window with a further window on the upper floor. Edward knocked lightly on the front door; he didn't want to attract too much attention. There was no response. He knocked a little harder and the door moved slightly.

'It's open,' Mallory said quietly.

'Yes.' He pushed the door open with his fingertips.

'Mrs Strange, may we come in?'

There was no answer. Mallory sighed and gently moved past Edward and entered the house.

'Mallory!' he exclaimed, 'what are you doing?'

'I'm doing what an investigator should be doing – investigating.'

'Mrs Strange, can I have a moment of your time, please?' she called out. An eerie silence followed. She took another few steps into the hall before Edward grabbed hold of her shoulder.

'Wait!' he commanded. 'If you insist on going in, stay behind me.' He moved to the front, they walked past the stairs and into the kitchen where a pungent odour invaded their nostrils. She wrinkled her nose in disgust.

'What's that horrible smell?' she asked, 'and what's that buzzing noise?'

'Flies,' he replied grimly. He glanced around the room and stopped as he saw a pair of feet through the open scullery door.

'Wait here,' he said tersely. Striding across the floor to the scullery, he observed the twisted body that had been bundled into a corner. He noted the bloodied head, the dried blood had attracted the flies and putrefaction had set in; flies were crawling all over her body. He knew she had been dead for some time. He turned to walk away but found Mallory behind him. He scowled at her.

'What is it?' she asked him.

'Mallory!' He scolded. 'I told you to stay back!'

'Yes, but I'm not the biddable type, Edward.' She made to go past him, but Edward firmly took hold of her arm.

'No, you will not take another step! Go, Mallory! Go home! Now!'

'But why—'

'Mrs Strange is dead! There's nothing we can do. I need to fetch the police, but I want you gone before I do that. Please leave now.' He let go of her arm.

'Can't I search John's room first before you call for the police?'

'What?' he thundered. 'Are you mad, Mallory? A woman has been brutally attacked and you want to search a room and not call the police?'

'Look, I'm only asking for a few minutes—'

'No! A crime has been committed, and you want to compound that by committing another.'

'All I'm—'

'No!' he rudely interrupted her. He took a deep breath. 'You don't know which room is John Kendle's, there could be other tenants,' he said clenching his jaw.

'Edward, I just—'

'Mallory! You can't be here when the police arrive. I will come and see you when I can.'

'I'm not leaving you to f—'

'For heaven's sake go!'

Placing his hands on her shoulders he turned her around and marched her towards the front door.

'Go! Get out of this street as quickly as you can – for once in your life just do as you're told!'

She swallowed back a retort and opened the door.

The street was empty. She wished they had asked the cab to wait but then realised it might have been noticed if it was sitting outside the house. Edward was right, her being there would only complicate matters. She needed to get back to Horseferry Road to find any chance of a cab. She walked quickly to the end of Bell Street and resisted the urge to look back to see if Edward had left to call the police. Another road led her back to the main road; she heard the police whistles as a passing cab answered her summons.

'Century Square, please,' she told the driver as she got in and closed the two doors in front of her. For the whole of the journey she worried over Edward – how would he explain his presence?

The house was empty when she arrived home. Gertrude answered her summons for tea. She sat in the drawing room thinking through the day's events.

'Ma'am?' Gertrude enquired, 'what is it?' She put the tea tray on the low table.

'Sit down, Gertrude, and pour tea for both of us.'

Gertrude passed her a cup and took her own and took the chair opposite her and waited for Mallory to speak.

'Have I managed to tell you yet about the two cases we've taken on?'

Gertrude shook her head as she sipped her tea.

'It's the second case that worries me the most.' Between sips of her tea, she told her of the recent visit to the landlady.

'She's dead?' Gertrude's mouth was open wide in shock.

'Yes. Edward stayed behind to call the police and told me to come home.'

'That was wise,' Gertrude replied, 'after the last time you came across a body and was arrested.'

'Don't remind me.' Mallory shuddered.

'What's happened to this John? Was his body there too?'

Mallory looked at her in surprise. 'I never thought of that! I wonder if Edward did?'

'Will he come here and let you know?'

Mallory nodded. 'That's what he told me. Has Ambrose arrived home yet?'

Gertrude shook her head. 'No, and Mr Finch is looking through heaps of journals and newspapers for Mr Weston. What's the first case about, ma'am?'

She regaled Gertrude with the details of the case and the visit to the mistress. She heard Ambrose's light step on the stairs.

'Ah, Mallory, how did you get on with the landlady?' He frowned. 'Wait a minute, you're back early – was she out or did it go badly?'

She bit her lip. 'Worse. She's dead, Ambrose!'

'What?' He threw himself into a chair.

Gertrude excused herself and hurried out with the tea tray.

'Tell me what happened,' he urged Mallory. She explained the circumstances and that Edward would return here later.

'What about John?'

'I don't know, Ambrose. Edward insisted I return here before notifying the police.'

'Thank God for his good sense and mine for insisting you don't go alone. That would take some explaining otherwise, unless it was Inspector Johnson.'

'He promised to come here and update us. I just hope they don't arrest him for her murder.'

'He will be able to talk his way out, he's a lawyer.'

Mallory looked apprehensively towards the door when the doorbell jangled. Edward appeared followed by Finch.

'Afternoon, Weston.' He nodded at Mallory and took a chair near them.

Finch cleared his throat. 'Sir, I have an idea with regards to your research. Would it be appropriate to share it now?'

'Not quite, Finch. There's been a complication, Mallory stumbled across another body.'

As he spoke Ruby entered the room carrying a tea tray. 'Begging your pardon, sir, I was asked to bring the tea tray up by Gertrude.'

'Put it down there, Ruby, and next time knock,' Finch replied, indicating the low table. 'You can return to your duties now and I will pour.' He gave her a meaningful stare.

'Yes, Mr Finch.'

Finch held up his hand to stop further conversation until he heard Ruby go down the stairs.

'You were saying, sir, about a body?'

'I think Sanderson had better inform us, he was there with Mallory when they found the landlady's body.'

'What happened after I left, Edward?'

'The police came fairly quickly; they searched the whole house and I waited with them until an Inspector appeared. I had a story planned that I was the lady's lawyer. Fortunately, I didn't need it as it was Inspector Johnson. So I told him the truth, that I was helping on one of your cases, but left Mallory out of it.'

'Thank you.'

He sighed. 'I think when the Inspector learns about John Kendle's disappearance it's likely he'll be wanted for murder.'

Chapter 9

Ruby rushed down the stairs and into the kitchen.

'Archie! Ma'am's stumbled across another dead body. I bet it's murder!' she said in a thrilled voice.

'Blimey! We got another case then?' Archie said delightedly. Gertrude walked into the kitchen.

'Ruby! I've told you before about eavesdropping.'

'I weren't!' she said with an injured air. 'The door was open, and I took the tea tray in – a job you asked me to do, so there weren't no eavesdropping!' She crossed her arms in front of her defensively.

'I weren't repeating gossip neiver, I heard sir say it, so it must be true.'

'I've told you before, what is said upstairs, stays upstairs.'

'Wot's that mean?' Archie was curious.

'It means, young Archie, that if you happen to overhear a conversation upstairs you do not repeat it downstairs. It's a private conversation, not to be repeated to anyone else.'

'So does the same fing 'appen if you overhear somefink down 'ere?'

Gertrude nodded. 'Yes, Archie, servants talk is not repeated upstairs. I would imagine Mr Finch will be down here soon, so we'd better get on with our jobs.'

'I 'ope we gets involved.' Archie grinned. 'I like detecting.' Gertrude gave him a look and sent him off to scrub some pots ready for Cook.

******

Edward stayed for dinner. They waited for the soup to be taken away before talking about the case.

'You haven't told us, Edward, what exactly the police have said.' Mallory asked as she sipped her wine.

'I don't think it's appropriate at the dinner table,' he replied. 'Shall we just enjoy our dinner first?'

'Agreed.' Ambrose much preferred to eat, rather than talk at the dinner table. Finch brought in a tray loaded with dishes of lamb chops and vegetables. They tucked into their meal and waited until coffee was poured for them in the drawing room.

'So, the police report if you please, Edward.' Mallory was not going to let him forget.

'Hmm. Mrs Strange appears to have been bludgeoned over the head. It looks as though she may have been dead for a few days before we found her. My advice is to tell the Inspector about your involvement with John Kendle, the sooner the better, but it's inevitable that John will become the prime suspect. Do you know if the young lady reported him as missing?'

'No,' Mallory admitted. 'That's something we didn't ask.' She bit her lip ruefully.

Ambrose replied. 'I think we will need to update our client with this news before going to the police.'

'We need to search his room,' Mallory said, 'there might be something the police have missed that might explain his departure.'

'That's something you will have to ask Inspector Johnson, I'm afraid.'

'I'll speak to the Inspector tomorrow, Lory, while you speak to Mary.'

She nodded. 'I presume this case takes precedence over the other one?'

Ambrose thought for a few moments, weighing up the options in his head. 'Yes, we have a week before the report is due to them.'

Mallory sighed. 'I also need to go back to their house, there is something I want to check out, but Mary comes first.'

She pulled out her fob watch and checked the time.

'What is it, Mallory? Why the sudden interest in the time?'

'It's Mary,' she replied, putting her watch back in her pocket. 'She finishes work at eight o'clock, if I time it right, I can catch her at the shop.'

'You're not going to tell her at work?' Edward looked horrified.

'Give me some credit. No, my plan is to speak to her whilst I take her home in a cab. Better to do it tonight before the Inspector knows.'

Dinner over; Mallory draped a shawl across her shoulders, although the day had been warm the night had cooled considerably.

'Would you like—'

'No,' Ambrose interrupted Edward with a smile. 'I think this is best left to the women.'

'Do you have plenty of handkerchiefs?' Edward solicitously asked her, 'I think you might need them.'

She smiled at both. 'Wish me luck!'

******

As Mallory neared Victoria Street, she heard a church clock strike eight. She frowned; how could it be eight o'clock already? She took out her watch and checked the time and blew out a sigh of relief – the clock wasn't keeping accurate time. A wry smile touched her lips, she supposed that it would ensure the timely arrival of worshippers. The cab stopped opposite the shop. Mallory, after asking the driver to wait, climbed down and crossed the road lifting her skirt to avoid the dust and debris. She briefly glanced at the elegant display of hats and fans in the window before entering the shop. An overhead bell clanged announcing her arrival. Mary was busy with a customer, so Mallory walked over to the walnut dresser. The shelves contained stacks of reels of ribbons in a variety of eye-catching colours. Vases of feathers filled the bottom shelf and sprays of wax flowers were carefully hung on the sides of the shelves. Opposite the dresser, wooden stands displaying a variety of elegant hats dotted the room. Some were veiled, other's adorned with roses, none of which were to Mallory's taste; she preferred the smaller, subtle styles. The drawers under the large counter, at the back of the room, held a variety of items. Behind the counter Mallory could see a desk where a matronly woman sat with a ledger.

Mary, tired shadows beneath her eyes, motioned her to come to the side of the counter. Mallory smiled politely at the other assistant but indicated she wanted to be served by Mary.

'Ma'am, what are you doing here?' Mary whispered. 'I'll be in trouble if they catch us just talking.' She inclined her head towards the desk, 'this supervisor is very strict. She'll fine me sixpence, given half a chance.'

'Well, we can't have that,' Mallory whispered back. She saw the supervisor frowning in her direction. In a louder voice she said, 'I'm looking for a plainish hat for my maid as a birthday present.'

'Yes, madam, I can show you a few.' She indicated the window. 'If you would care to follow me.'

As Mary took a straw hat from the stand Mallory informed her that she needed to talk to her and would take her home. Mary nodded. 'Would this suit? Do you have her measurements? We do this style in a variety of sizes.'

Mallory took it from her and held it up, turning it around in her hands to examine it in detail. 'I think this will fit her perfectly. Which ribbon trim do you suggest?'

She bought a yard each of the blue and lemon ribbons. By the time Mary had made a note of her address for delivery of both hat and fee, it was time to close the shop.

'I'll wait outside,' Mallory whispered to her. 'It's important we talk.'

Mallory pulled the shawl firmly round her shoulders and waited patiently for Mary to appear. A good five minutes passed before Mary appeared.

'The cab is over there.'

Together they crossed the road and clambered into the Hansom cab after Mary shyly gave the driver her address. Mallory waited until the cab lurched forward before speaking.

'I'm sorry, Mary, I'm bringing you bad news.' She clasped Mary's hands in hers. 'There is no easy way to say this, so I'll just explain what has happened.' She took a deep breath. 'John's landlady was found dead earlier today, unfortunately this will mean the police will treat John's disappearance as suspicious. He will be their prime suspect, if they find him they will arrest him for murder.'

Mary's eyes widened in horror. 'No! John wouldn't, couldn't have done that!' She began to cry. Mallory released Mary's hands and reached for a handkerchief from her bag and passed it to her.

'Mary, I'm assuming you informed the police that John was missing?'

Mary nodded. 'As soon as we discovered he hadn't turned up for work. They didn't want to know, just dismissed it as a lover's tiff.'

She stared at Mallory, anger in her eyes. 'What happens now? Are you going to walk away now my John might be a suspect?' Mary wiped away her tears.

'No! Heaven forbid! I'm just preparing you for a police visit. I'm sure the police will want to get in touch with you. When my brother reports John is missing he will inform Inspector Johnson that John had disappeared before the landlady was killed. Please stay strong for John's sake.'

The cab came to a halt. 'Oh, we're here now. I'm sorry I had to come to your place of work, but I thought you ought to know immediately.'

Mary sniffed back her tears. 'Thank you, ma'am, I'm glad you were the one to tell me and not the police. Oh, the police won't come to the shop, will they?' she said with a cry, her hand across her mouth.

'I've no idea, Mary,' she said with a frown, 'I hope not.'

'If they come to the house, the neighbours will have a field day, there's already talk about my John running away from our wedding.' She sniffed again. 'I'm sorry, it's just all too much at the moment.'

'Perhaps if you could visit your aunt at Mrs Fortescue's house every night when you finish work, we can let the police know and they can interview you there. That way it will be easier to get in touch if we have information.' She patted Mary's shoulder before leaning forward to open the doors for Mary.

'Century Square, please.' she called up to the driver before closing the doors. She settled back on the seat as the driver pulled away into the darkening night.

Chapter 10

'So,' Ambrose folded away his morning newspaper, and placed it on the breakfast table, before looking at his sister. 'We need to speak to Inspector Johnson, today if possible.'

'No,' replied Mallory, 'you need to speak to him. I am going back to Pinnerton Lodge to satisfy my curiosity. It's an ideal time as they are away.'

He raised an eyebrow. 'At the risk of repeating myself – not alone I hope?'

'Of course not, I will take a staff member.'

'Hmm. What exactly is it that you want to check out?'

'You will think me foolish, Rosy, if I told you.'

He sighed. 'No, I won't. If something has bothered you then you should trust your instinct, however foolish it may seem. I'm interested to see what you picked up that I didn't.'

They were interrupted by Finch who brought in fresh coffee.

'When we walked down the drive I turned back and thought I saw a face in an attic window. It disappeared so quickly that I wondered if I had imagined it. To be honest, I'm mystified by the house ... I ...' she hesitated, unsure of how to explain her feelings.

'I'm drawn to the house – like a moth to a flame. Something isn't right.' Her brow creased in puzzlement.

Ambrose nodded thoughtfully. 'Yes, I know what you mean about the house. I can't put my finger on it either. It may just be that we were unsettled by the strange reception we received.'

'Perhaps, but I'd like to find out more.'

Ambrose remained quiet. Finch poured them coffee, hovering discreetly so he could listen to the conversation.

'I think, Lory, you should go as any unexplained event should be examined,' he replied. 'You are not a person to give way to flights of fancy. I believe you did see something, so you need to see if it has a plausible explanation. However, you do need someone with you to witness it.'

Finch coughed. 'May I make a suggestion, sir?' Ambrose nodded.

'I think young Ruby should accompany madam, she is still feeling upset and driving the staff mad. It will make her day and give the rest of us some peace. Archie would also be useful, you may need his lock picking skills.'

'Excellent suggestion,' agreed Mallory. 'Would you be so kind as to inform them, Finch? I would like to go today as soon as possible.'

'I will check Bradshaw's for the train times.' Finch bowed and left.

'I shall try to see the Inspector and then go to my club,' announced Ambrose. 'I didn't get anywhere yesterday; the right people weren't there.'

'What do you hope to learn?' Mallory hurriedly sipped her coffee, hoping to make a point by putting her empty cup back on the table signifying she wanted to leave the table. Annoyingly her brother was taking his time, completely unaware of her needs.

'Well, I would like the Inspector to update us on the John Kendle case; I would also like an update as to the stolen necklace. I need it for my report. As for the club,' he took another sip of coffee, 'I want financial information on the Arlingtons. I do think they will try to avoid paying us a fee – even a reduced one.' He grimaced and swallowed the last of his coffee.

'I wish you luck, then.'

'Same to you, Lory.'

They left the dining room and went their separate ways.

******

Mallory had difficulty curbing Ruby and Archie's excitement.

'Ma'am, this is the most frilling thing that's ever 'appened to me,'

she said, beaming from ear to ear. 'And a train trip too!'

'I'm sure it is, but I need both of you to calm down,' she admonished them as they climbed onto the train, the hot sun beaming down on them. Archie ushered them into an empty compartment. It was late morning, but the train wasn't busy. As the train lurched forward Ruby couldn't stop herself from talking.

'Ooh, this is blooming exciting, I hope we finds a dead body or two!'

'Ruby! If you cannot keep quiet, I shall be forced to get off at the next stop and send you back.'

Ruby's face fell. 'Sorry, ma'am, please don't send me 'ome.'

'Then follow my instructions.'

Archie added, 'it's vital that we do as we're told, Ruby, otherwise we might all get into trouble. I reckon Miss knows what she's doing, and we gotta support 'er – got that?'

Ruby nodded, not daring to speak in case she said the wrong thing and was sent home.

'Good. Here's the plan.' She spoke quietly and made sure they understood. She looked out of the window for the rest of the journey leaving Ruby and Archie to talk in whispers. With a shrill whistle the train came to a standstill at Norwood Junction station.

'There will be a cart waiting outside, please leave all the talking to me.'

They obediently followed her through the station to the road. Just as she anticipated, Bob Miller's cart was there.

'Pinnerton Lodge, please.' She handed him the required coins and climbed on board, leaving room for Ruby and Archie to join her on the bench. They had the cart to themselves, which pleased Mallory as a talkative Ruby would not be good news for passengers. The horse snorted several times before Bob gently urged it forward; the rhythmic clopping of hooves blended with the smell of privet and lavender as they made their way along the road. Ruby looked anxiously around her; she was not enjoying the drive.

Bob dropped them at the beginning of the drive at Mallory's request, she didn't want the noise of the cart alerting anyone. As they walked up the drive, she stared at the attic window but could see no sign of anyone.

'This is scary, ma'am.' Ruby looked at her with big eyes. 'I ain't used to quiet, I like noisy London, I miss it already.'

'Then you will have to be brave, Ruby,' she whispered back. 'Can you do that?'

Ruby gulped and nodded.

'Good, I'm relying on your ingenuity to keep me safe.' Mallory smiled at her.

'Yes, ma'am, thank you.' Ruby cheered up immediately, it was nice to be needed.

They came to a halt at the front door.

'Do you want me to pick the lock, miss?' Archie asked hopefully.

'It might not be necessary. Archie, walk to the back and check for any sign of servants.'

Mallory waited for Archie's report.

'No sign, miss.'

Mallory tentatively tried the doorknob, it was unlocked. Who leaves an unlocked house unattended, she wondered, and immediately supplied the answer – unworthy staff.

'Archie,' she whispered, 'watch the house for me, if you spot someone, whistle a tune loudly to alert me, you'd better have a good cover story handy.'

'Leave it to me, miss,' he said grinning, and took himself off to a nearby overgrown shrub.

Silently, Mallory and Ruby entered the house. Mallory pointed to the stairs and Ruby nodded. The house remained silent as they quietly ascended the staircase.

'I don't fink anyone is 'ere, ma'am,' Ruby whispered.

'Just so,' Mallory murmured back, 'the Arlingtons are away this week.'

'Shouldn't there be servants though?'

'Yes,' muttered Mallory, 'one would have thought so.'

Once they reached the top floor, Mallory peeped into several rooms until she found the one overlooking the drive.

'This is it, Ruby.' She closed the door, and immediately the intense, suffocating heat hit her as she walked into the centre of the room. It seemed to have sucked out all the air. The sun poured through the window, dust particles dancing in its rays. She studied the room. It was a mixture of a servant's bedroom and storeroom. An old iron bed with a plain coverlet was placed against a wall with an old, scratched chest of drawers standing next to it – a china bowl and jug set upon its top. A rag rug covered the room's bare boards. Against the other wall, a pile of wooden tea chests and wicker baskets jostled for space along with some old lamps and covers; a broken hat stand lay across the floor. Altogether the room was cramped and musty; it didn't seem to be in use anymore. Mallory's nose began to itch with the dust, she could feel a sneeze forming, quickly she pressed her handkerchief to her nose to mute the sound as she sneezed. Beads of sweat had already started to appear on her face, even though she had only been in there a few minutes.

Ruby turned her attention to the bed. She pulled back the cover. 'Seems, ma'am, that someone 'as slept in 'ere recently. The sheet's all wrinkled, and the pillow's dented.' She pulled out a long grey hair.
'See?' She held it up for Mallory to see.
'So, I was right, there was someone here.'
'Bit of a strange bedroom even for a servant, I reckon. Why would a servant 'ave to share storage space? There should be uvver rooms to use as storage, there ain't enuff room to swing a cat, let alone sleep in.'
Mallory surveyed the room and picked her way across the debris to the window. She saw Archie hovering by a tree and waved to him.
'It must have been a servant I saw looking out of the window,' she mused out loud. 'Although it's an extraordinary thing for a servant to be in her bedroom just after lunch.'
'You seen enuff now, ma'am, can we go? I don't like it 'ere one bit.'
'Neither do I, Ruby, there's something about this place—'
Ruby interrupted her. 'It's haunted – that's what it is. Never again will I moan about me attic bedroom.'
Mallory turned towards her with a frown. 'Is there a problem with your room, Ruby?'

Ruby shook her head. 'Not now I seen this one. Me grandma always said I should count me blessings, and I do now.' She wiped her sweaty face with her arm. 'I don't like this 'ouse.'

'Then let's go.'

Ruby turned the door handle – the brass knob came away in her hand.

'Oh, ma'am!' she wailed.

'Hush, Ruby,' she said firmly, 'we need to keep noise to a minimum.'

'But ... but ...' she whined, 'the door won't open now. We're blooming stuck!'

'Just put the handle back into place and turn it.'

Ruby picked up the knob and pushed it in with such force that she pushed the handle out on the other side. The door was now unopenable, they were trapped in the room.

She wailed. 'Oh, I've gorn and broken the blooming thing, the 'andle's fallen out the other side. It's all my fault. We're done for now, there ain't no escape. We're going to die in this attic, from starvation and heat, the ghosts—'

'Ruby!' Mallory hissed at her. 'We are not stuck, we simply need to find another way out, that is all. I don't want to hear another word about death or ghosts.'

Ruby sniffed. 'There ain't anuvver way out.'

Mallory moved towards the window and opened the catch. Archie was still there. She motioned to him to come forward.

'We're stuck in this room,' she called down. He shook his head and pointed towards the drive, finger on his lip. She understood immediately, somebody had arrived at the house. Who could it be? The Arlingtons were away so it could only be servants. What were they going to do? How could they possibly come up with a story for being in the house, let alone an attic room? Archie came to their rescue however, he pointed up to the roof and the drainpipe. Of course! The question arose of how they were going to clamber across the roof in their long skirts. Archie melted back into the tree. They were on their own.

Sighing, she turned towards Ruby.

'Ruby, listen to me,' she said quietly. 'Somebody has arrived at the house, we need to get out of the window and down the drainpipe. We need to be quiet. If you have any ideas, now would be a good time to share but as quietly as possible.'

Ruby stopped sniffing and perked up. 'Down the drainpipe?' she squealed delightedly.

'Ruby,' Mallory hissed, 'you need to speak quietly!'

She nodded. 'Yes, ma'am, sorry, ma'am,' she whispered back. 'I did it a couple of times at 'ome to avoid me bruvvers.' Her eyes sparkled with delight. 'We just need to tuck our skirts and petticoats into our bloomers, so we don't trip.' She picked up the hems and started to stuff it into her white bloomers. 'Hurry, ma'am,' she urged.

They could hear a voice downstairs. Mallory quickly followed suit and climbed out of the window and slithered onto the decorative, narrow ledge. Ruby waited for Mallory to edge her way to the cast iron corner drainpipe, before climbing out and pushing the window closed without losing her balance. Mallory dangled one leg over the ledge until her boot rested on the rectangular hopper. Fortunately, there was plenty of ivy to cling on to. She tentatively put her other foot onto the hopper, it held. She slid her way down to the lower roof in comparative safety, despite snagging her bloomers on a sharp fragment of iron bracket. She sighed and looked down at the offending rip as she waited for Ruby. Gertrude would certainly notice it and require an explanation.

'All well, Ruby?' she asked softly as Ruby neared the end of the pipe.

'Yes, ma'am.'

'Then we need to get moving to the next drainpipe.'

They scrambled across the tiles to another ivy-clad drainpipe. Mallory heard Archie's voice beneath her as she half-slid, half-climbed down the pipe.

'Nearly there, miss, but hurry. I can catch you if you fall.'

She looked down and saw how near she was to the bottom.

'You don't need to catch me, so turn your back please.'

Concentrating, she slithered the last few feet to the ground. She shook off the ivy leaves that clung to her hands and her dirt-streaked bloomers, and quickly untucked her skirts and smoothed down the material.

'Can I turn round yet, miss?'

'No, wait for Ruby to land and restore her skirts.'

She gave Ruby a helping hand down the last few feet.

'Ready now, Archie.'

Archie turned and beckoned them to follow him.

'Best to sneak around this tree and through the shrubs to get to the drive,' he whispered. 'That part of the drive is hidden from the 'ouse. I checked it out earlier, miss, just in case of problems.'

'Cor, ain't this—'

'Be quiet, Ruby!' Mallory hissed at her, 'no talking until we reach the road.'

Walking quickly and quietly they made their way down the drive. Mallory heaved a sigh of relief as she saw the cart trotting down the road. There was no such relief from the stifling heat, however, she could feel her underclothes clinging to her. The air was heavy and oppressive, she could see the steam emanating from the horse as the cart approached. It needed another thunderstorm to clear the heat, and quite frankly she would have welcomed a heavy rain shower.

'Can I talk now?' whined Ruby. 'All I wanted to say was 'ow frilling it all was. Fancy me being an 'eroine and helping you down the drainpipe!'

Mallory smiled and resisted the urge to tell her it was the other way round. Let her have her moment of glory, she thought, as they climbed onto the cart ready for the journey home. However, once they were on the train, Mallory made it plain that they weren't to speak of today.

'Do I make myself understood?' she asked Ruby. 'Under no circumstances are you to mention about escaping down the drainpipe to anyone – ever! This is our secret, and if I hear our escape mentioned either above or below stairs you will regret it.'

'Why, ma'am? I ain't ashamed of it.'

'Because, Ruby, neither Mr Finch nor my brother would approve of it. It's not at all becoming to show one's bloomers, in fact it would … no I'm not even going to discuss it. The subject is banned.'

Ruby and Archie nodded, the rest of the journey was completed in silence as Mallory puzzled over the servant's attic room, it had only deepened the mystery rather than solve it.

Chapter 11

Ambrose unearthed Inspector Johnson in his office. Fortune had smiled on him as the Inspector was just about to go out.

'To what do I owe this pleasure, sir?'

'Glad I caught you, Inspector,' he replied as he sat on the proffered chair, his legs sticking out at an awkward angle due to the small space between desk and chair.

'I feel we should share information.'

'Is that so? Mr Sanderson did mention you had a case.'

'My sister and I have a client who reported that their fiancé was missing.'

'And why would that be of interest to me?'

'That person was John Kendle, his landlady was the murdered Mrs Strange.'

The Inspector whistled and leaned forward. 'I'm listening, you'd better tell me everything.'

'I see.' The Inspector remarked after listening to Ambrose's account. 'I am assuming you are also here to inform me that John Kendle is not the killer of his landlady.' A wry smile hovered on his lips.

'I am.'

The Inspector shook his head. 'The facts speak for themselves, sir. The landlady was cruelly murdered, and I discover John Kendle has disappeared. It is no co-incidence.'

'That will depend on when he went missing and when the landlady died.'

The Inspector frowned. 'Go on.'

'When did the landlady die, Inspector?'

The Inspector sighed. 'The body is over a week old.'

Inspector Johnson wagged his finger. 'No, no. Don't try to ruin my day by telling me that John Kendle went missing before that. You only have his fiancé's assumption that he did. Just because he didn't turn up for their Sunday tryst doesn't mean to say he was missing then.'

'Yes,' conceded Ambrose, 'but remember she went to his lodging on that day and there was no reply.'

'Indeed.' The Inspector grinned. Ambrose realised his error.

'Thank you for confirming my suspicions. That ties in with the date of her murder, and his sudden disappearance. I'm obliged to you.'

Ambrose sighed. 'Inspector, I really don't think—'

'If you want to convince me otherwise, you will need to show me evidence of his innocence. Have you any evidence?'

'No, but why would he kill his landlady, there is no motive.'

'He could have killed her in a drunken rage, his young lady said that he was upset.' He noted Ambrose's expression and sighed.

'I shall need to speak to the young lady, but I'm not making any promises.' He pulled a notebook towards him, a pencil already in his hand. 'Her address please and her place of employment.'

Ambrose cleared his throat. 'I think, Inspector, that it would be better not to visit her at her place of work, it may cost her job. I can't see her employer being happy about the police visiting its shop premises, can you?'

The Inspector raised an eyebrow. 'A shop, you say?' He thought it over. 'Perhaps not.' He looked keenly at Ambrose and said in a sarcastic tone, 'I presume you have no such objection to us visiting her at home?'

'Actually, I do.' He gave an apologetic smile. 'Imagine what the neighbours will think when the police bang on the family's door. The family does not need wild speculation adding to their troubles. No, Inspector Johnson, it won't do.'

'May I remind you, Mr Weston, this is a case of murder. I do not have time to worry about people's finer feelings.'

'Understood, but here's a compromise – why don't you interview her at Mrs Fortescue's house. Her cook is the girl's aunt, and Mrs Fortescue can act as chaperone. Miss Gage will call there every night when she finishes work at eight o'clock.'

'I'll think about it, but I'll take her address all the same.'

Ambrose sighed but gave him the addresses, it would be foolish to argue.

'It's possible I may have some other information for you, that might help with John's innocence,' Ambrose informed him.

'Go on.'

'It seems to me, Inspector, that if Miss Gage's version is correct, those friends may have the answers you seek. Perhaps they were involved with the murder rather than John. Unfortunately, I do not have any names, I'm sure, however, you will find out from the public house. In return for all this information may I ask your permission to search his room – I assume you have already completed a search?'

The Inspector nodded. 'Aye, you may as well, you might find something that my men have missed given that we didn't have this new information at the time. Well, you will have to excuse me now as I'm about to go out.' He rose from his chair and put on his jacket.

'Just one more thing, if you don't mind.'

The Inspector groaned and wearily sat down.

'Yes?'

'I'd like to know about the burglary at Miss Elowen James' house.'

'Why?' he asked bluntly.

'It has to do with another case we are working on.'

'Does it now?' He eyed Ambrose suspiciously. 'Has she employed you to find it?'

He shook his head. 'No, Inspector. She is not our client, but it does have an impact on our case.'

'Would you care to enlighten me?'

'Not at the moment. Suffice to say that we spoke with her, she mentioned the burglary and that she hasn't heard from you since.'

Inspector Johnson puffed out his cheeks. 'Well, I can't reveal anything about the case to you, but what I can say is that it seems our Miss James has a few financial worries.' He raised his eyebrows at Ambrose. 'Get my drift?'

Ambrose frowned. 'So let me get this straight, you are suggesting that the burglary is connected with Miss James' money problems.'

The Inspector smiled. 'I'm not suggesting anything, I'm just simply pointing out a fact. The other facts are that the house was empty and money and other valuables were left behind.'

'Interesting. You think it was an inside job?'

The Inspector held up his hands. 'Let's just say I don't believe in coincidences.'

'May I ask what steps you have taken to recover the necklace?'

'Is there a necklace to recover?' he countered.

'Perhaps you are at least able to tell me whether the necklace was insured?'

'Alas, I'm not at liberty to say.' He smiled at Ambrose. 'I would be interested, though, to hear about the connected case.'

'I, also, am not at liberty to discuss – at least not until a week has passed by.'

The Inspector gave him a quizzical look.

Ambrose laughed. 'Come to supper in a week's time, I may be able to tell you then.' He rose and took his leave.

Sauntering out of the station he hailed a cab. His thoughts turned to Miss James. If the Inspector was correct about her financial status, he needed to find out about her financial affairs – he hoped it wasn't true. Until he knew for sure, he would leave out this information in his report to the Arlingtons. Instantly he wondered how he had come to such a decision. It was not like him to withhold information to a client. He spent the journey home analysing his thoughts and was both disturbed and irritated to discover that he had a warm regard for Miss James, he had been dazzled by her demeanour and beauty. However, one thing he did know for certain, this would remain a secret – to be kept from Mallory at all costs.

******

'How did you get on with the Inspector?' Mallory asked her brother over supper.

'It was informative but tell me how your afternoon went.'

'Only if you promise to enlighten me about your visit.'

He nodded his agreement, so she told him about the attic room.

'So, there is a plausible explanation,' he replied.

She pulled a face. 'Yes and no. Logic dictates that it must have been a servant, but I'm still not convinced.'

'Why?' he frowned, 'it's quite clear that it's a servant's room – you said the bed had been slept in.'

'I know, but it comes down to this question: why would a servant be in their bedroom after lunch? It makes no sense, servants are busy all day long, they certainly don't have a rest in their room mid-afternoon.'

'Hmm. Let's ask Finch if that scenario is possible. The servants seem lackadaisical, if their butler was anything to go by.'

Finch was summoned and confirmed Mallory's viewpoint.

'Very strange, sir. The only possibility I can think of might be illness, but with the likelihood of their pay being docked it's not very likely. Will that be all, sir?' Finch left the room.

'You see my point?' she asked.

'I do.' He stroked his chin with his hand. 'Intriguing as it is, I can't see how this helps our case. However, I do have a little bit of information that might help. Miss James, according to the Inspector's hint, has financial problems. He isn't in a rush to investigate the burglary due to his belief that it might be an inside job.'

'You think she staged the robbery so she could claim the insurance money?'

'I am merely repeating the Inspector's thoughts.'

She gave him a thoughtful glance. 'You don't want to believe that Miss James could be guilty, do you?'

He avoided answering by passing on some information,

'The Inspector has agreed to let us search Mrs Strange's property.'

'That's quite a concession.'

Ambrose nodded. 'It is, so we'd better make the most of it.'

'There are some other actions that ought to be considered,' Mallory opined.

'Such as?'

'You've just mentioned one of them, we need further information on Miss James' financial position. That, I believe, is your line of expertise.' Her blue eyes bored into him, 'or would you rather have Edward look into that matter?'

He remarked stiffly, 'I shall make the necessary enquiries.'

'Will your judgement be clouded, though?'

He glared at her. 'What do you mean?'

She sighed. 'I believe you are quite taken with her.'

Ambrose shifted uncomfortably in his seat and glanced at his fingernails. 'I'm a professional, sentiment does not come into it.'

'If you say so.' She glanced at his mulish expression but said no more. She changed the subject. 'The other action is of course, the public house, The Rising Sun. Somebody needs to visit it, John's friends clearly frequent it.'

'We may not need to visit that establishment; it really depends on what we find in the rooms. We need to do that as soon as we can, in case the Inspector decides to rescind that invitation. If we do need to visit the tavern we need to give it careful thought.'

'We also have a report to write for the Arlingtons, the deadline is looming.'

'I know.' He drummed his fingers on the table. 'We can both go to search the house tomorrow morning, I shall then make my way to my club and see what information I can glean on Miss James.'

Finch came in with the tray of coffee.

'Finch, do you know anything about The Rising Sun tavern?' Mallory asked.

'The one in Southwark?' He glanced quizzically at Ambrose.

Ambrose sighed. 'Mallory thinks we need to visit it, I think we should wait until we have searched John Kendle's rooms.'

Finch frowned. 'Madam has a point, sir. That was the last place he was seen. It wouldn't hurt to assess it; I do believe I have a thirst coming on.' He put the coffee pot on the table and cleared away their plates.

'I suppose if you look at it in that respect, we could go tomorrow evening.'

Finch coughed discreetly. 'Pardon me, sir, for speaking out of turn but I do not believe you would blend in. You would be spotted immediately even if you dressed differently. I think this is a job for myself, sir.'

Ambrose laughed as he poured himself some coffee. 'You are probably right, Finch, however, let's wait to see what we discover in the search.'

'Very good, sir.' He bowed and left the room.

Chapter 12

It had rained overnight. There were still traces of dampness on some of the pavements which lay in the shadows, these would soon dry out as the temperature rose. It was going to be another hot day, Mallory noted as she looked at the blue sky, most of the clouds had now disappeared. Ambrose hailed a cab and soon they were threading their way through the traffic heading towards Horseferry Road.

The cab drew to a halt outside the house guarded by a lone policeman who looked suitably bored.

'Good morning, Constable.' Ambrose smiled at the man.

The constable touched his cap. 'Mr Weston?'

'Indeed. I assume Inspector Johnson has informed you of our visit?'

The policeman nodded. 'Yes, sir,' he inserted the key into the lock. 'Oh, it's already unlocked,' he scratched his chin. 'They must have forgotten to lock it before handing me the key. Go right in, sir.'

Mallory entered the house first followed by Ambrose. This time she was able to look around her. It was a narrow, dark hallway with one door to the left and the stairs to the right.

'She was found in the scullery,' she told him, waving her hand in the direction of the kitchen at the back of the hall.

'Yes, but we're going upstairs.' He gave her a brotherly shove towards the stairs away from the scene of the murder.

'Do you know which room is which?' he asked as they mounted the stairs. Three rooms led off the landing, two to the left and one opposite the stairs which was over the kitchen. She shook her head.

'Then we had better open all of them.' He tried the first door on the left, it opened into a shambolic room.

'What on earth?' exclaimed Ambrose.

A chair had been overturned, clothes and blankets strewn over the floor. The mattress, which had been pulled off the bed, rested precariously between the floor and the end of the bed. Drawers had been emptied and discarded.

'Surely the police haven't done this?' Mallory was appalled at the mess.

'We'll soon find out,' he replied grimly. 'Stay here whilst I have a word with the constable.'

He ran downstairs taking two stairs at a time.

'Constable,' he called as he stepped outside. The policeman turned towards him with a smile on his face.

'When did the police search the house?'

'They finished yesterday, sir.' He looked puzzled.

'Were you on duty yesterday?'

He nodded. 'Yes, sir. The Inspector put me on guard duty after his men left.'

'I see. It must have been a long day for you, just standing here. If it had been me, I would have sneakily taken a break.' He smiled at the constable. The constable smiled back.

'No break for me, but I was called away for a short while, so that broke the monotony.'

'Ah, that would explain it.'

'Explain what, sir?'

'I think you had better look upstairs. One of the rooms has been ransacked, I doubt very much it was the handiwork of your colleagues.'

The constable's jaw dropped, he dashed inside and up the stairs followed by Ambrose.

'No, no, no! This can't be possible!' The constable looked in dismay at the mess. He fingered the stiff collar of his uniform in agitation.

'So, this isn't the police's handiwork?'

The constable shook his head. 'No, they wouldn't leave a mess like this.' He surveyed the debris, misery etched on his face.

'The Inspector will have my guts for garters when he sees this. I had only been gone a short while. I swear!'

'Did you check the door on your return?'

The constable shook his head. 'No sir, why would I?'

'I don't think it was by chance you were called away.'

Hope shone on his face. 'Do you think so, sir? The Inspector's due here later, I've been told.' He glanced around puzzled.

'The lady, sir, where has she gone?'

Ambrose turned round and realised Mallory had disappeared. Heaving a sigh he replied, 'I'll find her, return to your duties for now.'

Mallory was in the room above the kitchen, which clearly had belonged to the landlady. It was a pleasant room neatly furnished with a bed and bedside table, a chest of drawers and a chair with a shawl hanging over the back. On the hearth stood a vase of faded lavender. She touched the stems, whereupon a shower of crumbly mauve fragments fell to the hearth. She sniffed the air, but their scent had long gone. A framed, embroidered sampler hung on a wall. She dusted off the bed cover with her lace gloves before sitting down on it. Pulling open the drawer in the little table she glanced into it just as her brother entered the room.

'I thought I said stay in the ransacked room.'

'You did but I saw no point in doing so when we have other rooms to search. Staying there would have contributed nothing. Why don't you make yourself useful and start looking through the chest of drawers?' She pointed to them before rummaging through the drawer.

'It's John's room that we need to search, why waste time on the landlady's?'

'We might uncover information on him, as a landlady she's bound to know something about him and it's possible she may have recorded it, even if it's in a diary.'

She pulled out a notebook and flicked through it.

'Oh, that's interesting!' She glanced up at Ambrose. 'It seems to be a rent book.'

'So?'

She smiled at him. 'She had another tenant besides John.' She held the book out to him. He took it and looked at the page.

Walter Yates
Middle room 5 shillings a week all in.

He looked at Mallory. 'So where is this tenant? Could it be him in the frame for murder?'

She smiled. 'You need to read a bit further. Look at the last date for payment of rent.'

He ran his gloved finger down the page.

Received 5/- May 15th, 1890.
Has lodgings with a new job at White's butchers, Brunt Street. Promised some sausages due to late payment.

'Oh, I see! He's out of the frame then. Not sure what use this will be.'

'Oh, Ambrose, use your brain! This Mr Yates may provide us with information on John. They had rooms next to each other, I'm sure they probably chatted to each other even if they only met on the stairs.'

'That is a good point. We need to find him, perhaps we could fit in a visit this afternoon.'

She sighed and shook her head. 'Rosy, you are not thinking straight. Is it likely that you would visit a butcher's shop rather than your man servant? Don't you think you might frighten him if you singled him out to speak with him?'

He laughed. 'When did you get to be so wise? I think we need to send Finch out to buy some meat.'

Mallory tucked the book into her bag, it might come in useful later, if not they could hand it over to the Inspector. Her glance landed on her coin purse as she shut her bag, a question beginning to form in her mind.

'Oh Ambrose! Where is her money? If she collected rent from her lodgers, she must have kept it somewhere.' Her brow furrowed trying to work out the answer. Ambrose walked around the room seeking a hiding place.

'She must have put their rent somewhere, in a place where she could access it daily to buy food,' she reasoned, as she put her bag back on the bed.

'In that case it would probably be in the kitchen.'

'Where her body was found – is that a coincidence, I wonder? Was she killed because she interrupted a thief stealing her rent money, Rosy?'

'That would certainly account for her body being there. I think we need to let the Inspector know about the rent book.'

They moved into the middle room. It was empty and clearly had not been re-let since the departure of Mr Yates.

'No point searching this room, I think, Lory. The landlady would have made sure it was cleared out ready for another lodger.'

Downstairs they heard the Inspector's voice and soon heard his footsteps on the landing. They followed him to John's room.

'What in god's name is going on?' He thundered, staring at the mess.

'Are you responsible for this?' he demanded of Ambrose.

Ambrose shook his head. 'I think you need to speak to your constable.'

'Harris!' he bellowed.

'Sorry, sir! It must have happened last night.'

Inspector Johnson glared at him.

'Asleep, were you?'

'No, sir! I was called away to an incident.'

'What incident? Nothing was reported at the station.'

'That's because there wasn't any incident in the end, sir.'

'I think you had better explain yourself! I'm not liking what I've heard so far.'

'Yes, sir. I was standing outside the front door when a lady came running up the street and told me I was needed at the pub at the end of the road – a fight had started outside. I told her to find another constable as I couldn't leave my post, but she began to cry and begged me to attend before somebody was killed.' He paused and took a deep breath aware that his account was sounding more fictitious as he recounted it.

'It sounded bad, sir, so I rushed to the pub. Two men were indeed fighting, throwing wild punches and shouting, but no knives were involved. It took a while to get them to calm down, then I returned to the house, and thought no more about it, until this gentleman told me the bedroom had been ransacked.'

Inspector Johnson breathed heavily, trying to calm himself down.

'It never occurred to you that you should have blown your whistle instead?'

'No, sir,' mournfully he looked at shoes, not daring to meet the Inspector's eyes.

'I shall deal with you later,' the Inspector told him in an ominous tone.

'It was a clever ploy,' remarked Ambrose, 'to use a woman to appeal to the constable. However, we have found something you might find interesting.' He felt sorry for the constable and tried to distract the Inspector from venting his rage at him.

'I hope it is good news, I could do with some right now.' He glared again at the constable before sending him outside.

'Mallory?' Ambrose nodded at her to produce the book. She handed the book over to the Inspector after opening it at the correct page.

'You will find, Inspector,' she informed him, 'that there was another tenant.'

'The body was found in the kitchen, was it not?' Ambrose asked him.

The Inspector nodded as he glanced at the book.

'Did you find any money on the premises?' he added.

The Inspector shook his head. 'Why?'

'Well, that book is a record of rent, where did she keep all that rent money? Isn't it likely to be the kitchen? Perhaps she was killed by a thief trying to steal the money.'

The Inspector pulled a face. 'I don't like it, but it fits,' he said grudgingly.

'No, wait, it doesn't!' Mallory glanced at them. 'Why would they come back and ransack Mr Kendle's room? It can't have been very much money, certainly not worth the risk of coming back and distracting the constable.'

'Now that's the reasoning I do like,' declared the Inspector. 'It's clear the murderer is after something specific as no other bedroom was touched. It doesn't take John Kendle out of the frame though. It could be he came back for something he'd left behind.'

'You are forgetting Mr Yates, Inspector. Although he left in May, perhaps he came back to murder Mrs Strange.'

'I haven't forgotten, Mr Weston, but John Kendle remains a suspect.'

'One fact we have learned is that a woman is involved,' Mallory reminded them.

'A woman or not, John Kendle remains a suspect,' the Inspector was adamant.

As there was nothing further to be gained they left the house and walked back to Horseferry Road to hail a cab. The sun blazed down on the blackened chimney pots of the grimy, terraced houses, Mallory shielded her eyes from the glare, she hadn't brought her parasol thinking it would be cooler after the rain, it had been wishful thinking. As she climbed into the Hansom cab, she felt the heat engulf her.

'Oh, it's stifling!'

'Are you talking about the weather or the case?'

'Both,' she replied as she looked at him. 'I'm not sure which is worse.'

Chapter 13

After dropping Mallory off at home, Ambrose went to his club.

He ordered a cognac from the steward and then wandered into the smoking room, the air heavy with cigar and pipe smoke. He spotted a member who frequented the opera.

'Hello, Dingle.' He sat opposite him and settled into the buttoned-backed leather chair. Dingle put down his paper and greeted Ambrose with surprise.

'My dear fellow, good to see you. Haven't seen you since ... well, you know ...'

'Yes.' Ambrose smiled at him, 'it's been a long time.' He waited for the cognac to appear before speaking.

'Been to any good theatre productions lately? I heard good reviews for that opera singer ... oh, can't remember her name — Jones? ... no ... James, that's it.'

'Ah yes, the lovely Elowen James.' Dingle smiled appreciatively.

'Beautiful, absolutely first-class singer. Do you know ...' he leaned forward and spoke softly '... I once invested in one of her shows.' He nodded at Ambrose.

'Oh really? Did it pay off?'

Dingle shook his head. 'No, unfortunately. Miss James had put her own money into the show, that's why I invested in it. Damned if I know why it failed though.'

'That's a shame, she's had such good reviews. I wonder how much she lost.'

'Ah, well, quite a bit if rumours are true.'

'Oh dear, let me buy you a whisky while you tell me about it. I've always wondered whether it was worth investing in the arts.'

The whisky arrived and Dingle settled back into his seat.

'Cheers, Weston! It is Weston, isn't it?' He peered at Ambrose through the smoke. 'Not much good with names, these days, I'm afraid.'

'Yes,' grinned Ambrose, 'you've got it right, it's Weston – guilty as charged!'

Dingle laughed and tapped his head, 'not totally lost the old mind yet then! Now about investing in the theatre—'

'Oh, you were going to tell me about Miss James' misfortune.'

'So I was, so I was.' He took a sip of his whisky.

'As I see it, she lost a fair bit, I only put in two hundred. Miss James, on the other hand, put in eight hundred – or was it a thousand?' He shook his head. 'I can't recall.'

'That's a big sum to lose.' Ambrose frowned. 'I think I read somewhere that she had a lover who gave her a valuable ruby necklace. Can't think of his name, though.'

'Lover?' Dingle snorted with laughter. 'He batted for the other side, if you get my drift.'

'A homosexual?' Ambrose widened his eyes in disbelief. 'I thought she was his mistress!'

Dingle shook his head. 'Good lord no! That was a front for him, to cover up his true nature. I think he loved her but as a friend.'

'Am I right about the ruby necklace though? I heard it from a good friend of mine.'

Dingle nodded. 'I believe so. It's worth a fortune apparently. If she sold it, she would not only recoup her losses but have a fortune to spend as well. Damn me, if I don't make a play for her – never thought about that. Got money of my own, of course, but well a fortune is not to be sniffed at, we could invest in a lot of operas.'

Smiling, he took another swig of his drink. 'Probably too old for her, but a man can dream.'

Ambrose smiled too. 'Indeed. Happy dreams, Dingle.' He clinked glasses with him, downed his cognac and bade him farewell.

******

Mallory explained to Gertrude exactly what happened to her bloomers. The offending garment was in the maid's hand.

'I see,' she said at last, fingering the rip. 'Never mind, ma'am, I reckon I can mend it. I'll send it to the laundry first and mend it afterwards. I just hope Ruby doesn't blab.'

Mallory shook her head. 'I've warned both her and Archie not to speak a word about the drainpipe business.'

Downstairs in the basement, Gertrude added the bloomers to the laundry list, with Ruby watching her.

'You see, Ruby, it's easy. You can write in capitals if you wish.'

'Not me Gertie—'

'It's Gertrude,' she interrupted. 'I am not Gertie, never have been, never will be, and don't you forget it.'

'Wot I was gonna say, *Gertrude*, is that I'll never remember all those letters.'

'Yes, you will. It's just practice. Look,' she produced a box of slips of paper. 'I've written all the names of the stuff we send to the laundry. Now you find the slip of paper that matches this garment. Go on.'

Ruby groaned and looked through the box and pulled out a slip.

'This is it, ain't it? B-l-o-o-m-e-r-s.'

'Well done, Ruby. You see you can do it.' She put the item in the large wicker trunk.

'Yeah, but it's gonna take me ages to do the list if I 'ave to keep looking at slips of paper,' she moaned.

'Then practice, Ruby,' Finch replied, walking into the room. 'Problems?' he asked, arching an eyebrow.

'No, only the rip in the bloomers, Mr Finch. We slid—'

'Ruby!' Gertrude hissed at her. 'The matter is not to be discussed.'

'I was only saying—'

'Ruby,' Archie hurriedly changed the subject. 'Is there any clean cloths? I've got the silver to polish,' he added proudly.

Gertrude smiled her thanks at Archie, who grinned back.

'Then you'd best get to it, Archie, and stop wasting time interrupting me!' Ruby glared at him, hands on her skinny hips. 'And while I'm at it, why does everybody keep interrupting me?'

she wailed. 'It ain't fair, I ain't speaking Dutch like them Frenchies do.'

Finch sighed. 'The people of France speak French, not Dutch, and don't call them Frenchies, it's disrespectful.'

'Well, they talks funny and I don't, so nobody should be stopping me speaking, and me pa calls 'em that, so why can't I?' She stomped off banging the door behind her.

'Is there something I should know about ripped clothes?' he enquired of Gertrude.

'No, not at all, Mr Finch. I'd better get on and take the tea to ma'am.' She left quickly before he could ask further questions.

******

'So did you hear anything useful, Rosy?' She took a seat in his study.

'I did, actually,' he momentarily paused his writing and looked across at her.

'Are you doing your report for the Arlingtons?'

He nodded. 'Time is running out, so I thought I'd better get it ready.' He returned to his work, his hand neatly moving across the page. Mallory watched him for a short while before continuing the conversation.

'So, what did you find out?'

Sighing, he put the pen back in its stand, blotted his work and then leaned back in his chair.

'I was in luck; I had a chat with an opera enthusiast. It seems our Miss James has been left with heavy debts.' He recounted the information he learned.

'Interesting.' She frowned. 'Do you think his parents knew about his ... preferences?'

'Hmm ...' he tapped his fingers on his chin. 'Maybe, they quickly changed the subject when we asked about his death and provided very sketchy information.'

'Is your information reliable though, or is it just a rumour about his sexuality?'

'A good question, Lory. It's difficult to say who I believe at this moment.'

'In all fairness to Miss James, she did say he wasn't the marrying kind.'

Ambrose nodded. 'Yes, I do remember, and I do believe that statement.'

'What about her disastrous investment, is that believable?'

'Oh yes. My acquaintance had also invested in it, though his loss was not as great as hers, so I do believe that to be true.'

'Then it's no wonder Lord and Lady Arlington are keen for the necklace to be returned to them. I presume that accounts for their prickly manner.'

'More than likely. Now if you have nothing further to say, I will get back to the Report. I wouldn't be at all surprised if I was to receive a letter shortly with the date of their intended visit.'

'What are you going to tell them regarding Miss James and the necklace?'

He sighed. 'I'm simply going to state that it was stolen in a burglary and leave it at that. There is no proof that it was an inside job. If they wish for further information they can contact the police.'

'Then our work is finished on that case.'

'I think so. We can concentrate on finding John Kendle. Talking of concentration – can you let me get on with the Report, please?'

'Certainly. I'm off to have a chat with Finch about buying some meat from a butcher.'

******

Finch and Archie made their way to White's butchers in Brunt Street, in the shadow of St Saviour's Church, Pimlico.

'Now, young Archie, do you remember what I told you?'

Archie grinned. 'Course, I do, Mr Finch. I ain't daft!'

Finch suppressed a smile and merely said, 'very well let's put our plan into action.'

They crossed the road and peered at the shop.

'Can you read the name, Archie?'

Archie grinned. 'I reckon so, but can I look at the window first?' He looked with interest at the window display. He'd never had a chance to have a proper look at a butcher's display, previously it was the pockets of the customers outside that had been interesting. This was a new experience for him. He liked what he saw, and immediately felt hungry. Hams jostled for position in the window with ribs of beef. Above the window on a row of hooks, pheasants and rabbits dangled along with legs of lamb and a side of pork. Lastly he looked at the name above the shop.

'Joe…Wh…ite…Fam…ily…But…cher?'

'Well done.'

Archie smiled proudly at the praise.

'Let's go in then and remember I'm relying on you to cause a distraction so that I can speak to Walter.'

Being a warm day, the door was open. The floor was strewn with sawdust soaking up any spilled blood. They would be swept up at the end of the day and replaced with a fresh lot in the morning. Archie traced a pattern in the sawdust with his boot.

'Morning, sir,' a man greeted him.

'I'm after some pork chops, please.'

The man squinted at him. 'Not seen you before sir, I take it you are not a regular?'

Finch shook his head. 'No, I come from Kensington, my master heard about your reputation so naturally he sent me here.'

'My assistant will serve you.' He nodded to his assistant and spoke to him in butcher's backslang, but Finch knew that old trick, a language used so that the customer couldn't hear that they were going to be overcharged. Finch replied in the same dialect to instruct them he would only pay the going rate. The butcher agreed before disappearing into the back to sharpen some steel knives on a strap. Saws of various lengths were hung on the wall. Archie was free to watch in fascination as there was no need for a distraction.

'Pork chops, was it, sir?'

'Yes, and at the correct price. Walter Yates?'

The assistant nodded, puzzled. 'Yes, sir?'

'I need to ask you about John Kendle. Can we talk here?'

'Yes, as long as you're buying.'

Walter loaded eight thick pork chops onto paper. 'These do you?'

Finch nodded. 'Do you know his friends? John has gone missing and I'm trying to trace his friends for any information.'

Walter carefully placed the paper onto the iron plate of the scales.

'He had three, sir. I can't say I cared for them.' He started putting a couple of brass trade weights on the opposite plate.

'Arthur Cripps, Fred Archer and Fergus Tate. They all used to meet at the Rising Sun in Shady Alley, just off Borough Road. Do you know it?' He added some more weights until it balanced evenly.

'I'll find it.'

Finch paid for the chops.

'I think you will find the police will want to talk to you.'

'Me?' Walter shot him a look of horror. 'What have I done?'

'Mrs Strange has been murdered, so naturally as a former tenant they will want to talk to you.'

'Blimey! That's awful!'

'Just thought I'd warn you, thanks for the information and chops.'

Archie picked up the parcel of chops and put it under his arm.

'We off to the Rising Sun now?' Archie queried, a spring in his step, hopeful that they were going to be doing a bit of detecting.

Finch shook his head. 'No, that's for another day if need be. We need to take this meat home.'

Archie's swaggering stance drooped; Finch hid a smile.

'There will be another time, my lad. We have three names to puzzle over, if our friend Walter is to be believed.'

Chapter 14

Mallory noted down the names that Finch had given them.

'How are we going to trace them?' she queried.

'I'm not sure yet,' Ambrose replied with a frown. 'The obvious place would be to go to the Rising Sun, but that's likely to send them underground. Finch's services are required, I think. It might be worth running those names past the Inspector, they might have history.'

'Have you heard from Lord Arlington?'

'Not yet, but I have a feeling it won't be long. I shall be glad to hand the report over and send in our bill. There is a lot to do in the John Kendle case. The longer he remains missing, the more I fear for a good outcome.'

The front doorbell jangled. Finch announced the Inspector.

'I shall bring refreshments, shortly.'

With a smile Finch took the Inspector's coat and hat and left the room.

'I hope I'm not intruding.'

'Not at all,' replied Mallory indicating a seat to the Inspector.

'So, what brings you here, Inspector?'

'I thought I would bring you up to speed.'

He took a chair opposite Ambrose whilst Mallory sat on the sofa.

'I have spoken to Miss Gage – at Mrs Fortescue's house, as suggested – and I am satisfied that she has no idea of where John Kendle is.' He held up a hand to prevent interruption. 'However, that does not mean John Kendle is off the hook. I know she believes wholeheartedly that her John is not a killer, unfortunately her beliefs are not evidence. Until such time as I receive it, he remains a suspect.'

'Then it's fortunate you came, for today we found the names of three of his friends; Miss Gage told us John would not let her meet them. May I run the names by you to see if you recognise any of them?'

Inspector Johnson nodded, so Ambrose gave him the three names.

'Ring any bells, Inspector?'

'Ah! Fergus Tate – petty theft, as for Fred Archer, he's of interest simply because he has an older brother well known for being a muscle for hire. Arthur Cripps ...' he rubbed his chin as he pondered the name. 'Hmm ...I don't recall that name at all.'

'Never mind, Inspector. These friends could be behind John Kendle's disappearance.' Mallory smiled at him. 'We need to talk to them.'

The Inspector pulled a face. 'If you're hoping this will save him, you're going to be disappointed. Think about it. If he's friendly with criminals, then it's very likely they are all involved with the murder. If he didn't kill her then he may well be an accessory to it. It doesn't look good either way.'

Finch entered bearing a tray of tea things and small cakes, freshly baked by the cook that afternoon. Sensing an atmosphere, he put the tray things down.

'May I make a suggestion, sir?' he asked as he poured the tea into cups.

'Please do,' confirmed Ambrose.

'Would an advert in the personal columns of newspapers bring information about the friends?'

The Inspector laughed. 'I don't think these lads read, let alone buy a paper!'

Finch inclined his head. 'Indeed, sir, but my point is somebody who knows them might, especially if a reward is offered. I understand that the personal columns are avidly read. You have nothing to lose but the price of the advert.'

'Thank you. Finch, it's certainly worth considering. Would you be able to place these adverts if we decide to do so?'

'I would be honoured, sir.' He passed the cups around, then made a move to go but was stopped by the Inspector's next words.

'I know your face from somewhere, I have a feeling we have met before.'

Finch turned round. 'Of course we have, you've been here on several occasions.'

The Inspector frowned. 'No, other than here.'

Finch assumed a sorrowful expression. 'It's my misfortune, Inspector, to possess one of those faces that people believe they recognise. It is not the first time I have been mistaken for someone else. A cake sir?' With the Inspector's attention being deflected to the cakes, Finch quietly left the room, a smirk on his face.

'What is your next move, Inspector?'

The Inspector brushed away the crumbs on his beard with his hand.

He took a sip of tea before answering.

'The friends, then possibly The Rising Sun. That public house has been brought to our attention before. I believe it has a certain … criminal element, we have yet to prove anything though, so this connection is certainly interesting. According to his fiancé, that was his last known movement. Someone might know where he went next. Yourself?'

'I have a report to give to my other client. I shall ponder our next move after that.'

'If you happen to see Miss James again, which I'm sure you will,' an amused smile hovered on the Inspector's lips, 'please tell her the police have not yet recovered her necklace.'

Swallowing the last of his tea, he got up to go. 'Thank you for the tea, Mr Weston, I will let you know if there are any further developments – in both cases.'

Ambrose rang for Finch to show the Inspector out.

'Will you place an advert as Finch suggested?' Mallory asked her brother. 'It may lead us up the wrong path.'

'I know, but the thought is tempting. It will be easier than doing the footwork to find them. Let me sleep on it.'

******

The next day dawned bright and sunny. It was very pleasant sitting in the dining room eating breakfast. Finch had opened the windows; a gentle breeze greeted them.

'I have decided we will put a carefully worded advertisement in the papers. I shall leave it to Finch to decide which ones.' Ambrose stirred sugar into his coffee.

'Well, I hope it brings a response.' She pushed away her empty plate and poured herself a cup of coffee.

'So do I, sister, so do I. It will be a long process otherwise, time I fear is not on our side. I am beginning to wonder if the Inspector is right, John is involved somehow with Mrs Strange's murder.'

'Surely not?' Mallory was aghast. 'Whatever has made you change your mind?'

'I wouldn't call it a change of my mind, more a case of being realistic. Despite our best efforts to uncover the truth, all the evidence so far has pointed to his involvement. That's difficult to ignore, Lory, I desperately hope I am wrong. We will have to find conclusive evidence if we want to find John and clear his name. Perhaps it might be an idea to have a word with Sanderson about the evidence. Let's invite him to dinner one evening.'

Finch was summoned for advice on the placing of the advertisement. He brought with him the early post.

'If I am not mistaken, this looks like Lord Arlington's handwriting.' remarked Finch.

Ambrose took the envelope and carefully slit it open and swiftly scanned the contents of the letter.

'They're coming here tomorrow afternoon. I'm glad I've got the report ready, though I think I might visit Miss James again today.'

'Shall I come with you, Rosy?'

'No! I mean … erm … there's really no need, Lory. I doubt Miss James will be in and I can go straight to my club, if that's the case. I only want to confirm a few details and pass on the Inspector's message.'

Finch and Mallory hid their smiles.

'Very well, I may visit Lady Marsham instead. I wonder if she knows anything about Lord and Lady Arlington.'

'Good idea. Now then, Finch, I want to take up your idea about those personal columns.'

'Very good, sir. What do you want to say?'

'Hmm ... nothing too wordy. Something like:
Possible reward for information on the whereabouts of Messrs. Arthur Cripps, Fergus Tate and Fred Archer. Apply 5 Century Square, Kensington.'

'Do you think that wise, sir? We could end up with some unwelcome visitors. May I suggest we use a Post Restante address?'

Ambrose shook his head. 'I want to draw them out, Finch. Using a P.R. address will add delay. You choose the exact wording.'

'As you wish, sir. I will make sure they go in tonight's edition of The Evening News and Post. May I suggest we wait for these results before using the morning newspapers?'

'Agreed. Oh, by the way, I shall be out tomorrow evening at my club, some fellow or other's birthday. Don't wait up for me.'

Finch nodded and left the room.

******

Finch announced that Mallory had a visitor.

'Are you at home to Lady Marsham?' he enquired, passing her the calling card.

'Of course! Please send her up immediately and bring some tea.'

Lady Marsham was shown into the drawing room. She clasped Mallory's hands in hers and smiled warmly at her.

'My dear, I'm so pleased you are in.'

They sat together on the sofa.

'I'm delighted to see you, Isabella. I was planning to visit you this afternoon.'

'Oh?'

'I was going to ask if you knew of Lord and Lady Arlington. We have been working on a case for them, hopefully that's now concluded.'

Isabella shook her head. 'No, I'm afraid not. However, I have something that may help.'

She rummaged in her bag and produced three invitations.

'There is a ball at Lady Hamley's house. I have secured invitations for you and Ambrose, and one for Mr Sanderson.'

Mallory raised an eyebrow.

Isabella laughed. 'I thought Mr Sanderson might make some useful introductions. Lady Hamley has some very influential friends; it might prove productive to Edward.'

Mallory was still puzzled. 'I see, but I was wondering how the ball might help with information regarding the Arlingtons.'

Isabella gave a girlish laugh. 'Oh Mallory! Someone at the ball may know of them, I mentioned she had influential friends, did I not?'

Mallory smiled. 'Ah, I see.'

'You will come, won't you?' Isabella pressed her for an answer.

'Of course!'

'I understand that Lady Hamlyn has engaged Miss James, the opera singer, to provide some entertainment.'

'In that case, I'm sure my brother will accept.'

Isabella gave her a look. 'Am I missing out on something?'

Mallory laughed. 'No, it's just that I rather think she has caught his eye.'

'How delightful!' Isabella smiled. 'I am so glad I procured these invitations.'

'However did you manage that?'

'I'm on one of her committees. She graciously allowed me to put forward your names.'

Finch brought in the tea tray. After pouring their tea, he bowed to them and left them to it.

'He's such a treasure. Wherever did Ambrose find him?'

'Oh, he's been with our family since we were small children.'

They spent a pleasant hour chatting before Isabella declared she must leave.

'Will you give Edward the invitation, or shall I take it?'

'Oh, I will go there now. Ambrose was thinking of inviting him to dinner one evening so I can deliver both invitations.'

As soon as Isabella left, Mallory rang for Gertrude.

'We're going out, Gertrude. If you could fetch me a suitable hat, we will visit Mr Sanderson. I have some messages for him.'

The cab dropped them outside his chambers.

The clerk recognised Mallory.

'I'm sure Mr Sanderson will see you. Please take a seat.'

'Shall I come in with you, ma'am or stay here.'

'I shan't be long; you may as well stay here and talk to the clerk.'

Soon Mallory was taking a seat, Edward solicitously pulled out a chair for her and waited for her to be seated before speaking.

'This is a nice surprise, Mallory,' he said as he returned to his seat behind the desk. 'It's always good to see you.' The desk was littered with documents, he lifted a pile and placed them neatly to one side.

'My clerk can deal with those.' He smiled at her.

'I've come bearing messages.'

She pulled out the invitation from her reticule.

'Lady Marsham has instructed me to give you this invitation to Lady Hamlyn's ball. She felt it would be beneficial to you.'

He gazed at her face for a few seconds before replying. 'Will you be going?'

'Of course! I believe Ambrose will accept his invitation, apparently Miss James will be singing!'

Edward grinned. 'Forgone conclusion then. I shall be delighted to attend. What do you hope to gain by going to the ball?'

She smiled at him. 'Can I not just go to a ball and enjoy it?'

'You could,' he agreed, 'but knowing you, I doubt it.'

She laughed. 'Very well, I hope to learn some information about Lord and Lady Arlington; on that note, Ambrose has invited you to dinner one evening. He didn't specify which, though.'

'Well, I shall be pleased to accept. You haven't forgotten my offer to show you the Italian Garden?'

'I haven't,' she replied, a smile hovering on her lips. She bade him farewell and returned to Gertrude who plied her with questions about which gown she would wear to the ball.

Chapter 15

Lord Arlington arrived at two o'clock the following afternoon. He pushed past Finch, throwing open the drawing room door without waiting for Finch to announce him. He strode into the room.

'Well?' he demanded. 'Have you got the necklace?'

'Please do take a seat,' Ambrose said politely.

'I want an answer – not a seat!'

'Nevertheless, do take a seat, your Lordship.' He waited for him to sit before continuing, 'the answer is no. There isn't a necklace, so it can't be returned—'

'What do you mean? Of course there's a damned necklace – are you an imbecile?'

Ambrose's eyes narrowed. 'There is no call to be offensive, Lord Arlington. If you had let me finish, you would have heard why. There isn't a necklace because it was stolen. Miss James suffered a burglary a few weeks ago.'

'That's absurd!' he thundered. 'I don't believe you.' He pointed a finger at him. 'You've got the necklace and are keeping it for yourself!'

'I'll pretend you never said that. The burglary was reported to the police. If you wish for further information, contact Inspector Johnson at Scotland Yard, he's dealing with the case.' He handed him a document. 'Here is my report, together with a note of our fees. You will see that I have reduced it right down as there was no further work. I expect prompt payment. Good day to you.'

He stood up indicating that the meeting was over.

'Now you look here, Weston!' Lord Arlington heatedly rose from his chair, 'if you wish me to pay this bill, you had better find that necklace.' He thrust the report and bill back at Ambrose.

'You wish me to take on further work, your Lordship?' He stared at him, breathing hard, trying to control his anger. 'That will incur further costs and expenses.'

His Lordship glared at him for a few seconds, then looked away and sighed. 'My temper is getting the better of me.' He held up his hand. 'I withdraw the accusation – it was unjust, my wife would be mortified. Shall we start this conversation again, as gentlemen?'

Ambrose agreed and took a deep breath.

'Indeed. We are happy to accept further instructions on the case, but it remains for me to point out that despite our best endeavours there is no guarantee of success. I am happy to contact Inspector Johnson to request details of the burglary. We will work with the police to recover the necklace. I must inform you though, the necklace will be returned to Miss James, the police will insist upon it. Unless, of course, you have a document to prove it belongs to you?'

'No, of course we don't have a document,' he replied crossly. 'I admit that it will be difficult to prove it to the police, but if the necklace is found, I expect you to make that … harlot give it back.' He stood up. 'Do we have an agreement, Weston?'

'Only if you agree that there will be a new fee covering the cost of tracing the necklace.'

Lord Arlington held out his hand. 'Agreed, providing it is reasonable.'

They shook hands.

'I will write to you at Pinnerton Lodge.' Ambrose informed him.

'I don't think that is a good idea.' He frowned. Mallory was fascinated by the serpent emblem on his gold ring – it flashed in the sunlight as his finger rubbed his chin.

'We are away a lot, we have a lot of engagements in the country, mostly parties at country estates – quite a bore most of the time, but we are obliged to attend.' He thought for a few moments. Mallory noticed his hooked nose and the tiny, jagged scar beneath it, and wondered what caused it, but she could hardly ask.

'I think it would be better if I write with a date to meet here. I think three weeks would suit. Expect a letter from me, and I expect some news in return. Good day to you. I will see myself out.'

He left the room without looking back. They heard Finch's voice as he opened the front door.

'Well!' was all that Mallory could say.

'Yes, indeed.' Ambrose raised his eyebrows in disbelief. 'I did not expect that. I thought that would be the end of the case. We're now in a tricky situation, running two cases and both will need our full attention.' He steepled his hands together and rested his chin upon them as he sat down, deep in thought.

'I can speak with Miss James, Rosy.'

He turned towards her, perplexed. 'Why?'

'We need to take details of all the staff at the time of the burglary. I've got a note of a maid's name but no other details. Given that the Inspector thinks it's an inside job, we had better investigate them.'

'Oh, yes,' he said, pulling a face, 'I hadn't thought about that. I can do that, it will be a good place to start, I shall then need to sweet talk the Inspector into letting me see the report.'

'I will remain here then, in case there are any responses to our advertisement last night.'

'Oh Lord! I've just remembered, I'm out at my club this evening. I promised I would attend a birthday celebration.'

'I doubt we will get any replies today.'

It was just Mallory for dinner in the evening. She rather enjoyed her solitary meal; it gave her a chance to think about the cases. She was going to suggest to her brother that they work individually on each case, but she realised that dealing with staff was not Ambrose's forte, and she would have to speak to Miss James's maid. If they each took a separate role, swapping over from case to case, it should work provided they communicated with each other. When Finch brought in her coffee, she asked him if there had been any replies to the advertisement.

'Yes, madam. There is a letter asking us to meet at the landlady's house at eleven o'clock this evening.'

'Oh, that's good, isn't it?'

He shook his head. 'I don't think so. I believe it is a trap. I did warn your brother that it was dangerous to put our address.'

'You and I will go, as we don't know when Ambrose will be home.'

'No, madam. That will leave our house empty, and that's my fear. It's a trap to lure us away from the house so they can burgle it. They could easily have written the information in the letter if it was genuine, and certainly wouldn't have chosen such a late hour.'

Mallory thought for a few seconds. 'What do you suggest?'

'We don't go.'

'I don't think we can ignore it, Finch. I will go, I know the house.'

He sighed. 'I would rather you didn't, the risk is too great, sir would never forgive me if something happened to you.'

'Nothing will happen to me. I shall simply turn up there and wait for a short while. I promise I shall return straight home if nobody arrives.' Finch gave her a steely glance before agreeing. Then let me prepare you, but I am not happy. I don't know who can rescue you.'

'I won't need rescuing! I can look after myself.'

Finch gave her another of his looks but simply said, 'very well, but dark clothing would be more suitable, the less conspicuous you are the better. When you are ready, come to the kitchen.'

Mallory no longer had her black mourning clothes; she had passed them on to her furious sister-in-law. She changed into a navy skirt and dark brown blouse. Finding a large black shawl at the bottom of a trunk, she pulled it out and examined it. Satisfied with its size, she tied it around her.

'You look like a gypsy,' Gertrude declared with a worried frown.

'Then so be it. I need dark clothing. At least this skirt has deep pockets.' She smiled at Gertrude. 'Don't look so worried, I shall be perfectly fine, Finch will make sure of that.'

She made her way down to the basement. Finch was waiting along with Archie.

'Can't I go with miss?' Archie asked.

'No, I shall need you here, I do hope you haven't told Ruby.' Finch replied.

Archie shook his head. 'It's our secret.'

Finch unwrapped a cloth and produced a small pocket pistol, with a bronzed handle. 'Take this. Do you know how to use it?'

Mallory nodded. 'I think so.'

'Let me remind you. You need to cock the hammer before firing. It only has five bullets. It doesn't have a large range, so make sure you are near to the person if you must shoot. I hope to heaven you don't need to.'

Mallory nodded. 'Anything else?'

He handed her another weapon. 'Hide this on your person. I don't anticipate you will need it, but I would rather you were prepared.' He took both her hands in his.

'Get there early and have the advantage.' He pulled out his watch to check the time, nodding, he advised her it was time to go. 'I'll fetch a cab. Good luck, madam.'

The cab pulled up outside 9 Bell Street. She paid the driver who patted his horse before trotting away. She listened to the clip of the horse's hooves until it faded. Silence reigned, she felt utterly alone and vulnerable. She glanced in both directions but with just one gas lamp at the end of the street and a clouded moon it was difficult to see clearly. Somewhere in the distance a drunken man started singing. She shivered. This won't do, she told herself, you need to move. She took a deep breath before checking her pocket watch. She would be there before them – if anyone came, of course. She patted her other pocket to check she still had the pistol; it was comforting to know it was there – a friend in a time of need. She tried the door, it was unlocked. Hmm. Either the police hadn't locked it or ... she didn't want to think about the alternative. She opened the door and crept in. Total darkness, as she had suspected. In which room was she supposed to meet? Finch hadn't said. Slowly and quietly, she tried the kitchen and peered into the darkness.

Dim moonlight peeped through the narrow window, faintly illuminating the table. As her eyes adjusted to the darkness, she picked out a shape on the table. She moved nearer and saw the outline of a candlestick. Further exploration yielded a box of matches, lighting the candle with shaking hands, she watched the flame take hold of the wick and immediately felt calmer. Feeling more confident, she decided to explore upstairs, it would be far better to do something active than just sit and wait. With one hand holding the candlestick and the other hitching up her skirt she climbed the stairs. A faint moaning reached her ears as she neared the landing. She stopped and listened carefully; there it was again. Without further thought she made her way to the noise and realised it was coming from John's room. Could it be John, injured? She pushed open the door and thrust the candle into the space. In front of a tiny fire grate lay a body. Holding the candle further towards it she could see a skirt and boots. Not John then. Warily she moved towards it then stopped in shock.

'Mary? What are you doing here?' Putting the candle on the floor she saw Mary had been bound. Tucked in her boot she had a folding knife, silently she thanked Finch for his preparation. She paused, gazing at the ropes before cutting through them. Pushing the ropes to one side, she gently helped Mary sit upright.

'What happened?'

'After I finished work, I came to see if I could find the letters I had written to John. It occurred to me that my address may be on them, I didn't want anyone bothering us at home. I mean, whoever hurt John could come after me.' She gulped.

'Can you stand?' Mallory asked her.

'I think so.' Mallory helped her up.

'While I was searching someone grabbed me from behind and tied me up. They took my candle. What are you doing here, Mrs Wynter?' She rubbed her legs above her boots where the rope had been tied.

'Someone sent a note asking to meet them here, they had information on his friends. I think we had better leave before they arrive.' She looked around the room.

'Is there a way out from the back, in case anyone is watching the front?'

Mary nodded. There's a little alleyway off the back yard.'

Mallory was puzzled. 'How did you get in, by the way?'

Mary gave her a sad smile. 'I knew where Mrs Strange kept the spare key, in case her lodgers forgot theirs.'

'We'd better hurry.'

With the candle lighting their way, Mallory and Mary entered the kitchen, Mary led her through the scullery.

'Do you know how I can get to Horseferry Road from the alley?' Mallory asked as she unlocked the door.

Mary shook her head. 'I've no idea, I don't go in that direction. It's better for you to go the way you came, these alleyways are a maze, one leads into another, you can easily get lost. I only know the way John showed me.'

Mallory sighed, the chances of her finding her way out of a labyrinth were slim, especially late at night. She wished Mary luck.

'Thank you, Mrs Wynter.' Mary slipped into the darkness as Mallory locked the door. She headed out of the scullery into the kitchen and came to an abrupt stop.

Leaning against the far kitchen door which led into the hall, a young man with his arms folded watched her.

'I see you got the message.'

'That's why I'm here.' Turning, she put the candlestick on the dresser and took a deep breath to calm herself. At least she had a weapon.

He grinned. 'And that's just where you're gonna stay, for some time.'

'I beg your pardon?' Haughtily, she drew herself up to her full height.

'You can beg as much as you want but you ain't going nowhere, lady,' he sneered.

'Oh yes I am!' Mallory replied as she slipped the tiny pistol out of her pocket and pointed it at him.

'If you don't want a bullet through you, I suggest you let me leave.'

'You think I'm scared of that little thing – shoot peas, does it?' He laughed. 'It's this you need to be scared about.' Brandishing a large knife, he moved towards her. She held her nerve and waited until he was about six feet in front of her. She cocked the hammer with her thumb then fired.

Screaming, he fell to the floor clutching his bleeding thigh, the knife clattering to the ground.

'Bitch!' he yelled, as blood poured through his fingers onto the floor. Mallory kicked him hard in the face before kicking away the knife and pocketing the pistol. Stepping over him she made a bid for freedom. At the kitchen door she turned back to make sure he hadn't got up. A stinging blow to the back of her head sent her spinning, blackness engulfed her as she slumped to the floor.

Chapter 16

As soon as Ambrose stepped into the upper chamber of his club, he regretted it. The revelries were in full swing, and he could hear the carousing. A bottle appeared in front of him.

'Come on Weston, take a drink and join in the fun, it's party time.' The man swayed, unsteady on his feet, as he held the bottle.

Ambrose raised an eyebrow and looked around the room. Most of the men were drunk and the others were well on their way, slapping each other on the back and swigging from champagne bottles, white bow ties dangling from their necks. A great cheer emerged as one man downed the last of the bottle.

'More! More! We want more!' they chanted as a harassed steward hurried over to them.

'I say, Weston, you don't look the part, its formal evening wear.'

'So I see.'

'Never mind, old chap, have a drink anyway.'

The bottle was once again thrust towards him. He pushed it away.

'Perhaps later,' he replied.

'Suit yourself.' The man shrugged and stumbled across to a group gathered round the billiard table. Ambrose came to a decision. Time to leave, no-one would even notice. He would call in at Sanderson's chambers and see if he was free for supper. He returned to the front desk and signed out.

'I'm not attending the party, please make sure I'm not billed for it, I've only been here a few minutes,' he told the steward in charge.

'Yes, sir.' He made a note against Ambrose's entry.

'Much obliged to you.' He nodded at the steward and left.

Edward was indeed at his chambers. He was putting some documents into his leather case and looked up as Ambrose entered the room.

'I was just about to leave.'

'I wondered if you would like to go out for supper, unless of course you have a prior engagement?'

'Only with my case notes! Of course, I'll come. I presume you want to talk about one of your cases?' he said with an amused smile.

'Not really, I just wanted some intelligent company. I've just come from my club; a rowdy party is taking place.'

'Let's go then. Where shall we eat?'

They settled on The Cheshire Cheese in Wine Office Court, just off Fleet Street, an old-fashioned chop house famous for its rump steak puddings.

'How is your practice going?' Ambrose asked as his meal was set before him.

'Not bad. I have had some successful outcomes for several high wealth clients, at long last I'm beginning to make a name for myself.'

'Ah! You can pick and choose then.'

'To some degree, I still take on poorer clients, injustice is what motivates me. I adjust my fee accordingly.'

Edward tucked into his steak pudding.

'Talking about fees,' began Ambrose, 'I have a very strong feeling that my current client will avoid paying them.'

Frowning, Edward wiped his mouth. 'Why? Am I allowed to ask who?'

'Lord Arlington. Heard of him?'

Edward shook his head. 'Not that I recall.' He swallowed the last of his beer. With satisfied sighs they finished their meal and pushed their plates to one side.

'Would you like to come back for a nightcap?'

'Excellent idea. I'm sure you want to talk about your case, can we call at my place to pick up a bag, then I can stay overnight if it's going to be a late night.' They paid their dues and caught a Hansom back to Century Square.

'That looks like a cab outside your house,' remarked Edward as their cab slowed down.

'We've missed whoever it was,' replied Ambrose, 'it's pulling away.'

Frowning, he asked the driver to wait.

'Expecting trouble?'

'I don't know, I put an advertisement in the personal columns so it might be in response to that.'

Edward rolled his eyes but said nothing.

As soon as they entered the hall, Finch met them with a worried look on his face.

'Who was our visitor?' Ambrose asked as Finch took Edward's bag.

'No, visitor, sir. It was Mallory going out. We received a note asking to meet at the landlady's house at eleven o'clock, if we wanted information. I'm so sorry sir, I did try to persuade her not to go.'

'You should have gone with her, Finch! It's bound to be a trap.' Ambrose gave an exasperated sigh and glared at Finch.

'I didn't, sir, because I firmly believe this house is the target, and the meeting is a mere decoy. I couldn't risk leaving the house unattended,' his face a picture of misery.

'I did my level best to protect her by giving her a gun.'

'A gun?' Edward was aghast. 'Mallory with a gun? Oh, for God's sake, I'd better go after her. I know the address.'

'She knows how to shoot, sir.'

'I don't doubt it, that's what worries me.' Edward dashed out of the house into the waiting cab.

'Do you really think this house is the target?'

Finch nodded as he took Ambrose's hat and cane. 'I do sir, I feel it deep in my bones. The only thing I'm not sure about is why.'

'Burglary?'

'That or worse.'

'Let's hope it's burglary then.' They moved upstairs to his study.

'You'd better bring me a whisky and get one for yourself. We've got a lot of thinking and planning to do. I just hope Sanderson gets to Mallory first.'

******

Edward was furious that a road had been blocked due to an accident, unusual for an evening; they had to take an alternative route. When they finally arrived, he asked the driver to wait. He jumped out of the cab and ran into the house. Darkness met him; however, he knew the layout of the house. Hearing voices, he resisted the urge to shout Mallory's name, preferring instead to remain silent. He caught a snatch of conversation coming from the kitchen, a small gleam of candlelight showing near the door.

'You alright, Joe? Can you 'ear me? We gotta move.'

'The bitch got me! I reckon she's broken me jaw.' The voice was whining. 'I didn't know she 'ad a gun, Arthur, she got me in the thigh, mate.'

'Surprised a female got the better of you.'

'Look, she took me by surprise! I was expecting a gent, not a bleeding bitch of a female.' He moaned in pain. 'Me leg mate, I'm bleeding to death.'

''Ere, take me neckerchief and tie it round your leg. Told you I 'ad your back. Got 'er good and proper. She ain't going anywhere.'

A muscle in Edward's cheek twitched, he clenched his fists and moved silently forward.

'What about the bitch upstairs? I left her tied up.'

'We need to scarper quick. Can you walk?'

'Just about, me jaw 'urts where she kicked me.'

'Come on.'

Edward heard, rather than saw, them coming. Their footsteps echoed on the tiled floor. The flickering candlelight revealed shadows moving towards him. He stepped to the side by the stairs and as they drew closer, drove his fist into the face of the nearest man. In his rage he picked up the man and slammed him against the wall. The other man was in no fit state to help his friend, he hobbled away shouting curses.

'Who are you?' Edward growled, holding him by his collar.

The man managed to punch Edward's stomach, as he released his grip the man took his chance and ran from the house.

'Mallory, where are you?'

Running towards the kitchen he almost stumbled over her body.

'Mallory?' He gently put his arm around her and stroked her face to wake her.

'I need you to wake up!'

Slowly she opened her eyes and stared at him in confusion. 'Edward. What are you doing here? Ooh, my head hurts.' She closed her eyes briefly to clear them.

'Are you hurt? Let me see.' He reached up for the candlestick with his other arm and put it on the floor so he could see more clearly. Brushing her hair away from her face he checked for any injury.

'There are no cuts, so that's something.'

'I was hit from behind, Edward, that's why. Can I get up now please?'

'They mentioned another girl, where is she?'

'Gone. It was Mary, I helped her escape. Help me up please.'

He gently placed her on her feet.

'I don't think walking is a good idea, you look very pale. Let me carry you to the cab.'

'No, I'll be fine. I just need a few minutes to clear my head.'

'Hand me your gun.'

'Why? Are you going to shoot me?'

He gave her an exasperated look. 'To make sure it doesn't go off, if you faint.'

He took the pistol from her and put it in his jacket pocket.

'What on earth are you wearing, you look like a gypsy!'

'I do not!'

Her head spinning, she held onto the wall to steady herself. Dizziness engulfed her, she squeezed her eyes shut determined not to faint. After taking a deep breath she gingerly tried taking a few steps but sank to the floor, overcome by giddiness. Muttering an oath, he picked her up.

'Put your arms around my neck, in case you faint,' he said as he carried her out of the house.

She rested her head against his shoulder and sighed. 'You didn't need to carry me; I just needed a few minutes for my head to clear.' She muttered to him. 'The air has helped tremendously, so you can put me down.'

He ignored her and continued to carry her across the road to the cab.

'Why don't you listen to me?'

'It's you that needs to listen,' he replied firmly, as he deposited her on the seat. 'You're in no fit state to make demands, and by the way a thank you wouldn't go amiss.'

'For what?' she demanded as the cab pulled away.

'For coming to your rescue.'

'I didn't need rescuing! I shot a man in the thigh before he could knife me.'

'What? He had a knife?' He turned to glare at her. 'You could have been killed!'

'Well, I wasn't because I shot him. Do keep up, Edward – and I'm the one with the fuzzy head!' She put her hand to the back of her head and winced as her fingers touched a large lump.

'Oh, so you admit you're not compos mentis at the moment?' he said with a smirk. She couldn't see his smirk, but she heard it in his voice, and had to stifle the urge to hit him. It was difficult to argue with a lawyer at the best of times and impossible when your head was hurting.

'I've just got a headache, that's all, so save your rhetoric for court, where it might be more appreciated.' She closed her eyes for the rest of the journey. Edward glanced down at her and smiled, if she was up to arguing then her injury couldn't be serious. He relaxed back into the seat.

Chapter 17

Finch debated whether to lock the front door while waiting for the return of Mallory and Mr Sanderson. He was finding it difficult to concentrate on his tasks, worried that Mallory would be hurt and feeling partly responsible. She had always been the most stubborn of the twins. He checked the kitchen clock – eleven-thirty. He reasoned that a burglary would take place after midnight, it would be too risky before with staff still about. As the grandfather clock in the hall chimed the half hour, he heard the front door open and shut with a bang. It must be Mallory; a thief wouldn't make that much noise.

He rushed upstairs and saw Mr Sanderson carrying her.
'Is madam injured?' Concern etched upon his face.
'Just a head wound, concussion I think, she was knocked unconscious. She needs to be taken to her bedroom.'
'Indeed. I will fetch the laudanum.'
'I will submit to the laudanum, but I shall walk upstairs. Please put me down, Edward. You are making a fuss over ... ' she swallowed hard, suddenly she felt very sick, ' ... over nothing.'
'Not a chance. I will set you on your feet once we have climbed all the stairs. Despite what you say, you should not be walking until your head is better.' He carried her up the first flight of stairs.

At the sound of conversation, Ambrose flew out of his study.
'Mallory, are you alright, you look awful!'
Before she could reply Edward answered him.
'She was knocked unconscious, I think it's just a concussion, it should clear after a few days of rest.'
'Ignore him, Ambrose, I'm absolutely fine ... ' she began, but stopped as another wave of nausea engulfed her. She pushed the feeling away by screwing up her eyes. 'I can walk the rest of the way, thank you,' she said in a small voice.

Edward sighed and set her gently on her feet. 'Just stand there until your head clears,' he advised her gently, he held on to her until he was sure she wouldn't faint.

'I'm fine now, you can let go of me.'

She walked to the staircase and gripped the rail tightly; she was determined not to keel over or be sick. Nobody was fooled, however.

'Enough, Mallory!' Ambrose called as she attempted to climb three steps. 'You are far from fine; you are extremely pale and wobbling all over the place. Let me at least help you.'

He put an arm around her shoulders. 'Come on, lean on me, little sister.' He gently guided her upstairs to her room. Gertrude soon appeared, followed by Finch with the laudanum.

'I'll take it from here, sir.' Gertrude took hold of Mallory's arm and the bottle of laudanum.

'I'll stay with her during the night,' she said quietly as she closed the door.

******

Finch locked the front door and took the brandy decanter into the study.

'I shall do my rounds in a minute or two, sir. Soon it will be midnight and we need to put the plan into action.'

Returning to the kitchen he peered under the table.

'Archie, it's time to do the locking up.' He watched Archie crawl out of his makeshift bed.

'You're getting too big to sleep under there now, we need to find you a proper bedroom.'

'I like it under there, Mr Finch, I ain't used to a bed.'

'Nevertheless, my lad, I can't have you sleeping there permanently. You've been here a few months now and grown taller, so we need a permanent room for you. Leave it with me. Now go and lock up.'

Finch prepared for the plan. He produced rope, candles and lanterns. He picked up a wooden truncheon and the black umbrella with the hidden swordstick.

'All locked, Mr Finch.'

'Good, we'll check them every half hour. Go and fetch the silver salver from the hall table and bring it in here, it will be safer.'

Archie scooted off and Finch gathered the items and took them to the study.

'We'll need a lantern each. I've got rope in case we need to apprehend the villain. We'll need a weapon each too.'

'Here's Mallory's gun.' Edward produced the pocket pistol and put it on the table.

'Choose your weapon of choice then gentlemen,' advised Ambrose.

'You go first, sir.'

Ambrose, looking at the choices, chose the pistol.

Edward removed the umbrella sword and placed it by his side.

Finch picked up the truncheon with a smile.

'If it is burglary they were planning, they are likely to search the drawing room, I'll sit in that room,' Ambrose confirmed.

'Shall I stay here in the study?' Edward asked.

Finch nodded. 'I'll stay in the basement area, so I can cover the ground floor if necessary.'

'Are we agreed with the plan?' They all nodded. 'Good. Let us take our places then.'

Finch did another check of the locks. The first door he checked was the hall back door. The handle turned when he tried it, the door began to open. He locked it, a thoughtful expression on his face. Young Archie had said he locked everything, had he missed this door? With a growing concern he crept into the kitchen and spoke softly to Archie who was back under the table.

'Archie, was the back door definitely locked?'

Archie poked his head out. 'Course it was, Mr Finch, I locked all the windows and doors, just as I do every night.'

'Then we have a problem. It's unlocked.'

Quickly he made his way to the front door, his worst fears were realised – that too was unlocked. Either Archie hadn't done his job at all, or the happening had started. He shook his head; Archie was diligent in all his tasks. He went back down to pick up his truncheon.

'It's started, Archie. Stay under the table.'

Finch crept upstairs, truncheon in hand. He didn't bother with the lantern; its light might alert the intruder and he knew every nook and cranny of the house. Quietly he checked the morning and dining rooms – there were no signs of intruders. The grandfather clock struck one o'clock. In the stillness of the night, the chime had an eerie ring to it. Like a shadow, he stealthily moved upstairs. On the top stair he paused, listening for any sounds. He thought he heard soft voices coming from the drawing room. He opened the study door and faced the point of the umbrella.

'It's me, sir,' he hissed to Edward.

Edward immediately withdrew the umbrella.

'What is it?'

'It's started, I think it's happening in the drawing room.'

Edward clicked on the umbrella clip to release the sword. He nodded at Finch.

'I'm ready.' He picked up the lantern.

Finch filled his pockets with bits of rope. Cautiously they moved to the drawing room. Archie not wanting to miss out on the action had followed Finch. He placed himself at the top of the stairs, unseen by all.

Chapter 18

Ambrose sat in a chair in the corner of the room, the lantern at his feet covered by a cloth, he didn't want the room to glow. He placed the pistol on his lap, and stretched out comfortably, it could be a long night. He was glad in a way that Mallory was indisposed, she would have insisted on taking part, it was one less worry. The house had its own noises at night which he knew off by heart, but there was one noise that was different. He listened intently, yes there it was again, a shuffling noise. He moved his legs back from their relaxed position and picked up the pistol. It would take but a moment to cock it, but for now he trained it on the door.

His hearing was excellent, he picked up whispering outside the door. So, there were two of them, he thought. It would be interesting to see how this would pan out. The door began to open slowly, two dark figures crept in.
  'Let's try this room, we'll strip it bare, bound to 'ave something valuable.'
  A glow of light suddenly appeared in the corner. Horrified, they turned towards it.
  'Good evening, gentlemen, I've been waiting for you.'
  Ambrose levelled the pistol at their chests.
  'Don't even think about moving. I'm an excellent shot. There are four bullets in this gun, the odds are against you leaving this room alive.'
  'Www ... what do yer want?' a gruff voice asked whilst the taller man attempted to retreat through the door.
  'It's not your day,' Finch remarked as he clobbered him over the head with the truncheon. It barely had any effect on him. He shook his head and barged them aside and made for the stairs.

Archie was too quick for him. He stuck out his foot and tripped him; the man toppled head over heels down the stairs, landing in a heap. Finch ran down the stairs and held him down while Edward tied his hands and his feet with the rope. Dazed, the man looked up.

'Who the 'ell are you? Bleeding magician?'

'More to the point, who are you?' Edward replied.

'Archie, fetch a policeman.'

'What I want is your name,' Ambrose stated. The man had stood petrified when Finch burst through the door. He had gained a bit more courage since he'd found himself alone.

'You ain't getting it, you'll 'ave to shoot me instead. Then they'll 'ang you.' he sneered.

'Oh, I wouldn't be so sure. I believe someone has gone to fetch the police. Inspector Johnson is a friend of mine. Now, let's try it again. Who are you, and what are you doing in my house?'

'Yer weren't supposed to be 'ere,' he snarled.

'I know that, now tell me something I don't know – your name.'

He shook his head. 'Yer gonna 'ave to shoot me!'

'Oh, it would be a pleasure, I assure you, but Inspector Johnson would rather I keep you alive.'

Edward appeared with more rope. 'It's two against one now, hands behind your back.' Edward secured his wrists tightly.

'Finch wants to put them in the cellar until the police arrive.'

Ambrose and Edward escorted their prisoner to the cellar, made him sit down, then tied his ankles together.

******

Breakfast was over by the time Inspector Johnson arrived, and Finch hastily made him a bacon sandwich.

'You'd better come clean and tell me what's been going on.' He bit into his sandwich, the butter oozing out of the bread.

'My sister received a note stating they had information on the friends, and to meet at eleven o'clock at 9 Bell Street.'

'The landlady's house?'

'Yes,' replied Edward quickly, to stop Ambrose giving too much away.

'As Ambrose wasn't there – he was out with me incidentally – Mallory decided to go. She is not a fool, Inspector, she knew it could be dangerous, so she took her mother's little pistol as protection. To cut a long story short, she was attacked by two men with a knife, and shot one in the thigh as self-defence. She had been knocked unconscious when I found her.'

The Inspector groaned. 'I will need a statement from her.'

Edward shook his head. 'Not today, she is badly concussed. She did, however, hear their names – Arthur and Joe.'

'I see, and where is this gun?'

'Here it is.' He handed it over. Ambrose flashed Edward a grateful look.

The Inspector sighed with relief and finished his sandwich before replying.

'In that case, I won't need to bother her. It's not a gun, just a close protection pistol, so it's of no interest to me.' He wiped his hands. 'Where are these burglars then?'

Inspector Johnson surveyed the prisoners with a critical eye as he entered the cellar.

'Oh, I know these two alright! The big one is Dick Archer, a muscle for hire and Fred's brother. The skinny one, well that's Fergus Tate, finally they have been caught red handed, so I can charge them. It's turning out to be a good day.'

'Then these are John Kendle's so-called friends.'

The Inspector nodded. 'And they are going to tell me exactly where Mr Kendle is.'

'Never 'eard of 'im!' Dick Archer immediately responded.

'Me neiver!' Fergus Tate confirmed.

'That's a shame, in that case I am going to charge you both with Mrs Strange's murder.' He eyed them both with a gleam in his eye.

'What? You can't pin that on me, I weren't there!'

'Me neiver!'

'Oh, but we can, as Joe ratted on you.'

'Me bruvver would never do that!' Dick was confident.

'Wouldn't he? Your brother was shot last night.'

'Shot?' Alarmed, Dick forgot to be clever. 'I never did trust that weasel, Arthur Cripps.'

'So, Arthur was there with your brother last night?' the Inspector grinned.

Dick saw his mistake and tried to bluff his way out.

'Yer said 'e was. I distinctly 'eard yer.'

'Yeah, I 'eard 'im too!' Fergus backed him up.

The Inspector shook his head. 'No, I didn't, because ...' he leaned forward to gloat at them, 'I didn't know they were there, you've just confirmed my suspicions.'

'Then yer was lying about me bruvver being shot.'

'Course 'e was Dick, don't listen to 'im.'

'No, he was shot alright.'

'Me bruvver ain't dead 'is 'e?' Fear gripped Dick.

The Inspector pulled a face and said nothing.

Dick put his head in his hands. 'Me little bruvver killed! I wish to God 'e 'adn't listened to that weasel. Will yer get Arfur for me if I tell yer what 'appened?'

'Don't do it!' yelled Fergus. 'Can't yer see 'e's lying?'

'I don't care abaht anyone 'cept Joe! It were Arfur who decided to kill 'er. She found them ransacking the 'ouse so she 'ad to die. Joe told me abaht later, as 'e were upset by the killing.'

'And John Kendle?'

'Don't know, all I knows was 'e were their friend.'

'Yer should've kept yer mouth shut!' whined Fergus. 'The Inspector didn't say Joe was dead!'

Crestfallen, Dick looked at the Inspector.

The Inspector grinned. 'He was shot in the thigh, but we'll get him and Arthur.'

A howl of rage emerged from Dick.

'Take them to the station and lock them up.' He nodded at the constables.

'I hope your sister recovers soon, Mr Weston.'

He made a move to leave but Ambrose waylaid him.

'About Miss James' burglary, can I read the report please? I have been commissioned to find the necklace.'

The Inspector eyed him thoughtfully. 'Have you now? I'll see what I can do.'

Chapter 19

Mallory felt better, although her head still hurt it was nowhere near as painful as yesterday. She tenderly sat up, expecting a wave of dizziness to swamp her senses. Surprised to find it didn't occur, she gingerly got out of bed. Gertrude had disappeared, presumably to fetch her some breakfast. She walked around her room, moving slowly, testing out how fast she could walk before she felt woozy. She discovered it only happened when she turned or moved quickly – excellent news, it meant she could go downstairs and be useful.

Gertrude, bringing her a late breakfast, was shocked to see Mallory walking around.
'Ma'am, you should be in bed!'
'No, I shouldn't. I'm fine and I don't need any more laudanum. If I walk carefully and don't turn quickly, my head is fine. What's for breakfast?'
Gertrude offered her toast, marmalade and coffee, which she accepted gratefully.
'It seems, ma'am, that we missed an eventful night. We had burglars!'
Mallory looked up in surprise. 'Finch was right, the house was the target. Help me get dressed, I want to hear more from my brother.'

Duly gowned she made her way down to his study. She had guessed right; he was in there along with Finch and Edward.
'What are you doing up?' Ambrose asked her in concern. 'You need to rest.'
'I've had all the rest I need, thank you, there is nothing like boredom to make you feel instantly better. I hear I missed an eventful night – shame.'
Ambrose filled her in. Edward added to it.
'Mallory, I told the Inspector that your pistol belonged to your mother and that you shot in self-defence as you were attacked by

two men. I would advise you to stick to that story if he should ask you, otherwise it might cause awkward questions as to how you had the gun.'

'But Finch gave—'

'No!' Edward told her sharply. 'Both your brother and I have said it was your mother's, to say anything different would amount to perjury by us. The Inspector is happy with that explanation, do not muddy the waters.'

She nodded acceptance. 'If they killed the landlady, could they have killed John Kendle?'

'It's a possibility, certainly. However, I believe the Inspector still thinks John had something to do with it, there's no evidence to the contrary.'

'Then we need to visit The Rising Sun, somebody might have seen something.'

'We will at some stage, but let's see if the Inspector can get more out the prisoners – he may even be able to trace Joe and Arthur.'

'Our next move should be to visit Miss James.'

'I need to visit her; you will stay here and rest.'

'Do not tell me—'

'No arguments, Lory! Stay here in case there are other replies to the advertisement.'

'I'll stay with her to prevent her dashing off if another note arrives.' Edward confirmed.

Mallory sighed. 'Honestly, you are all making too much of my headache, but I accept it would be sensible to wait in for other replies – but that is the *only* reason I shall stay here.'

'Good, that's sorted then.'

******

Ambrose rang the bell at Miss James' house in Symon's Mews. Shyly the maid let him in. He removed his hat and gave it to her along with his cane. She looked a little lost as to where to put it.

'I'm sure a hat stand would suffice,' he suggested gently. She smiled in relief and asked him to wait.

'Miss will see you now.'

Elowen was sitting in the same chair as before, artfully chosen so that the sunlight fell upon her face.

'Do sit down, Mr Weston. How may I help you this time?'

'I have spoken to the Inspector, he asked me to relay to you that the necklace has not yet been found.'

'Why are you involved? I understood you would be advising your client that I would not be returning the necklace once recovered.'

'My client now wishes me to trace the necklace. I have explained to him that if it is recoverable the police would take charge of it.'

She frowned. 'Why? The necklace belongs to me.'

'The police will hold it as evidence until the culprit is charged.'

'I see.' She remained silent.

'There are a few questions I would like to ask you, please don't take offence at them, but they may help to find your necklace.'

'You are not disputing it's my necklace?'

'No, I am not, Miss James.'

'I have previously asked you before to call me Elowen.'

'Elowen, I really will hand it to the police, you needn't have any fears on that score.'

She sighed several times as though unable to make up her mind, then after a keen glance at Ambrose she replied.

'Very well, ask away. I can't promise to answer though.'

'Firstly, my sister would like to know about your ex-maid.'

'Her name is Kitty Bunbury.' She frowned. 'I believe you already have a note of that.'

'Yes, we do, but we need to know more about her. Did she live here, or do you have an address for her?'

'None of my staff live here – may I call you Ambrose?' He nodded.

'Kitty only worked part of the week, I didn't need a full-time maid, she either worked days or evenings depending on whether I was performing.'

'Do you have her address please?'

'No, why would I?'

Ambrose sighed. 'I thought that might be the case, but it was worth asking. Who else did you employ around that time?'

Elowen frowned once more. 'There was a handyman, but ... he was only here for a few days. Kitty complained about something not working, so I told her to find someone to fix it. I briefly saw him once as I left for rehearsals, I only remember because he was kind enough to hail a cab for me. That's it, apart from a cook, she has been with me for a long time though.'

'Could you tell me about the failed opera. How much money did you lose? An acquaintance of mine invested in it too, although his loss wasn't great.'

She stiffened. 'That is my business, Ambrose.'

'Indeed, I don't wish to cause offence, but it must have been devastating for you, it is hard to recover financially from a great loss.'

'It is hard, but nothing is impossible. Now do you have any more questions?'

'Was the necklace insured?'

She pursed her lips, her annoyance evident.

'With respect, Ambrose, that is my business, not yours. I would appreciate not being asked such personal questions. Shall we talk about something else or is that the end of the interview?'

Ambrose knew it was better to end the interview on a pleasant note.

'I understand you are singing at Lady Hamley's ball.'

She smiled. 'Yes, I'm looking forward to it.' She looked curiously at him. 'You seem to be very well informed about my movements.'

He laughed. 'No mystery, I have received an invitation from Lady Hamley for her ball, so I shall be there along with my sister.'

They talked for a little while about operas until regretfully Ambrose decided he must return home. Sitting in a cab he reflected on her answers. She seemed to know very little about her ex-maid, Kitty, or was that a ploy? Why was she refusing to say whether it was insured? How much did she really lose in the failed venture – enough to commit fraud?

Chapter 20

Mallory was sitting in the drawing room sipping tea with Edward, whilst Gertrude was sitting at the back of the room with her mending basket. She heard the jangle of the front doorbell and wondered who the visitor was.

'There is a young man downstairs in reply to the advertisement, madam.' Finch informed her. 'Where would you like to see him?'

Before she could reply, however, Edward spoke.

'I shall sit with Mallory, Finch. I do not think the drawing room is appropriate.'

'Very well, sir, I will show him into the morning room.'

'What's wrong with seeing him up here, may I ask?'

'It's a large room, Mallory, it might make him tongue-tied. You will need to put him at his ease, to get the most out of him.'

She conceded the point. 'Could you fetch me my notebook please Edward. It's in the bureau.' She got up carefully, pleased to find her headache no worse.

'Hold on to my arm, if you need to.'

He solicitously walked by her side down the stairs, ready to steady her if she stumbled. She didn't.

'His name, madam, is Billy Ashe. He works at the Rising Sun,' Finch announced as he opened the door for them.

'Hello, Billy. You have some information for us I believe?' Mallory smiled briefly at him, noting the wax stains on the lapel of his jacket. 'Take a seat please.'

'I'd rather stand, if it's all the same to you, miss.'

'Well, what information do you have?' Edward asked him.

'It's like this. I work shifts at the Rising Sun. Those names you mentioned, they are regulars there. Thick as thieves they are, never see them apart. They 'ave anuvver mate, 'is name is John Kendle. He ain't quite so regular, only comes a couple of times a week.' He stared at them, his cap hanging out of his pocket.

Edward was used to hesitant witnesses; he had plenty of experience of coaxing information from them. He gave him an encouraging smile.

'Please continue.'

'Well, one night this John fella wins a prize. He and the others celebrated by getting him shickered, begging your pardon miss, I mean very drunk. He was real shickery after a bit so they said they would take him 'ome. I ain't seen 'im since, mind.'

Mallory scribbled down the information.

'Do you know where they live?'

'Near Redcross Court, Southwark.'

'Where is the Rising Sun?' Edward frowned, he wasn't liking the area, too many criminal gangs, Red Cross Court was well known for it, even the police were wary of visiting it. He liked it even less when Billy told him.

'How do you know where they lived, you must have lots of customers.' Edward was sceptical, how much of this was the truth? Billy had been a bit evasive with some of his answers.

'Oh, they got a little business going, dropping parcels off to people. I think that might be 'ow John Kendle knew them, I think 'e did a bit of side work for them, if you know what I mean.'

'No, I don't,' Mallory replied, 'you will have to be a bit clearer.'

Billy looked at Edward in surprise.

'Just answer the lady.'

Billy shrugged. 'Well, 'e 'ad a main job, I understand, but 'e needed a bit extra like, so 'e did some parcel dropping for them as well.'

Edward folded his arms. 'Let me get this straight, how do you know all this from being behind a bar?'

Billy looked at his shoes. 'I did a bit meself for them.' He looked up with a fierce expression. 'But then I got this job, they knew the landlord you see, so they stopped asking me to do parcel runs.'

'There's something you're not telling me,' Mallory looked him in the eye. 'I shan't be satisfied until I know.'

Billy fingered the cap in his pocket and sighed. 'The Rising Sun ain't the best of places, miss, some of the regulars are criminals, but not all of them. This friend of the three men, he were nice. I don't like those three, though; I thought I might be able to earn meself some money from this information, and get away from the Rising Sun.'

'That I believe, but what about their address – is that bit true or a lie?'

'None of it is lies! I knew their address from doing them parcels. I always 'ad to meet them at a place just off Borough High Street, but I saw one coming from the direction of Red Cross Court. If they knew I was 'ere I'd lose me job. Those fellas are in with the landlord so I gotta be careful.'

'What was in the parcels?' Edward frowned. This conversation was not going in a direction he liked.

'Dunno – and that ain't a lie, you didn't dare ask questions.'

Mallory had a question. 'What was the raffle for?'

Billy gave a wry smile. 'Oh, it were a regular thing. The landlord was always pleased to 'elp local causes so we often 'ad a raffle to raise money for them. One of the prizes was always a keg of beer. 'E can be good like that, but in uvver ways 'e can be a right ba—'

'Mind your language,' Edward interrupted him.

'The paper said there was a reward.'

'Can you read?'

'A little but I'm not very good, a bit slow.'

'Then,' Edward asked him icily, 'how do you know what the paper said?'

Billy sighed and shifted his feet. 'Because the landlord can read. Someone left a newspaper behind. Don't know who, but the landlord picked it up and was looking through it when 'e saw the advertisement. 'E called to the three fellas and read it out loud to them. I was behind the bar wiping the glasses and overheard 'im.'

'Wait here please,' Mallory informed him. She and Edward moved into the hall. Finch was by the door.

'Did you hear it all?' she enquired of Finch.

'Most of it, madam.'

'Should we pay him?' she asked them.

Finch nodded. 'You might need him again.'

'If you are too generous though,' warned Edward, 'you might find he will keep coming back with made up stories.'

Finch had a solution. They both nodded. She winced at the movement. Edward noticed.

'I'll deal with this,' he told her.

'This is a one-off payment,' he informed Billy as they re-entered the morning room. 'There will be no further payment, even if we need your services again. Do you understand?'

Billy nodded. He held out his hand.

'How much do you get paid each week?'

'Eighteen shillings usually, if I work every night.'

Edward raised an eyebrow.

Billy shuffled his feet. 'Alright, fifteen then.'

'Do you work every night?'

Billy looked at his feet and mumbled, 'not usually.'

'Here is ten shillings.' Edward handed him five florins. 'I don't want to hear of any more requests for payment, this payment includes all future information.'

'Thank you, sir.' Finch showed him out.

'Doesn't do to be too generous,' Edward told Finch as he handed him the other five florins. Finch smiled and nodded approval.

Edward and Mallory returned to the drawing room.

'When your brother returns, I will go back to my chambers. Will you be alright, Mallory?'

'Of course! Why would I not be?'

'Hmm ...' he said drily as he took a seat near the window. 'You still look pale and your head is hurting. Are you sure about going to the Ball?'

'I shall be perfectly fit for the Ball.'

Ambrose came in at that moment. 'Glad to hear it, Lory. Elowen is going to sing several arias.'

'Is she now,' Mallory was amused. 'Did you get answers to the questions?'

'Some. She was a little cagey on the question of the failed opera and insurance.'

'We had a visitor whilst you were out. Another response from your advertisement.'

'Oh?'

Edward repeated the information.

'We'll have to pass that information to the police, next time we see the Inspector, but do you think he is a reliable witness? Can we use him again?'

Edward nodded. 'It was a fairly honest account; I think it was just his expectation of the reward that was at fault. At least you will have an informer inside the public house.'

'I wonder what was in those parcels?' mused Ambrose.

Edward got up. 'I shall return to my chambers, Weston, if you need my services just come and fetch me. Otherwise, I shall see you both in a few days for the Ball.'

'Ah, about that,' Ambrose said, 'Lady Marsham is collecting both Mallory and Mrs Fortescue. How about you and I share a cab?'

'Glad to. I'll come here.'

******

On the day of the ball, Finch took some time out in the morning to visit a friend for an update on Elowen's maid. Several days had passed since his initial enquiry. His friend could usually be relied upon to provide background details, but this time he had drawn a blank. That was suspicious. There is always a trace if given the right information. However, his friend assured him that just because the first search had failed it didn't mean she couldn't be found. A deeper search would be necessary, which would take longer. Sadly, time was of the essence to Finch, the longer the case dragged on the less successful the outcome and of course payment. He was well aware of Lord Arlington's displeasure at the amount of the fees. Nevertheless, he requested his friend to start the search, he also asked about local fences, if the necklace was stolen then a fence would have been used. He hoped Mr Weston would approve.

He returned to the house only to find Ruby complaining in the kitchen.

'It ain't fair, it just ain't fair, why was I not told about them burglars?' she demanded of Archie and Gertrude.

'I'm always the last to know about anyfink around 'ere,' she continued. 'If you'd 'ave told me I might 'ave been able to 'elp catch them, I'd 'ave shown them a fing or two. Look 'ow I 'elped madam down the drainpipe!'

'Ruby, yer weren't supposed to speak of that!' Archie declared horrified.

'What's this about a drainpipe?' Finch asked her.

'Nuffink, Mr Finch.' He glared at her.

Hurriedly she went back to her moaning. 'Anyway, I should 'ave been told about them burglars. I could 'ave 'ad me precious 'air clip stolen! Me grandma must be turning in 'er grave at the danger I was in.'

She drew a breath, before she could carry on ranting Finch intervened.

'You were not the only one who didn't know, Ruby,' he said firmly. 'Madam and Gertrude were also unaware. I suggest you get on with your duties.'

Ruby, disappointed she was going to be deprived of her audience, went into a sulk and stomped off.

'What is this about a drainpipe?' he asked again, with a steely glance in their direction. They remained silent.

He sighed. 'Never mind, I shall pretend I never heard it. So, Gertrude, is everything ready for madam for the ball this evening?'

'Yes, Mr Finch, it's just a case of getting her dressed. I'm ever so pleased that her head is much better.'

'I'm pleased to hear it. I shall be concentrating on sir this evening, so we'll eat after they have left for the ball.'

He watched them depart to their various duties aware there was a secret between them. He didn't like secrets amongst staff, it led to unpleasantness, he would have to watch and see how it played out.

Chapter 21

Gertrude fastened the back of the silk, peacock-blue ball gown and adjusted the off-the-shoulder sleeves.

'You look a picture, ma'am, it makes the most of your blue eyes,' she said with a proud smile. Mallory's copper-coloured hair was piled at the back of head and cascaded down in neat coils at the back of her head and pinned firmly into place at the nape. Several little blue silk flowers had been carefully placed in her hair; the effect was stunning.

'Thank you, Gertrude, you are so clever, I don't know what I'd do without you.'

Gertrude blushed. 'You will need a wrap, ma'am, it will be chilly late at night.'

She placed it round her shoulders and smoothed out any creases, standing back to see the results.

'Hmm. You still look a little pale, if you pinch your cheeks, ma'am, it will put a little colour in them.' Mallory did as she was told.

'Better?'

Gertrude nodded. 'Much better. Be careful when you walk, I don't want you tripping over the back of the skirt as it trails a bit.'

She helped her downstairs to the drawing room. Ambrose did a double take.

'Goodness, how beautiful you are, sister dear. Your dance card will be full.'

'I'm not sure I want to dance all night. I plan to sit and watch most of the time.'

He shook his head smiling. 'That won't happen.'

'We'll see.'

Finch arrived to announce the carriage had arrived.

'I'll help you into it, Edward should be here shortly.'

Lord and Lady Marsham greeted her as Ambrose closed the carriage door.

'You look marvellous,' Isabella declared, admiring her gown.

'We will call for Mrs Fortescue, there should be enough room, despite our gowns.'

Lord Marsham's eyes twinkled. 'Always ready to have a gal sitting on my lap!'

'Linus, really!' Isabella laughed, a light tinkling sound. 'There will be plenty of room for our gowns if you tuck in your long legs!'

He chuckled and drew his legs in. 'That suit you, my dear?'

Mrs Fortescue was duly collected, and they made their way sedately through the traffic to Lady Hamley's house.

Ambrose and Edward were on the front steps waiting to greet them.

Ambrose smiled at them as they descended from the carriage. Edward offered his arm to Mallory whilst Ambrose escorted Mrs Fortescue, followed by Lord and Lady Marsham.

'You look ...' Edward began, searching for the right word.

'Like a gypsy?'

'Most certainly not like a gypsy!'

'I'll take that as a compliment then.'

'Please do,' Edward smiled as they made their way to the ballroom. Lady Hamley greeted them by the door. 'Please feel free to wander the grounds and any rooms on this floor. We have an excellent library.'

'It's very grand, isn't it?' remarked Edward as they entered a large room. Intricately carved mouldings surrounded the blue wallpapered panels giving relief to the cream walls. Several large chandeliers hung from the ceiling. Against the far wall, a small dais held several musicians busy tuning their instruments.

Mallory received her dance card. Linus immediately requested the first dance.

'My love,' he said to Isabella, 'I shall have the third dance with you. That will be the end of my dancing, you will be pleased to note.'

Isabella laughed. 'I must warn you, Mallory, my husband might tread on your toes.'

'May I request the third dance, Mallory?' Edward enquired.

'Be careful, Lory, do not over-tire yourself, you are still recovering.'

Mallory rolled her eyes.

'That's very good advice, my dear', Lady Marsham replied, 'both myself and Mrs Fortescue will insist upon it.'

Mallory gave in with good grace. She duly marked her card with her partners names.

'Do not offer me the last dance, Rosy,' she warned her brother, 'you should instead be offering that to Miss James. She might wish to dance after her performance.'

'What an excellent idea!' confirmed Mrs Fortescue. 'I spotted her over in the corner. Come along, Mr Weston, you can introduce me to her.' Left with no choice other than to obey, Ambrose followed Mrs Fortescue.

The orchestra struck up and the dancing began. The dance floor was crowded. The less energetic sat on chairs at the edge of the room watching the flashes of breathtaking gowns, as twirling couples swirled to the strains of the music. Isabella was true to her word and rescued her after the first dance.

'Are your toes still intact?' smiled Isabella, as she insisted they sit out the next dance.

'Of course! Lord Marsham was step perfect.'

'Well, that will be a first!' laughed Isabella. 'How are you feeling, my dear?'

'I'm perfectly well, thank you. Everybody is making far too much fuss for my liking.'

'You can't be too careful, Mallory. It is beginning to get hot and stuffy and will not help your head.' Both unfurled their fans and used them to waft some cool air around them. Mallory waved her fan near her cheeks; she was feeling slightly flushed. She cooled down by the time Edward came to fetch her for his dance with her.

It was the Viennese Waltz. The floor was once again bursting with vibrancy and movement. Edward noted her flushed cheeks as he expertly navigated her through the throng of dancers, holding her firmly around her waist.

'I paid a visit to the library, it has a Burke's Peerage volume,' he said in her ear as he twirled her around. 'It's so crowded in here, what say you to waltzing our way to the terrace and going to the library. We can enter it from the terrace. Nobody will notice we are missing.'

Mallory rapidly agreed, she was already tired from the dancing, but wasn't ready to admit it. Edward waltzed her across the room and out onto the terrace.

'Oh, thank you, it's nice to get some air.' She stood still for a few seconds to catch her breath. 'That was some waltz!'

He smiled. 'It was rather fast wasn't it! The library is the second door on the left. I thought you might want to look up the Arlington family. I had to admit to your brother that I knew nothing about them. Maybe we can change that after looking them up.'

'That's an excellent suggestion, thank you.'

Mallory entered the room as Edward closed the glass door behind them. She glanced around the room and noted the floor to ceiling bookshelves and green leather chairs; Edward was locking the main door.

She frowned at him. 'What are you doing?'

'I wanted to spend some time alone with you, is that so wrong of me?'

She put her head to one side as she considered. '... no,' she concluded. 'Please unlock the door, Edward, it's making me uncomfortable.'

'I apologise,' he replied. 'That wasn't my intention.' He unlocked the door.

'What was your intention?'

'Just to stop anyone intruding on my time with you.' He moved towards her.

'The only way I seem to be able to spend time with you is by getting involved with your cases.' He gave her a meaningful look. 'I am a patient man, Mallory, but my patience isn't infinite. I won't play second fiddle for long.'

'What?'

'I'm not going to insult your intelligence by explaining.' Looking at her nonplussed face, he sighed, crossed the room to the far bookshelf and pulled out a volume.

'Here it is.' Edward directed her to a pair of green leather club chairs next to each other, she sank into one gratefully. She took the volume from him.

He pushed his chair against hers so the arms touched. She ran her finger down the listings for Arlington.

'Oh, that's odd!'

'What's wrong?'

She put the book on the arm of the chair and Edward leaned across to look at it, their heads touching. He breathed in her delicate perfume.

She shook her head. 'I don't recognise any of the names.'

'How do you mean?'

She glanced at him. 'Well, my notes differ.'

'Perhaps they don't want you knowing about their ancestors, especially if there are skeletons in that particular cupboard.'

'Oh, I see.' She gave him a rueful smile. 'Yes, that would explain it and their reticence to talk about them.' She smiled at him. 'Thank you, Edward.'

'My pleasure. Why don't you summarise the case for me, begin with Lord Arlington's appearance.'

He gently took the book from her and closed it. 'I don't think this is going to provide any further information.'

He listened intently as she detailed his clothing, serpent ring and his watch, followed by his demeanour.

'A man with impeccable taste.' Edward remarked with a smile. She returned his smile before recounting the case.

'You think that there is something wrong about this case, yet you cannot put your finger on it,' he concluded.

'Yes exactly.'

He gave her a questioning look. 'What are you most worried about?'

He gazed at her as she gathered her thoughts, smiling at the way she wrinkled her nose as she thought.

'Pinnerton Lodge, I think. That house is hiding something, almost as though it has a secret.' She looked at him. 'I suppose you are going to laugh and say it's my imagination.'

He shook his head. 'No, I'm not laughing. Sometimes I feel that about a witness's statement, gut instinct tells me something isn't accurate, yet everything seems to be correct.'

'What do you do to solve it?'

'I scrutinise every single word. My advice is to keep evaluating it until something begins to make sense.'

She nodded. 'Thank you, Edward.' She smiled across at him.

Edward nodded. 'I'll make some enquiries for you. But now,' he added looking at the carriage clock on the mantelpiece, 'it's time for supper.'

He held out his hand to help her out of the chair, his dark eyes searching her face.

'I won't wait forever, Mallory,' he whispered after gently raising her to her feet. Smiling, he offered her his arm as they made their way to supper.

******

Supper was a splendid affair, plenty of food and drink. It needed to be for the dances were energetic. As they finished their ices, Lady Hamley announced that Miss Elowen James would be starting her recital in a few minutes. There was a rush for the ballroom. Seats had now been arranged in rows and the small orchestra were preparing their instruments ready for the recital. Miss James entered the room to a rapturous applause.

'Thank you.' She nodded to the audience, gracefully making her way to stand by the grand piano, a musician already seated in front of the ivory keys. Mallory was seated next to her brother, she smiled as she saw the delight on his face, but decided she would not comment on it.

Miss James had a beautiful voice, each song brought out different depths and range to her voice. She was definitely a star in the making, Mallory thought, as they stood to give her a standing ovation.

Lady Hamley walked to the front and asked for quiet, waiting for everyone to be seated before giving a short speech.

'Thank you, Miss James, for that wonderful recital. It gives me great pleasure to present you with a bouquet of flowers. I think I speak for everyone when I say what a privilege it's been to hear you.'

Again, there was a round of applause.

'Well, that's going to be difficult to top for future hosts,' announced Mrs Fortescue as she politely clapped. 'I pity the person that tries.'

People mingled in small groups chatting whilst the servants returned the chairs to the sides of the room ready for non-dancers to sit and watch the spectacle of the dances. The orchestra had taken a quick break whilst the re-arranging of the room took place.

It had been a beautiful evening, full of warmth and laughter. Now it had come to the last dance, Elowen was still chatting with Ambrose when Edward asked Mallory to dance.

'Can we get some air instead?' she pleaded.

'I really think that's a good idea, Mr Sanderson, poor Mallory is fatigued.'

He smiled. 'Of course, shall we all take a turn in the garden to cool ourselves off?'

'Good idea. It's about time we took a walk, Isabella my love.' Lord Marsham offered his arm to his wife.

Mrs Fortescue declined the walk. 'Oh, I shall stay here and try to spot Miss James and Ambrose dancing. I will let them know where you all are if the dance finishes before your return.'

Careful to avoid the dancers they made their way to the terrace for a late-night wander.

'A stroll is such a good idea, it will cool us down before we make our way home,' Isabella declared. As they walked Isabella and Mallory chatted, with the men dutifully following behind them. Lord Marsham touched Edward's arm.

'I believe I saw a decanter of whisky in the study, Sanderson, how about a nightcap and leave these ladies to their gossip.'

'Gossip?' Isabella replied, turning around. 'Linus, we don't gossip, we talk.'

'If you say so, my dear,' he said affably. 'How about it, Sanderson?'

Chapter 22

Ensconced in comfortable chairs, Lord Marsham poured them each a generous measure of whisky. Edward raised his eyebrows at the size of the measure as he was handed the glass, and decided he wouldn't drink it all.

'Well now, this is cosy, ain't it?'

Edward smiled and took a tiny sip of his whisky, so small that barely any liquid touched his lips.

'Indeed. I was just hearing from Weston about his latest client – Lord Arlington.'

'Oh him!'

Edward was taken aback. 'You know him?'

'Not personally. Years ago, I went to a shooting weekend with a colleague and Lord Arlington was there. Strange fellow, made rather a fuss about the gun not being cleaned properly, used it as an excuse for his poor shooting.'

'You must have an excellent memory.'

Lord Marsham smiled. 'Yes, I have, handy if you work in the Foreign Office.' He sniffed the whisky before taking a sip. 'It's a fairly decent malt.'

He eyed Edward. 'So, what is Weston doing for Arlington – or is it hush hush?'

Edward laughed. 'I don't think it's hush hush, but he didn't reveal what it was, just asked me for advice on a legal matter. I believe he had been to see him at Pinnerton Lodge in Norwood.'

'Pinnerton Lodge you say? How odd?'

Edward raised an eyebrow. 'Why odd?'

'I seem to remember a club member talking about that place.' He frowned. 'I recall it because the name reminded me of a winning horse, I once had a wager on – I haven't had many of those, though,' he conceded, 'as I don't place many wagers.'

'Why was Pinnerton Lodge mentioned?'

'Hmm.' He took a large sip of the whisky. 'I think it may have been in connection with one of his clients … he did mention a name, what was it?' He tapped his fingers on his glass. 'Ah yes! I recall it its—'

The chiming of the clock interrupted him.

'Dear me, is that the time? I think we had better fetch the gals. Drink up, Sanderson, and I will tell you on the way.'

Edward was obliged to take a mouthful before Lord Marsham rose from his chair. Following his lead, he stood and discreetly pushed his glass out of sight.

******

At breakfast the next morning, Mallory told Ambrose about her discoveries.

'That's certainly interesting,' he said. 'Though I'm of the same opinion as Sanderson, there's bound to be a satisfactory explanation.'

She sighed. 'Well, it's a puzzle I'm not sure how to solve.'

'Then don't, wait and see what evolves.'

She poured herself a cup of coffee.

'How's the head today, Lory?' He took a swirl of butter and spread it on his toast. He glanced at her, concerned about her appearance; she looked a little pale this morning, but he knew better than to point that out to her.

'Marvellous.' She sipped her coffee.

'When I had concussion earlier this year, I felt grim for quite a few days, not to mention the rope burns I had when Finch pulled me clear.' He buttered the other slice.

'Oh!' She frowned and paused sipping her coffee, her cup still in mid-air.

'What is it, Lory?' he became alarmed when she didn't respond and simply stared into space.

'Lory?' The butter knife fell from his hand and clattered onto the plate. The noise brought a reaction from her, she shook herself and put her cup down.

'Whatever is the matter?'

She looked at him, her eyes wide with surprise.

'Your remark reminded me of something, if only I can recall it. I have a feeling it's important.'

She put her hands on her head leaning her elbows on the table and groaned. 'Oh, why can't I remember? I'm sure it's important.'

'Can you remember what it was in connection with?'

She frowned. 'I'm sure it's to do with that night at the landlady's house, but I can't for the life of me remember why.'

'Then leave it for now, Mallory,' he instructed. 'It won't do any good forcing it. It will make your headache ten times worse.'

She rubbed her forehead.

'Do you need some laudanum?'

'Heavens, no! I will soak a handkerchief in lavender water, that should help.'

He eyed her with misgiving as he munched his toast. Mallory actually admitting to a headache was cause for concern.

'I will ring for Gertrude.'

'I can manage to soak a handkerchief, Ambrose. I am not that inept.'

'Hmm …'

'What does that mean?'

'It means I think it's best that Gertrude does it for you whilst you just rest.'

She was about to protest when he added, 'it's amazing what rest can do to clear the thought processes.'

She sighed. 'If that's the case, then I will submit to resting. Tell Gertrude I will be in my room.'

The lavender-soaked handkerchief worked its magic, Mallory soon fell asleep. She woke to the sound of the front doorbell jangling. Opening her eyes, she realised her head felt much better. As she stared at the fireplace, she remembered something puzzling. She rushed downstairs and found her brother in his study. She pushed open the door.

'I've remembered something, Rosy,' she said as she shut the door. She was surprised to see Edward smiling at her.

'Good afternoon, Mallory.'

'Afternoon? How long have I been asleep?'

'A while,' replied her brother grinning. 'What have you remembered?'

She took a deep breath. 'I remember finding Mary tied up.'

He frowned. 'Yes, you told me, had you forgotten you told me?'

She shook her head. 'No, but something in my bedroom triggered a memory.'

Edward was curious. 'What memory?'

'Not a memory exactly, more of a feeling.'

Both men looked at her, waiting for her to continue.

'There was something odd about her rope bonds.'

'What was odd?'

She shook her head and sighed in exasperation. 'That's what I can't remember.'

Chapter 23

'Edward, how was your chat with Lord Marsham? Isabella was rather hoping to leave on time, she was quite tired.'

'Lory, that was what Edward was about to reveal.'

'Then I suggest we sit in the drawing room.' She looked around the study. 'There isn't a spare chair unless I sit at the desk, and I would rather like something to eat. There is simply not enough room here.'

They moved to the drawing room, Finch was summoned to bring tea and cake for Mallory.

Edward waited for refreshments to be served before speaking.

'I asked him if he knew Lord Arlington. It appears he knew him slightly in that he once attended a shooting party with him.'

'At least that's a start.' Ambrose replied.

Edward nodded his head. 'This next bit you might find interesting, the Arlingtons do not live in Pinnerton Lodge, according to Lord Marsham.'

'They don't?' Mallory was perplexed. 'How does he know?'

'Because he knows who does live there – Mrs Thornton.'

Ambrose frowned. 'Forgive me for asking but how does he know the lady?'

'He doesn't, a fellow member of his club does.'

'How very odd!' Mallory's brow puckered as she thought.

'I hope you are not thinking, what I think you are.'

Mallory smiled. 'Quite probably, Rosy. That's now my next move.'

Ambrose groaned. 'I thought so. That's not advisable.'

'I see no harm in paying her a visit. I shall take Gertrude, of course.'

'You know nothing about this lady, Mallory,' Edward cautioned, 'let me make enquiries first.'

'Don't be absurd, Edward! I shall be perfectly fine.'

'You are suffering from concussion,' he admonished, 'you need a few more days to recover. In the meantime, I can make enquiries.'

'That makes sense, Lory.' Ambrose flashed her a sympathetic look.

'No, it does not. Recovering from concussion does not prevent one from travelling on a train. It is just a mild headache. The only enquiries made will be mine!' She put her empty plate back on the tray and looked at Edward.

'It was kind of you to bring us that news, Edward.'

He acknowledged her thanks with a nod of his head.

'Now you owe me a visit to the Italian Gardens.'

'I know,' she sighed, 'I haven't forgotten, but the case takes precedent.'

'Actually, it might do you the world of good to step back from the case just for a day,' Ambrose suggested. 'You might start remembering more details about your attack, which would be extremely helpful given that something is puzzling you.'

'No.' Edward was firm. 'Mallory's mind will be on the case, not on enjoying the garden, therefore the visit can wait.'

She beamed at him, the smile lighting up her face. 'Thank you, Edward, you are perfectly correct. It will be a waste of a visit.'

He threw her an amused smile before replying.

'What will you do with this new piece of information?' he asked.

'Well,' began Ambrose but Mallory interrupted him.

'I'm going to Pinnerton Lodge! The answer lies there.'

A muscle twitched in Edward's jaw.

'That could be dangerous.'

'If it makes you both happier, I shall take precautions.'

'Not the pistol!'

'Very well, if you insist. Though it was very effective.'

'I managed to get you off the hook once,' warned Edward, 'but it's unlikely to work again.'

Mallory sighed. 'I have no expectations of needing your help, thank you. I shall ask Finch to equip me. That I hope, gentlemen, will allay your fears.'

After a hurried consultation with Finch, they caught the late afternoon train to Norwood. As the train rattled its way along the tracks with the odd blast of its whistle, Gertrude asked Mallory about the visit.

'Should I be concerned? Mr Finch gave me some instructions about protecting you.'

Mallory turned towards her in surprise. 'Protecting me? Whatever for?'

'That's what I'd like to know, ma'am.' Her plump face puckered with concern.

'All we are doing is paying a visit to the house, to see Mrs Thornton.'

'Can I ask why?'

'Because we need to know why Lord Arlington told us he lived at Pinnerton Lodge. Why we met his wife there, appears to be a mystery. I don't like mysteries or secrets, and I can't help feeling that the house has a secret.'

'How, ma'am, are we going to introduce ourselves? It does seem rather odd to turn up if we don't know her.'

'I know, which,' she sighed, 'is a problem I need to solve whilst we travel. I need peace and quiet to think, Gertrude.'

The slamming of the doors and the hissing of the train brought Mallory out of her reverie.

'Thought of something, ma'am?'

Mallory nodded. 'Yes, thank goodness, as I think it's our station next.'

She glanced out of the window and saw the sun shining down on rooftops, despite the afternoon drawing to a close. She fanned herself with her hand.

'It's still hot. I wonder when the weather will break again.'

'Shall I try to open the window?'

Mallory shook her head. 'No, we are nearly there now.'

The train pulled into the station with a hiss, clouds of steam billowing into the air. Gertrude opened the door, allowing a porter to help them down.

'Follow me, Gertrude, we will take the local cart to the house.'

148

Bob Miller pulled the cart to a standstill at the top of the drive. He helped them down as he took the coins that Mallory held in her lace glove.

He touched his cap. 'Thank you, miss, I will be back in time for the next train.' With a flick of the reins, he urged the horse forward and trotted down the drive.

Mallory glanced once again at the frontage of the house, before pulling the bell.

'It's impressive, ma'am, isn't it.'

Mallory nodded and was about to reply when the door opened, a graceful, grey-haired old lady stood before them.

'Yes?'

'Mrs Thornton? I wonder if I might have a word. I'm a private investigator.' Smiling, she pulled out a calling card from her bag. Mrs Thornton glanced at it and frowned.

'I'm not sure how I can help you?' She peered at her again. 'I didn't know women were detectives.'

Mallory smiled. 'I'm not a detective, I investigate on behalf of clients. It's about one of my cases that I'm here.'

'Oh, I see. What an unusual occupation for a lady, how very courageous of you. Please come in.' She opened the door wide and ushered them into a room. 'I'm afraid my maid only comes in twice a week, she's not a patch on my last one.'

The room, Mallory was pleased to note, was not the same one she visited before. This time it was the room on the left-hand side of the hall, not the one with the obstructed view.

'Do take a seat,' she swept a hand towards a sofa. 'Just take the dust cover off. As it's only me here, I only uncover the furniture that I need. Old houses are notorious for dampness and dust, so I just keep everything covered for preservation.'

Gertrude promptly removed the cover so that they could sit.

'I would offer you refreshment, but as I said my maid isn't here and it takes me an awfully long time to make tea.'

Gertrude turned towards Mallory. 'Shall I make the tea, ma'am?' She raised her eyebrows in an unspoken question.

Mallory smiled, immediately understanding, Gertrude would have an excuse to wander around the house.

'Would you like my maid to make the tea, Mrs Thornton?'

'Oh, would you mind?' Mrs Thornton smiled at Gertrude.

Gertrude, already on her feet, bobbed a curtsey and left the room.

'Now how can I help you?'

Chapter 24

Smiling, Mallory took a small leather notebook from her bag.

'I'm investigating a missing person, and one of my enquiries led me to this address.'

'How very odd! Well, there is only me here, apart from an unsatisfactory maid. Oh, wait a moment ...' she looked keenly at her. 'Yes, your face seems vaguely familiar. Have you been here before, my dear?'

'Yes, Mrs Thornton. I came here very recently, but it wasn't you that I saw. I saw Lady Arlington.'

'Oh, now I remember. I briefly saw you from an attic window. I'm afraid I somehow got locked in the room. The handle fell off and I was unable to get out for quite some time. My maid came to the rescue.'

'How well do you know Lady Arlington?'

'Not at all! I received a note requesting access to a room for an hour, the next day. It was very short notice, but my maid pointed out that the money would come in useful. Though I am a little annoyed that they haven't sent payment.'

'How much did they offer?'

Mrs Thornton shook her head. 'They didn't say, just that I would be compensated. That's how I came to be in the attic, you see. My maid said the attic was getting a little overcrowded, so I thought it would be a good time to peek inside. Fortunately, there was a bed I could rest on until I was rescued.'

'Ah, that would explain the link to this house.'

Gertrude brought in the tea, and very quietly left to start exploring.

'I'm so delighted by your visit, Mrs Wynter, I get very few visitors. Do you take cases about missing jewellery?' She took a delicate sip of tea. 'Oh, this is delicious, far better than either my maid or I make.'

Mallory smiled. 'My maid is very well trained.'

Mrs Thornton sighed. 'Unlike my new one. My old one left to take up a new position that was better paid.' She sighed and took a sip of her tea.

'Is it very selfish of me to want her back?'

Mallory shook her head. 'No, Mrs Thornton, it's not. How long has your current maid been with you?'

'Not very long. A month or two? Oh dear, I really have no idea, time doesn't seem to mean anything when you are old. I would advise you not to get old, Mrs Wynter.' She smiled as she sipped her tea.

'There's still time for your maid to return, I assume she must have been taken on for a trial period.'

'Oh, do you think so? I never thought of that, how clever of you! Thank you for brightening my day.' She smiled happily.

'You asked me about jewellery,' Mallory reminded her.

Mrs Thornton nodded. 'Oh yes, I did, didn't I? I seem to have mislaid some of mine. I noticed the other day that my jewellery box seems somewhat depleted. I can only assume I have put them somewhere else. What advice can you give me on how to find them?'

Mallory sipped her tea thoughtfully. 'How much has gone missing?'

Mrs Thornton shook her head. 'I'm not quite sure. You see, I sold some of it. I don't socialise very much these days, so I saw no point in keeping it all.' She thought for a few moments before continuing.

'I can't find a diamond ring my late husband bought for me when I was much younger. My fingers are now too small to wear it, so I kept it in my box. I had a silver bangle, though I'm sure I've seen that recently,' she mused.

'I owned a sapphire peacock brooch and a pearl necklace too.' She frowned. 'But I can't be sure that I didn't sell those. Oh dear, I am hopeless without my old maid, she would have known exactly what was sold.'

'Did she write a list?'

'I would imagine so, but where she put it, I have no idea. The maid I have now, is not as efficient.'

'When did you notice they had gone?'

'Let me see, my previous maid kept the box under lock and key in her room in the basement, then when she left she handed me the key. I had no need to look in it until recently. I needed something from the box.'

'You found it empty?'

'Not quite empty, there were still some earrings and other minor bracelets and necklaces.'

'Do you think your previous maid took them?' Mallory suggested gently.

'Not at all!' Mrs Thornton was shocked. 'She had been with me for ten years, she helped me through my husband's death, she was my rock. The new position came out of the blue, she had a poorly sister and the new position would be nearer to her. I could offer her more money, but I couldn't compete with the location. I trust her completely.'

'Then I think the best thing to do is let my maid search your house. She is very good at finding things, I often mislay items and she has always found them. Do you have the key to your jewellery box? Maybe you have returned them.'

'Oh, that would be wonderful and so very kind of you. I keep the key in the lock so I don't lose it.'

'Do you have any other staff?'

Mrs Thornton shook her head. 'I have an occasional gardener, but he hasn't been well, so the gardens are rather bedraggled.'

'Then I will leave you to your tea and help my maid. When is your maid expected?'

'I never really know; she can only manage two or three days a week, so I leave it to her to sort out the days. She occasionally stays overnight.'

'Do I need a key to any of the rooms?'

Mrs Thornton shook her head as she poured another cup of tea, delicately balancing the silver tea strainer on the china cup.

'All the rooms are unlocked but be careful of the attic room with the loose handle.'

Gertrude had completed a quick tour of the layout of the house.

'I can't find any evidence of servants quarters, there is a room with a bed which I presume her maid uses, I don't think there are other servants.'

Mallory agreed. 'Yes, she confirms it's just the one. Mrs Thornton mentioned that some of her jewellery has been mislaid, so why don't we search for that, it will give us an excuse to look thoroughly at the house.'

'For what?' Gertrude queried.

Mallory had to admit she didn't know. 'We might come across something interesting,' she said lamely.

They searched the basement first. They found the room where the jewellery box was kept, surprisingly the box was locked but no sign of the key. Mallory frowned; didn't Mrs Thornton say she kept it in the lock? She closed the cupboard.

The final room of the basement was a storeroom. One part of the room stored wooden crates that held apples, but it was what was beneath the shelves of jars of jam and chutney that caught her attention. She wondered why an old lady kept two beer barrels, she couldn't imagine her drinking beer, but then again, they could have belonged to her husband.

'We need to check the bedrooms, if it's jewellery we're after,' Gertrude pointed out.

'Good idea.'

Mallory found Mrs Thornton's bedroom. As she made a quick search of the bedside table, she noticed a bracelet on the floor. She picked up a silver bangle with a slight dent in it.

'This might be one of the missing items from her jewel box.'

As she pocketed it, she heard a noise on the stairs. She turned around to Gertrude.

'Did you hear that?'

Gertrude nodded. 'Mrs Thornton must have come upstairs.'

A door banged shut. Frowning, Mallory nodded towards the other doors as they returned to the landing.

'We'd better check them in case Mrs Thornton is stuck. There might be other loose handles.'

The first door they tried was locked.

Gertrude looked at Mallory questioningly. Mallory shook her head.

'She told me none of them were locked.'

She knocked on the door, expecting to hear Mrs Thornton's voice, but there was no reply.

'Strange,' muttered Mallory. 'Perhaps we had better check if Mrs Thornton is still downstairs.'

Mrs Thornton was still in the same position where they left her – drinking her tea.

'I heard someone go into a room,' Mallory said as she sat on the chair.

'It must be my maid, I heard her come through the basement.'

'I think she has locked herself in a room.'

'Really?' She sighed. 'She's a very odd maid, however, when she stays overnight I do sleep remarkably well. We have a routine, she makes me cocoa, and I fall asleep until morning – normally I am a light sleeper. It's a shame she doesn't stay here for the duration of her weekly duties, I do so enjoy that cup of cocoa. I shall have to ask her to show me how to make cocoa for myself. Do you need to speak to her at all?'

Mallory shook her head. If the maid had locked herself in, then she clearly didn't want to be disturbed.

'It would be useful to know her name though.'

'Ellen Ward.'

Mallory pulled the bangle from her pocket and offered it to Mrs Thornton.

'Is this the missing bangle?'

'Let me see.' She peered at the bangle. 'Yes, it's got a little dent in it. Now I remember why I needed it. I was hoping the local jeweller would be able to fix the dent. Where did you find it?'

'In your bedroom, on the floor by the bedside table.'

'I must have knocked it off the table. Thank you so much, Mrs Wynter. I'm sure the other pieces will turn up somewhere.' She took the bangle and placed it in her bag.

Mallory took out her pocket watch and checked the time.

'It's time for us to leave, I'm afraid. It was lovely to meet you and thank you for supplying the answers to my questions.'

'Do come again, it's nice to have visitors.'

Smiling their thanks, they made their way out of the house and down to the road in time for the cart.

'Why did the maid lock herself in a room?' queried Gertrude. 'It seems very strange.' She shuddered. 'I don't like that house, ma'am, it gave me the shivers. I wouldn't be surprised if the maid was a ghost.'

Mallory smiled. 'That's nonsense, Gertrude, we heard the maid's footsteps. There is something mysterious about the house, I grant you, but it's not ghosts.'

After clambering onto the train, Mallory settled back in her seat and reflected on the meeting. What had she learned? Lord Arlington requested a room – how did he know about Mrs Thornton? The second fact that struck her was that there was a similarity to Miss James's situation – a new maid. So, two maids had been replaced recently. Could that be a coincidence?

Chapter 25

At breakfast Mallory relayed to Ambrose the details about the visit to Pinnerton Lodge.

'Altogether it's a very odd situation, Rosy. The burning question for me is how does Lord Arlington know Mrs Thornton, and why did he want to use her place to meet us?' She spread marmalade over her toast.

'I don't know, Lory, there must be a link somewhere. Your point about two maids being replaced is a good one. We need to bear that point in mind because presently the explanation eludes me.'

Finch brought in the first post of the day, on a silver salver.

'Several letters, sir, one I recognise as Lord Arlington's handwriting.'

He proffered the tray. Ambrose picked up the letter knife and sifted through the post until he came to Lord Arlington's letter.

'You might as well stay and hear what he has to say, Finch,' Ambrose slit open the letter. He glanced over it and frowned.

'He says he will be calling upon us at two o'clock for an update.'

'Why?' Mallory placed the remains of her toast back on her plate. 'I thought he said we had three weeks, and isn't he supposed to be away?' Mallory replied.

'Yes, it's certainly curious.'

'By the way, Finch,' she informed him, 'Mrs Thornton has a replacement maid called Ellen Ward. It might be worthwhile if you can find information about her.'

'Very good, madam.' He bowed and left the room.

'What do we tell Lord Arlington?'

Ambrose shrugged. 'The truth, that the investigation is ongoing. Let's not mention the Mrs Thornton business, we'll keep that to ourselves for the moment.'

Mallory could see the point in keeping quiet, it wouldn't do to reveal your hand. Ambrose picked up his newspaper and turned the pages whilst she poured coffee for both of them. He whistled in surprise.

'Something caught your eye?'

He nodded and grimaced as he took a sip of his coffee. He picked up another sugar lump with the tongs and stirred it into his coffee. 'Let me finish reading it and I'll explain.'

She sipped her coffee patiently.

'There's an article in here about a spate of jewellery thefts, across London.'

'From shops or houses?'

'Both, though mainly houses. According to the paper, it's believed to be the work of a gang.'

'Inspector Johnson didn't mention it to you?'

He shook his head. 'No, he didn't but then I was only interested in Miss James' theft.'

'Do you think the theft of her necklace was the work of this gang or do you believe in the Inspector's theory that it was an inside job?'

He sighed. 'Unfortunately, I can't rule her out considering her financial losses. I desperately hope it is the work of this gang.'

She gave him a curious glance. 'Do you like Miss James, Ambrose?'

He stiffened. 'That is none of your business.'

'Isn't it?' she asked softly. 'You are my twin brother; we had a pact that there would be no secrets between us.'

'That was when we were children. We're adults now; I don't expect you to pry into my business.' He returned to the newspaper, indicating the conversation was over.

'Yet you pry into my life.'

'That's different. You are my little sister.'

'No, I am not!' Nothing riled her more than inequality. 'I am your twin and equal and don't you forget it!' She rose angrily from the table and threw her napkin onto her plate. 'I'll be back in time for Lord Arlington.'

'Where are you going?'

'That's my business, not yours, as you said – we're adults now.' She stormed out of the room.

Mallory walked out into the sunshine after picking up her parasol and bag. She didn't quite know where she was going but she needed to clear her head. She had been deeply hurt and shocked by Ambrose's remark. As twins they had always been very close, even after her marriage the strong bond hadn't been broken. Yet here he was denying it, regarding it as a childish action; it was as if a limb had been torn from her. Tears pricked her eyes; she hurriedly blinked them back. Was it possible to feel both pain and anger at the same time? Why did everyone feel she needed protecting? Just because he was born five minutes before her, did not give him rights to be superior. She was still fuming when she hailed a cab. Her thoughts turned to finding a house she could move into. Nothing that was available was suitable, yet she couldn't remain at her brother's for much longer. By the time her cab drew to a halt she had resolved to look further afield, widening the area might help.

Looking out of the window she was startled to find herself outside Edward's office. As she climbed out of the cab, she put up her parasol to fend off the sun's rays. What on earth was she doing outside his office? What was she thinking of? It was not one of her brightest moments; she turned and started to walk away, then changed her mind. A walk might cool her temper and numb the pain – as long as she wasn't by herself to brood.

Shutting her parasol, she opened the door to Edward's chambers. Edward was talking to his clerk.
'Mallory? Is something the matter?' He immediately led the way to his office.
'There is nothing the matter, thank you,' she forced herself to say. 'I found myself in this direction and wondered if you were free for a walk, perhaps the Italian Garden.'
'Hmm ... I see.' He eyed her thoughtfully. 'I thought you said the case took precedent?'
'It does, but I just happened to have some spare time and was in the area.'

He gave her a wry smile. 'Really? It did not occur to you that I may not have some spare time?'

She bit her lip. 'I just called on the off chance in case you did.'

'I see.' He glanced at her again. 'I'm sorry, but I don't.'

'Never mind, another day then. Goodbye, Edward.'

She turned towards the door.

He sighed. 'Why don't you tell me why you are really here, Mallory? You're not here for the garden visit.'

She spun around. 'Aren't I?'

'No.' His brown eyes gently rested on her face. 'I wish you were, but you are not, so let's not play games, Mallory, I am not a fool. What is troubling you?'

She lifted her chin determinedly. 'Nothing, can I not visit you without a problem?'

'Frankly, that's unlikely.'

'Goodbye, Edward.' Giving him a tight smile, she turned heel and made for the door.

'Mallory!' She ignored him and made for the stairs.

'Mallory!' An arm grabbed her.

'What is going on? I'm not letting you leave until you have calmed down.' He gently pushed her back into his office and closed the door.

'This is not like you.' He folded his arms, his back against the door. 'Who has upset you?'

'I am not upset.'

'I know you too well.'

She glared at him. 'No, you do not! Why does everyone think they know me better than I do?' She pointed towards the door, reluctantly he moved away allowing her to walk downstairs, this time he didn't follow her.

She turned right out of the office and tried to open her parasol – it was jammed and wouldn't open. She pushed harder to no avail.

'Let me do it.'

She turned in surprise to see Edward behind her.

'You're going in the wrong direction for home.' He took the parasol and opened it for her.

'Why don't you walk with me across the square, it's not the Italian Garden, but there is a cabbie stand on the other side of it.' He steered her across the road through the traffic to the square.

'I can spare you five minutes, which is enough time for you to tell me what is wrong and reach the cabs.'

'There is nothing wrong, Edward.'

'Do not lie to me, Mallory, there clearly is and don't give me one of your furious looks, I'm immune to them – I have had plenty of practice in court.'

They entered the square; Edward took her arm and guided her along the path to the left.

'I presume from your silence that it is a personal matter, and therefore it must be to do with your brother.' They passed under a lime tree, the sun glinting through its leaves.

'I once had a half-sister,' he advised her.

'Once?' She turned her face towards him. 'Is she no longer alive?'

'Sadly no. Amelia was much older than me, born from my father's first marriage. She made some bad choices in her life and my father washed his hands of her, she died a few months later. It's one of the reasons I took up law, to get justice for those that need it.'

'I'm sorry you lost your sister.'

'I blame my father entirely for not taking enough care of her, he wasn't interested in a daughter. When she needed his help, he turned his back.'

He pointed to the cabbie stand on the opposite side of the road.

'There's the stand. A word of advice Mallory,' he turned and faced her. 'Do not get annoyed with people for wanting to take care of you – the alternative is far worse.'

'Well, thank you for the lecture, Edward,' she replied drily.

'Here is another one for you.' He frowned. 'Stop hiding behind the shadow of widowhood, one bad marriage doesn't define you, if anything it should make you stronger. Don't bother to tell me it wasn't a bad marriage, because the only person you would be fooling is yourself.'

He sighed. 'I really do need to go now; I have a court case to prepare for tomorrow.' He turned and started walking towards his office.

'Edward!' she called to his retreating back, 'I really do want to visit the Italian Garden with you.'

He raised his arm to show he heard but continued walking without looking back. She watched him until he disappeared from view.

Sitting on a bench she put her thoughts in order. His words had stung but she knew deep in her heart that perhaps he was right. Her marriage had turned sour through no fault of her own. She bit her lip, she had worn widowhood like a second skin, she wasn't sure she would be comfortable shedding it, yet if she wanted to step out of its shadow, she must. She frowned; the word shadow immediately reminded her of the case. Her thoughts flew to Pinnerton Lodge, it had a shadow hanging over it too. It seemed to be the centre of the case; did it hold the answers? She needed to go back there but first she needed to go home for Lord Arlington's visit. She got up and crossed the road to the stand and got into a cab.

******

At precisely two o'clock, the front doorbell jangled. Mallory was already in the drawing room; Ambrose joined her just as Finch opened the front door.

'Good afternoon, Weston, Mrs Wynter.' Lord Arlington nodded in their direction as he took the proffered seat.

'I believe you are wanting an update?'

Lord Arlington nodded. 'Correct.'

Ambrose rubbed his chin. 'I understood you would be expecting an update in three weeks' time.'

'I did, but as I found myself unexpectedly in London, I thought I would see if there were any updates.'

'There isn't much to tell at the moment, the investigation is ongoing, we are making headway but only slowly.'

Lord Arlington stiffened. 'Slowly?' He glared at him. 'I'm not paying you by the hour if that's what you're hoping for!'

Ambrose glanced at him coolly. 'Our fees are not charged by the hour, but by the amount of work involved. You have already agreed upon our fees, there will be no extra charge beyond expenses.'

'Glad to hear it!'

'Is there anything in particular you are concerned about?' Ambrose asked.

'Yes, as a matter of fact.' He got up and wandered across to the window, looking out at the trees as he spoke.

'There is something that perhaps I should have mentioned at the beginning.'

'Yes?'

Mallory could see he was uncomfortable, he fiddled with his necktie as he turned towards them. What was he going to reveal?

'The reason I was reluctant for you to visit our home is because ... technically it isn't our home – not anymore.'

'Do go on.' Ambrose kept his voice neutral.

Lord Arlington licked his lips before continuing. 'Pinnerton Lodge, or Hall as I prefer to call it, was expensive to run. We preferred our other smaller residence anyway, so we did the sensible thing and leased it to a very reputable couple – Mr and Mrs Thornton. We never met them; it was all arranged through our respective solicitors.'

'So how come,' Mallory asked, 'that we met you there?'

'Mrs Thornton – we recently learned that she had become a widow – was kind enough to allow us use of her home for that meeting, even though it was short notice.'

'Why not just simply use your real home?' Mallory was confused.

'As I explained before,' he replied pompously, 'I do not like or want visitors to my home. We live a quiet life, and do not like the imposition of visitors. I thought it better to use something ... a little grander.'

'Thank you for your explanation, though it was unnecessary, we do not judge clients by their homes.' Ambrose looked thoughtful.

'Is there anything else that troubles you?'

Lord Arlington shook his head. 'No, my wife did not feel comfortable deceiving you, so I thought I would come clean. However, my question still stands – why is it progressing so slowly?'

'Tracing a necklace is always difficult, but we are making headway. If you would care to give me your address, I will write to you once we have further information.'

'I do not want a letter – damn you – I want the necklace!'

Ambrose rose and moved towards him, matching him height for height, and stared directly into his eyes.

'Then' he commanded, raising an eyebrow, 'how do you suggest we contact you, or should I just hold onto the necklace until such time as your Lordship pays us a visit?'

Mallory was impressed, Ambrose could be intimidating at times.

'You seem to be in a hurry to find the necklace, so I need a way of contacting you in a hurry.'

Lord Arlington, breaking eye contact, turned towards the window once again.

'Place an advertisement in the personal columns of The Times – "I have news for A, please make contact", that sort of thing.' Dismissively he waved a hand towards them without looking. 'I shall then write to you to make an appointment, or if I am in town, I will simply call in at my earliest convenience.'

Still looking out of the window he pulled out his gold hunter watch and checked the time. 'I am late for another appointment. I shall wait for your advertisement.'

Ambrose flopped into a chair as Finch showed Lord Arlington out.

'Well,' he blew out his cheeks and sighed, 'that explains Mrs Thornton.'

'I find it a little odd that he won't reveal his address to us.' Mallory was frowning. 'Why all the secrecy? I don't like it, Rosy, not one bit.'

'Neither do I, but we will have to accept his explanation.'

'How is he going to pay, if we don't have an address to send the fee note?'

Ambrose nodded. 'Good question, being cynical, I would say that is entirely why he is not providing an address. I really don't think he will pay up.'

'No, if he had to lease Pinnterton Lodge, it's likely they are experiencing financial difficulty.'

'Agreed.'

'So, do we drop the case?'

'No!' Ambrose clenched his jaw. 'We can't leave it unsolved, Miss James' reputation is at stake, so either we have to prove her guilt or her innocence.' He stared at Mallory. 'Don't force me to take sides.'

She glared at him. 'I would never dream of forcing you to do anything, I find it insulting that you think I would. All I pointed out to you was the danger of overlooking facts. You would have said the same thing to me.'

He had the grace to look abashed. 'True, I'm sorry.'

Mallory nodded acceptance.

'About this morning—' She held up her hand to stop him.

'Shall we just concentrate on the cases instead?' After clearing her head earlier, she had no intention of revisiting the past even if it was only a few hours ago.

'No, Mallory. I need to clear the air. I upset you and I apologise. You are right, we are twins and therefore equal, but that doesn't mean I stop worrying about you. One of Father's last instructions to me was to take care of you.'

She sighed. 'Thank you for your apology, that means a lot. However, I also worry about you, so bear that in mind next time before shutting me out. It's not prying, just sisterly concern.'

Ambrose smiled. 'Back to being twins again, sharing and caring?'

'Agreed. So back to the necklace.'

'We keep investigating, Lory, let's not have an unsolved case.'

Mallory sighed, she felt they were chasing shadows on both cases. An image of rope in candlelight flooded her brain.

'Oh,' she jumped up excitedly, 'I've just remembered why I was puzzled over Mary being tied up!' She began to pace the room.

He looked up at her. 'Do sit down, Lory, and explain.'

'I noticed,' she replied ignoring his request, 'that when I cut the ropes that bound her, they were loose.'

'Strange! Did you not ask her?'

She shook her head. 'There was no time, I remember being puzzled as I freed her. Clearly Finch was correct, it was a trap, so I needed to get her out safely.'

He nodded. 'I follow your reasoning. I think it's about time we spoke with Mary again, don't you?'

Chapter 26

Finch now had two names to research. He slipped out of the house to update his friend on the new information.

'Ellen Ward, eh? I suppose there is no other information?'

Finch shook his head. 'She is currently a maid at Pinnerton Lodge, Norwood, employer is Mrs Thornton.'

'Ah well, that might help as she is still employed. I'll see what I can do. As it happens, I do have some information for you on possible fences.'

'Excellent news, my friend.' Finch congratulated him. At least he would have something concrete to show his employer.

'One or two names have cropped up in connection with fences – although they could just be associated with them. Most of the fences are in Cheapside, but I have two names and addresses for you that are outside that area – so might provide you with a starting point. I'll write them down.'

Finch knew his friend was right about Cheapside and kicked himself for not thinking of it. He cast his mind back to the layout of Cheapside – a large, busy thoroughfare, with lanes and alleys running off it. Westwards lay Oxford Street and Holborn, towards the east lay Bishopsgate and Leadenhall. It had a constant stream of traffic, often grinding to a halt due to the number of carriages and cabs that used the road. Pickpockets worked the streets and lanes, often their pickings appeared for sale in the less reputable shops within an hour of acquisition. He nodded to himself, where else would you find a fence? Jewellery shops were in abundance, from large prosperous ones on the main thoroughfare and lanes with the smaller dingy shops hiding in the narrow, back alleys. Finch knew it would be these narrow, twisted alleys that would contain the kind of jewellers that would fence stolen jewellery. Why did he not think of that? His friend passed him a piece of paper.

'Usual Rates?'

Finch nodded his agreement. He looked at the list and smiled, a fissure of excitement growing, he recognised one of them, at least the place anyway. Pocketing the paper, he made his way back to the house.

******

Ambrose and Mallory sat in Mrs Fortescue's drawing room waiting for Mary to visit. The clock chimed eight times and Mrs Fortescue smiled.

'Oh, she won't be long now. Shall I stay or not? I'm not sure of the protocol when it's not a member of your own household.'

Mallory laughed. 'I wouldn't want to deprive you of your comfortable room, and Mary might feel more at ease in a smaller room.'

'Ah! I understand, perhaps the morning room would do?'

'Excellent suggestion, Mrs Fortescue, thank you.' Ambrose replied.

They talked of the ball and future invitations until Mary's presence was announced. They found Mary sitting around a small circular table. They joined her with a smile.

'Thank you for coming, Miss Gage,' Ambrose said, 'I appreciate you must be tired after your long day.'

'Have you got some news for me?' she said eagerly.

'Not yet, but we just needed to clarify a few things.'

'Oh.' Her face dropped, 'I see, yes of course I'm happy to oblige.'

'Thank you. I'd like you to cast your mind back to that night I found you at the landlady's house, please,' Mallory asked her.

'Yes?'

Ambrose frowned as he watched Mary gulp nervously.

'When I cut the ropes that were binding your hands and legs, I couldn't help noticing that the knots were loose.'

Mary shut her eyes and bit her lip before nodding.

'Yes,' she whispered, 'they were fairly loose.'

Mallory and Ambrose waited in silence for her to continue.

After several deep breaths she broke the silence.

'I suppose I had better tell you the truth as you are bound to find out.'

'That would be wise, it might help us.' Ambrose told her gently.

She nodded. 'He didn't have a chance to tighten the knots as he heard a noise and went to investigate. I heard the front door close, and he never came back. I had just managed to loosen the ropes on my feet when I heard someone come up the stairs. It was Mrs Wynter.'

Mallory thought through the events of that night before asking another question.

'You told me a lie, didn't you, when you said you were worried that your letters to John would reveal your address.'

She nodded and bit her lip again, before wiping away a tear.

'Did you know the person who tied you up?' Ambrose asked her.

Again, she nodded, not trusting herself to speak.

'So, you knew his friends, despite your claim that you didn't.'

Mary wiped away some tears.

'Why don't you start again from the beginning, only this time tell the truth no matter how bad it sounds.'

Two deep breaths later she was ready to speak.

'Before I met John and before I started at the hat shop, my mother grew sick, and father struggled to afford her medicine. He was ashamed that he couldn't provide for her when she was ill. We were all contributing every penny we had, but it wasn't enough. I knew if we didn't find the extra money she would die, so the only option for me was to sell myself.'

'You mean a dolly mop?' Ambrose queried. Mallory was confused by the terminology.

'Part time prostitute,' he informed her.

Mary winced but nodded. 'Yes, but at the last minute I couldn't bring myself to do it. I couldn't bear the thought of the shame and humiliation my parents would feel because I had to sell myself to pay for the medicine. I think my mother would have preferred death if she'd known.' She gulped and twisted her handkerchief between her fingers.

'Anyway, one of the girls took pity on me and told me there was another way out. She knew of some men that needed a courier, all I had to do was drop a few parcels off to people.' She shrugged. 'I'd got nothing to lose.'

'What happened?'

'I thought I would only have to do it two or three times as they paid quite well, I would be able to cover the extra cost of the medicine.'

Mallory guessed who they were. 'These were John's friends I presume?'

'Yes, that's how I met John. I thought it would be three trips at the most and then I could leave.'

'But that wasn't the case, was it?' Ambrose asked her.

Mary shook her head. 'No, that's when the trouble started. John stuck up for me, he was the one who gave me the parcels and routes. They refused to let me go and said how I was part of a criminal gang. John told them I was unreliable and a liability anyway and to let me go. So eventually they did, then I got this job at the hat shop. It's slightly better paid than my last job but it's not great.'

'How is your mother now?'

'She's better now thank you, the medicine worked. I don't regret my actions – not for a minute!' she said defiantly. 'If I hadn't worked the parcels, I would never have met John. He and I started walking out after that; I discovered that he is really a kind man. When we got engaged, he promised that after the wedding he would stop the couriering, he wanted to earn extra money for our wedding and a place to rent.'

She looked at Ambrose. 'He would never hurt anyone; he hated the couriering but it was well paid.'

'What was in the parcels?' Mallory was curious.

She shrugged her shoulders. 'We never knew, not even John. We all knew that if we asked we would be beaten. We were given a route and a place to put the parcel and that was it.'

'Thank you for being honest,' Ambrose told her. 'It would have helped if we knew this from the beginning.'

'I know I'm sorry, I was frightened that you might not help if you knew the truth.' Mary bowed her head.

'We will have to mention this to the police, Mary,' Ambrose added gently.

She nodded. 'I know,' she whispered back. 'It will make things worse for John though, won't it?' she added miserably.

'Perhaps.'

After a few seconds of awkward silence, Mallory asked a question.

'What were you really looking for in John's room, the night I found you?'

Mary sighed. 'John kept a secret list of the places for the drops and knew some of the customers' names. He said it was his insurance in case things turned nasty when he left.'

'You thought it might help you to find John.'

She shook her head miserably. 'No. My name was on that list. I didn't want anyone to know that I had been a courier, the police or somebody else might come across it. I didn't find the list, although I didn't have time to search thoroughly. I wasn't expecting anyone to be there.'

Mallory looked at her brother to see if there were any further questions. He shook his head.

'Just one thought, Mary,' Mallory added, 'where would John hide anything important?'

She bit her lip, reluctant to say.

'I know you believe it will make things worse for John, but the sooner this gang is stopped the better.'

She shook her head. 'I don't know for certain and it's only a wild guess. I'm not landing John in it over a guess.'

'The truth is you are making it worse for John.' Ambrose suggested gently. 'The fact that the list wasn't there indicates John has it, the police will view that as evidence against him.'

'How?' Mary was indignant.

'It could be assumed that the landlady found out about his criminal activity and confronted him. That list would support that theory.'

Mary bit her lip but remained silent.

Mallory knew it would be pointless to persist at this stage, so instead she thanked her and watched her leave.

'What now? Do we search?'

'It's not going to help in finding John, the police have searched his room anyway. Let's leave it for now. Come on, I could do with a nightcap, we have a lot of thinking to do. Let's go home.'

Finch brought them a tray of drinks.

'I have some news, sir. My friend has given me two names with connections to fences.' He handed Mallory a glass of Madeira wine.

'I think you will find one name in particular very interesting.' He handed the glass of whisky to Ambrose. Ambrose sipped his drink as Finch produced a note from his waistcoat pocket. He handed it to Ambrose who studied it with a puzzled expression.

'Not the name, sir, look at the place!'

Ambrose gave a grin. 'Well, well, well. That is interesting. The question is what do we do about it?'

'That, sir, is what we need to work out.'

Chapter 27

Inspector Johnson called on Ambrose and Mallory in the morning.

'Thought I would update you on the Southwark friends,' he said as he sat down in the drawing room. 'Dick Archer and Fergus Tate will be charged soon. However, they are keeping quiet about the other two, Joe and Arthur appear to have gone to ground.'

Ambrose nodded. 'We have something for you, Inspector. It seems Mary and John were working for the Southwark friends as couriers.'

'Oh?' The Inspector processed this information before continuing.

'Then it must be something criminal. What were they couriering?'

Ambrose updated him with Mary's responses.

'I can think of only two things they would be delivering – drugs or the Yellow Trade.'

Ambrose frowned. 'Yellow Trade?'

The Inspector nodded. 'Counterfeit money. London is being flooded with fake coins and to some extent bank notes. It's the coins that are hardest to control. They are faking the smaller coins – shillings, florins and half crowns.'

'How?' Ambrose asked.

'Public houses and music halls are some of the main distribution points for counterfeit money. Agents use these places to pass the forged coins to Utterers who put them into circulation.'

'Utterers?'

'Don't worry about the terminology, it's not important, but how they do it is.'

'I don't understand how they make a profit.' Mallory queried. 'A shilling hardly seems worth the effort.'

The Inspector smiled. 'There's a big profit to be made from just a shilling. Think about it: the forger sells a pack of 30 forged shillings for 20 real shillings. It has only cost him a few pennies to make them, so 20 shillings for an outlay of perhaps sixpence, that's a big profit of 19 shillings and sixpence for one pack. Multiply that by many packs and you will see it's very profitable. The agent obviously gets a cut from that profit. The Utterer who bought that pack from the agent now has 30 fake shillings to spend, giving them a profit of 10 shillings which they need to use wisely.

'I presume they would need to swap the bad shillings for real shillings as quickly as they can in order to maximise their profit,' Ambrose reflected.

'Correct. They would have to be very careful how they distributed those coins, probably one at a time. All they need to do is ask to swap the shilling for some smaller coins whilst they're buying, if they chose the right moment when it's busy nobody will check the coin. Public houses and shops are the usual targets as they deal in a lot of cash.'

Mallory thought this over. 'That would make sense for those parcels. Mary and John could be taking parcels of coins to the Utterers.'

'Indeed, Mrs Wynter. The coins are usually wrapped in newspaper to stop them chipping. They chip and break easily, that's how you can tell they're fake. So, it would be easy to parcel up a newspaper containing lots of fake coins and easy to carry.'

'That's a very good reason for John's disappearance, perhaps he's hiding from them. Perhaps he knew too much and became a liability. It would account for why the landlady was killed.'

'How do you mean?' The Inspector frowned; he couldn't follow that line of reasoning.

'According to Mary, John kept a list of not only the couriers but those who took delivery of the parcels. If the landlady caught them searching for that list ...'

'I see where you're heading. You could be right. It's certainly turned the case on its head. Counterfeiting carries a far greater sentence than burglary. I'd rather charge Dick Archer and Fergus

Tate with counterfeiting than burglary. I need to speak to those two again. Thank you, Mr Weston, you've been very helpful. I'll be in touch.'

'Well, that was useful knowledge. I must start examining my coins.' Ambrose exclaimed.

Mallory smiled. 'We might be using forged money. Seriously though, it does explain John's disappearance and the murder of the landlady.' She bit her lip. 'Should we tell Mary?'

'No, not at this stage, not until there is proof, we are rather assuming his innocence. This new information could also work against him. He could be the perpetrator of the counterfeit coins, perhaps something went wrong, and he is hiding until things settle.'

'This case gets trickier by the minute, and still no joy in sight for the necklace.' Mallory took a deep breath. 'It's hard trying to run two cases at once, I thought it would be easy to do so but it's not. As we take one step forward, we take another back, or find ourselves having to swap to the other case.'

'We'll find answers, I have no doubt of that, but it can take time. However, a man's life is at risk the longer we take. We do need a breakthrough quickly.'

'I still think we should search the landlady's house again. I wish Mary would tell us where she thinks he may have hidden that list.'

'Do you want to do that?' He looked at her. 'I rather think I need to dig deeper into the finances of all those involved. At the moment, I can't see any other course of action, unless the Inspector gets a confession.' He paused and looked at her again.

'Lory, I've changed my mind. Don't go to the house. It's too dangerous.'

'Why?'

'Look what happened last time. Joe and Arthur are still at large, who's to say they're not still watching that house? They may be getting desperate if they are after that list. They're certainly searching for something, if only we knew what it was.'

Mallory nodded glumly. 'You might be right, Rosy. I'll take your advice. There is no point in courting danger on a whim.'

He glanced at her in concern.

'You're admitting I'm right?'

'No, I'm just being sensible.'

'Hmm ...' He glanced at her serene face and decided against further comment.

'Rosy,' she added as an afterthought, 'talking about cases, we haven't any further information on Elowen's necklace. We still have no communication from her about insurance. Why is that?'

'I don't know, but it's not necessarily a sign of guilt.' His jaw tightened. 'I really can't see her faking her own burglary.'

'I agree, she doesn't seem the type, she's quite open on other matters.'

He nodded grimly. 'I need to find evidence of her innocence, and the only way to do that is find the necklace.'

Chapter 28

Ambrose was up early the next day. He had already eaten his breakfast when Mallory appeared in the dining room.

'Good morning, did you sleep well?' he asked her as he poured her a cup of coffee.

'Quite well thank you. You seem remarkably cheerful this morning.'

He nodded. 'A good night's sleep does wonders for the brain.'

He opened his morning post as Mallory ate her breakfast. She watched him as he opened a letter, a smile on his face which he quickly hid. She was amused.

'Care to share?'

He looked up. 'Oh, it was a letter from Miss James. She wants to visit this afternoon.'

'I expect she wants an update.'

Ambrose nodded his head and eyed her anxiously. She immediately understood and smiled.

'I shall be out, Rosy. I want to go back to Pinnterton Lodge.' She thought she detected a sigh of relief, but his face remained neutral.

'Why? You heard Lord Arlington's explanation.'

She nodded. 'I did, but something still puzzles me.'

'About the case or the house?'

'The house. I'm convinced it holds the key,' she replied.

'What are you looking for?'

'I don't know, it's holding a secret, I'm sure of that.'

'Old houses have lots of secrets. It may have nothing to do with the case, be careful you don't upset anyone with what you find.'

She nodded. 'I know. I'll take Gertrude with me. Mrs Thornton is eager for visitors, maybe if I let her talk I might find a clue as to its secret. If not, at least I will have made an old lady happy.'

Gertrude was delighted at the prospect of another visit to Norwood.

'Is this part of the case or just a social visit?'

'Both, I think. I'm hoping to find some answers to some puzzles. If we get a chance, I would like to explore the basement and attic in more detail. Is it possible you can think up an excuse for us to explore?'

'I will certainly give it some thought, ma'am.'

Mallory donned a small lightweight straw hat, the weather had still not broken and she was expecting it to be hot outside. She wasn't wrong.

On the now familiar train journey, Gertrude had time to think up an excuse.

'It will be easy if her maid isn't there, ma'am, you can simply ask if it's convenient to look at some of the features in the basement as your staff have requested some alterations to ours. Not sure about the attic though, it wouldn't work for that.'

'That's a clever idea, Gertrude, well done. If the maid is there, we will simply have to turn it into a social visit.'

Bob Miller's cart was waiting as usual. He deposited them at the bottom of the drive this time as there were quite a few passengers for various areas. Gertrude rang the bell and glanced anxiously at Mallory.

'What if no-one is in?'

Before she could reply they heard the door opening. It creaked open to reveal Mrs Thornton.

'Hello, Mrs Thornton, thought you might appreciate a visit. Is your maid not here again?'

Mrs Thornton shook her head. 'Tomorrow, I believe. Where are my manners, do come in. It's such a pleasure to see you.'

Mallory took off her gloves and placed them with her parasol on the hall sideboard, the only piece of hall furniture that was uncovered. Gertrude followed suit.

'Shall I make the tea, Mrs Thornton?' Gertrude smiled at her.

'Oh, thank you so much. I'm not sure if there are any biscuits. I must employ a cook soon but every time I mention it to my maid, she says there is no need for the extra expense. I feel equally sure that if I were to interview for the position, she would deliberately put them off. I really don't know what to do.'

'I would put an advertisement in the Lady magazine, and make sure your maid is not here when you are interviewing. If you are unhappy with your maid, perhaps you could advertise for both posts?'

'Oh, I hadn't thought of that. I shall give it some thought.'

Gertrude brought in the tea tray.

'No biscuits, I'm afraid,' she said as she put the tray down. She faced Mallory.

'Ma'am, is it possible for you to come to the basement?'

Mallory smiled as Mrs Thornton looked puzzled.

'Our basement needs updating, and I think Gertrude has spotted a feature that might be useful.'

'Oh, how exciting to have some remodelling done. Do please feel free to go to the basement, though I'm not sure how an old basement will help.'

'Thank you.' Mallory turned her head towards Gertrude.

'We'll go after our tea.'

Gertrude poured the tea for all of them and sat discreetly on the furthest chair.

'Now, do tell me whether there are ghosts in this house, Mrs Thornton. Gertrude thinks there is. Of course, most old houses have shadows.'

'Oh, not as far as I'm aware. Yes, you're right about shadows. Once I came down the stairs during the night because I needed some water. I thought I saw shadows in the basement, but it was just me being silly.'

Gertrude shivered. 'My dear, I can assure you I have never met a ghost in this house.'

'There you are, Gertrude, I told you there were no ghosts here. It's funny how shadows always make you think the worst. Old houses have so many secrets, don't they?'

Mrs Thornton nodded as she sipped her tea.

'I would imagine so. If only walls could talk, I'm sure there would be a wealth of stories, some good some bad.'

It wasn't quite the answer Mallory was hoping for, she had hoped by steering the conversation in that direction it would disclose some interesting facts which might prove useful. She tried again.

'The house I lived in as a child had many secrets, one of which was a hidden room, at least I thought it was hidden, until I saw my father open it one day. It turned out to be just a storeroom that he kept his best wines in.'

Mrs Thornton laughed. 'I'm sure this house holds a fair few, but alas I have yet to find them.'

Defeated, Mallory changed the subject. 'Have you found your missing jewellery?'

Swallowing the last of her tea she shook her head. 'No, my dear, I think it's likely I sold them.'

Mallory finished her cup too. 'Would you mind awfully if we visited your basement now? I confess I'm keen to know what Gertrude has spotted that would work in our basement.'

'Of course, I shall just sit here and pour myself another cup.'

Gertrude opened the door to a storage room.

'What are we looking for, ma'am?'

'I don't know until I see it. Perhaps something that doesn't fit in. Let's just keep looking, I just feel that we will find answers here.'

They searched the shelves but found nothing out of the ordinary.

'There's them barrels, ma'am,' she said pointing to two barrels in the corner.

'Oh yes, I remember those from last time. It struck me as odd that an old lady would drink beer.'

'Doesn't have to be beer. They could contain dry goods such as flour or salt – anything in fact.'

'Shall we take a look anyway?'

Gertrude fetched a candle so they could see the inside properly. There wasn't a great deal of light in the room, certainly not enough to see inside a barrel.

The lid of the first barrel came away easily and was empty. They tried the second barrel. It took a few hefty tugs from Gertrude before it loosened enough for them to lift the lid. As Gertrude held the candle above the lid, it caught the gleam of something bright.

'What's that?' Mallory turned towards her. Gertrude put her hand in and pulled out a silver candlestick. She passed it to Mallory in surprise. She held the candle directly over the opening.

'Ma'am, you need to see this.' She passed the candle to her.

Mallory was amazed to see items of value including a pearl necklace that had been caught around another candlestick. She passed the candle back to Gertrude.

'What's it all doing in a barrel?' Gertrude asked, perplexed.

'I've no idea,' Mallory replied. 'I saw several necklaces in there as well as a carriage clock.'

'Shall we empty it out?' Gertrude asked her.

Mallory shook her head. 'No, we don't have time, in case Mrs Thornton decides to come and find us. Let's put the lid back on and just mark the barrel, if we can, and tell my brother when we get home.'

They looked around for something to use as a marker. Gertrude found a coal bucket and picked up a small piece of coal.

'I'll do it, ma'am, or you'll get dirty hands. If you could just help lift the barrel slightly, I'll mark the bottom.'

Between them they managed to slightly tilt the barrel.

'If you could just hold it there,' Gertrude said, panting, 'I can put a cross underneath.'

Righting the barrel, they were both out of breath. Gertrude put the coal back. Waiting until both had regained their breath, they made their way back upstairs after Gertrude washed her fingers in the sink.

'Did it help?' asked Mrs Thornton putting her cup down.

'Yes, thank you. I rather like the idea of the alcove shelves. Do we have alcove shelves, Gertrude?'

Gertrude shook her head. 'No, ma'am, that's why I wanted to show you them, that and the extra sink.'

'I'm so pleased I was able to help you.'

Mallory smiled. 'It was enlightening, thank you. We really ought to be going now. May I bring my brother back to see it? He makes all the decisions as it's his house.'

'Of course! You will be welcome anytime. I would so like to meet your brother.'

Picking up their gloves and parasols they walked outside into the bright sunshine towards the bottom of the drive, for the cart.

'Will he come, do you think, ma'am? I'm sure we've missed the next train.'

'I think you'll find he'll come past again knowing we didn't make the train.'

Her prophecy was correct; they could hear the clopping of the horse's hooves on the road.

The station porter helped them find a carriage. As Mallory rewarded him with sixpence, he asked her if she had visited the old lady in Pinnerton Lodge again.

'She is a nice lady, miss. I do hope her new maid is suiting her.' He pocketed the sixpence.

'You know the maid?'

'Only that she were looking for a job and asked me if any houses were taking on maids. Poor woman had been to several houses without any luck. Now if I can do someone a good turn, I will.' He nodded at them and moved on to the next compartment.

As the train pulled out of the station, Mallory sat back on the seat and stared out of the window. Why was a barrel of expensive goods in the basement of Pinnerton Lodge? Had they been stolen, or did they all belong to Mrs Thornton? If so, why store them in a barrel? She frowned, had she uncovered the house's secret?

Chapter 29

Elowen James was sitting drinking tea in the drawing room with Ambrose. Ruby was hovering outside listening to the murmur of their voices.

'Haven't you got work to do Ruby?' Finch whispered in her ear. She jumped.

'Thought Miss James might like a … whatcha call it … a …' she screwed up her face in an effort to recall the word. '… Chapawhatsit,' she replied in hushed tones.

'Chaperone?'

'That's it, Mr Finch.'

'If a chaperone hasn't been requested, then it's not our place to insist.' He eyed her firmly. 'Return to your duties.'

She huffed at him and sloped off, muttering under her breath. The front doorbell jangled, and Finch sprinted downstairs to answer it before Ruby got there, Ruby in a bad mood was not conducive to a polite welcome.

Mallory handed her outdoor accessories to Gertrude.

'Is Miss James and my brother in, Finch?'

Finch nodded. 'Yes, madam, I'll bring another cup, the tea will still be hot.'

He looked at her concerned. 'Is something the matter? You look worried.'

She nodded. 'I found out some information, but I'm not sure what it means. It might be of interest to you, Finch.'

'Ooh, can I bring up the extra cup, Mr Finch?' Ruby's eyes shone, her bad mood forgotten, here was a chance to learn what was going on and repeat it to Archie.

'No, Ruby.' Finch glared at her. 'Your duties lie below stairs.'

'That ain't fair! It just ain't f—'

'Ruby! If I hear one more word …' Ruby stomped off; Mallory could hear her footsteps stamping down the stone steps that lead to the basement.

'I will be up shortly, madam.'

Mallory knocked lightly on the door before entering. Taking a deep breath, she smiled brightly as she entered the room.

'Good afternoon, Miss James.'

'Please call me Elowen.' She put her cup down and smiled at Mallory.

'I thought you were going to see Mrs Thornton,' Ambrose frowned. Mallory was amused to see that he had dressed rather more nattily than usual. Although the weather was very warm he had kept his jacket on, but it was his cravat that was the crowning glory – a splash of deep, rich burgundy silk tied under his collar wings pinned into place with a gold tie pin.

'I did,' she replied, 'and that's why I need to speak to you.'

'Can't it wait?' he said with a touch of impatience.

'No, not really.' She noticed Elowen attempting to make ready to leave.

'Oh, please do stay, Elowen. This might be of interest to you.' She sat on the nearest chair. Elowen picked her cup back up.

Finch knocked and entered, a cup and saucer in his hand which he placed on a side table by Mallory.

'You wished me to stay, madam.'

She nodded and turned towards her brother. 'Gertrude and I were able to examine the basement. In the storeroom were two barrels.'

Ambrose frowned. 'Go on, I fail to see the urgency at the moment.'

'Well, you will, Rosy, when I tell you that one of the barrels was filled with jewellery and other valuable items.'

Elowen gasped and quickly put her cup down in case she dropped it.

'What?' Ambrose's frown deepened.

'Gertrude put a mark on the bottom with a piece of coal so that we should know it again.'

Ambrose thought for a few seconds. 'Now I see the urgency.'

He turned towards Elowen. 'Perhaps your necklace is amongst it.'

Mallory continued. 'There is a chance of course, that they are Mrs Thornton's possessions.'
'In a barrel?'
Mallory nodded. 'You have seen how bare the house is, she is quite eccentric.'
'You really don't believe that do you? Otherwise, you wouldn't rush back to tell me.' He stared at his sister.
'No.'
Finch coughed discreetly. 'I believe there was something in the paper about a spate of burglaries.'
'Yes, I read that too.'
'No, sir, that was a different item. This one centred on burglaries in the Norwood area. I'll fetch the article.'
'That would make sense,' Ambrose said.
'How so?' asked Elowen.
'If houses were being burgled in Norwood, they would need somewhere to store the items before taking them back to the city.'
Elowen nodded. 'Yes, I understand now.'

Finch returned with a copy of the newspaper, already folded to show the article.
'It's halfway down the page, sir.' He passed it to Ambrose who read aloud the first few lines.

OUTRAGE IN NORWOOD
A spate of burglaries in Norwood has baffled the police. Ten houses in as many days have outraged residents ...

He didn't bother reading the rest, he handed it back to Finch.
'So, it seems that Pinnerton Lodge is the hiding place. We will need to act quickly. Finch, please inform Inspector Johnson by telegram to meet us at Norwood Junction.' Finch nodded and left.
'What if it's no longer there?'
'That's why we need to act now, Lory. Please stay here with Miss James.'
'No!' She looked at Elowen. 'I'm so sorry, Elowen, but I have to be a Pinnerton Lodge, Mrs Thornton doesn't know Ambrose.'

185

'I agree.' She turned to him. 'Mallory is right, she is your way in. I will return home. '

'But your necklace might be amongst it.'

'No, Ambrose, it won't be.' She declined to say why. 'I bid you both a good day. I very much hope you will keep me abreast of the situation.'

After consulting his Bradshaw's Timetable, Finch fetched a four-wheeler cab.

'I informed the Inspector as to what train we would be catching,' he said as he opened the door and helped them inside. Finch was insistent that he join them. Ambrose didn't argue.

At the station, Ambrose purchased the necessary tickets whilst Finch led Mallory to the platform. They could hear the train coming by its whistle. When the train pulled in with a screech of brakes and belching out smoke, Finch found them an empty compartment; they waited for the train to depart before speaking.

'What is your plan, Rosy? I think even Mrs Thornton will be upset that we are accompanied by a police inspector.'

Ambrose turned to Finch and raised an eyebrow.

'Yes, madam, you are right. The Inspector will have to enter secretly. What excuse did you use for looking in the basement?'

'That we were remodelling our basement and Gertrude had spotted one or two things that might prove useful.'

Finch nodded. 'Good, then we will continue with that theme. I have no doubt that the servant's entrance will be unlocked, if it isn't I came prepared. The Inspector and I will use that entrance and Ambrose can meet us in the basement. Madam, if you could remain with Mrs Thornton and keep her talking until Ambrose comes to fetch you.'

'What if her servant is there. She mentioned she might arrive tonight as sometimes she stays over.'

'Interesting!' Ambrose thought for a few seconds. 'We will have to deal with that if the case arises. Tell me, Lory, do you think Mrs Thornton is involved?'

'Oh, I hadn't thought of that!' She looked at him wide eyed.

'Surely not?'

'As you reminded me, we cannot overlook facts, however much we like the person.'

Mallory pulled a face and sighed. 'You are right. It is a possibility.'

The rest of the journey was spent in quiet contemplation. Mallory really hoped that Mrs Thornton wasn't complicit in the burglaries.

The smell of burning coal filled the air, as Finch helped her down onto the platform. The platform, besides being engulfed in smoke, was noisy, she could hear the fireman shouting to the driver.

'Where's the Inspector?' she coughed.

Through the smog, Mallory saw some shapes emerge as the smoke cleared, she recognised the inspector accompanied by two colleagues.

'So where are we going?' he asked disgruntledly. 'I hope this is not going to be a waste of time.'

'There's usually a cart waiting outside which will take us to Pinnerton Lodge.'

The cart was indeed waiting in its usual spot.

'Back again, miss?' was all Bob Miller said.

'Indeed, same place please, Bob.'

The cart trotted off, the horse swishing its tail as it clopped along the street. Thankfully being summer, the nights were still light, although the heat had died down for which Mallory was grateful. Before leaving home she had draped a silk shawl around her shoulders as a precaution against an evening chill; you could never tell with the summer weather, and she had felt the suggestion of a breeze as she had climbed into the cart. She pulled it tighter around her shoulders, she knew the house would be cold.

As usual, the cart deposited them in the driveway of Pinnerton Lodge.

'I'll be passing by as usual.' Bob took the coins and nodded as he urged the horse on.

'So, this is it?' Inspector Johnson eyed the ivy clad house with suspicion.

'The servants' entrance is towards the back of the house, Finch.' Finch nodded. 'Shall we Inspector?' They moved off, the Inspector kept one of his men back to watch the place from the shrubs.

Mallory pulled the bell and waited patiently – who was going to answer?

The door creaked open, and the head of Mrs Thornton appeared.

'Oh, Mrs Wynter, I wasn't expecting you back so soon.' She opened the door fully. 'Is this your brother?'

Mallory introduced Ambrose to her.

'Oh dear, where are my manners! Please come in, both of you.'

They followed her to the drawing room, Ambrose looked discreetly around as he took a covering off a chair. It was similar to the room where they had interviewed Lady Arlington, except perhaps that it contained a few more chairs and paintings, but other than that it was soulless.

'I assume your maid isn't in?' Mallory gave her a sympathetic smile.

'No, not yet. I had hoped it would be tonight. I could do with another good night's sleep. I'm so sorry I cannot offer you refreshment.'

Ambrose waved away the apology.

'No need to apologise, Mrs Thornton, it is us who should be apologising for disturbing you.'

'Oh, that's quite alright, dear. I do love visitors and I told your sister I would be delighted to meet you.'

'Speaking of staff, our butler is waiting by the servants' entrance. Would it be possible for my brother to admit him?'

Ambrose gave her a charming smile. 'This is very kind of you, Mrs Thornton. I'm sorry to have come with staff, but my butler was insistent. However, if you would like some cocoa I'm sure my butler will oblige.'

She smiled back delightedly and clapped her hands together. 'Your butler must see it; he will be spending all his time in the basement after all. He will be invaluable in your decision making, though what my humble basement has to offer I cannot fathom. Yes please, Mr Weston, cocoa will be delightful, thank you.'

'Old houses often contain a wealth of features that sadly some townhouses lack.' He rose and nodded his thanks, still smiling.

'I'll find my way there and thank you.'

He found his way by heading towards the back of the house. There was a separate set of stairs leading down to the basement. He found Finch and the police already there.

'Over here, sir,' Finch called out, recognising the footsteps.

Finch, the Inspector and his man were standing in the middle of the storeroom.

'Finch, can you make cocoa for Mrs Thornton please?'

'So, what is it you want to show me that is so vital that it disrupts Scotland Yard's evening?'

'I believe barrels are involved.' Ambrose replied smoothly. He pointed to the corner of the room where two barrels were tucked discreetly amongst some empty crates.

'If we could just lift one, I believe one of them has been marked by my sister.'

They tried the first one without success. The Inspector was growing grumpier by the minute. 'I warn you Weston, if you are wasting my time—'

'Sir, there's a mark on this one.'

'Well get it open, man, we haven't got all night!' Between them they tugged open the lid.

'Some light would be helpful,' the policeman muttered.

Ambrose fetched a candlestick and lit the candle.

Gingerly they tipped the contents onto the floor, expecting to be flooded with liquid. Instead, they found themselves staring at a hoard of valuable items, including jewellery and a carriage clock.

'Satisfied now, Inspector?' Ambrose asked with a grin.

He whistled in surprise. 'What have we got here?' He picked up a gold hunters watch and turned it over to read the inscription.

'This, if I am not mistaken,' he said to his colleague, 'is one of the stolen items from the Norwood robberies, the inscription confirms it.'

'What do you want to do about it?'

The Inspector sighed. 'We need to take it to the station, but I also want to follow the trail of its destination. Let me think.'

Finch, after taking the cocoa upstairs, wandered through the basement rooms until he came across the butler's room. He looked inside the cupboard and dismissed the jewellery box; it was the top shelf he was interested in. It held an old account book and a bottle of red ink. Under the bed was an old carpet bag. Picking up the bag and the ink he made his way back to the storeroom.

'Would this be of service to you?' He held out his finds. The Inspector merely grunted and grabbed hold of them.

Between them they stored all the stolen items into the bag.

'What we need is a stick to mark the barrel with the red ink.'

Finch obligingly went in search of one, finding some twigs outside the back door. He held out a few of various sizes.

'I wanted one, not a forest!' complained Inspector Johnson. He pulled one from Finch's hand and dipped it into the pot of ink. He marked the base with a tiny PL by the ridge. He waited until it was dry to see if it darkened, the last thing he wanted was for it to be obvious. Satisfied that it had darkened enough he stood the barrel upright.

'What do we replace the contents with? It needs a fairly similar weight to fool them.'

They partly filled it with coal before replacing the lid firmly.

'Sir, at which brewery do we think it will end up?'

'That is the problem, Lennox.'

Finch cleared his throat and looked at Ambrose. Ambrose took the hint.

'May I suggest The Rising Sun?'

Inspector Johnson swore under his breath. 'Not the one in Southwark?' Ambrose nodded.

'I was hoping there would be another one,' he said unhappily. 'I think I told you that it's come to our attention before?' Again, Ambrose nodded.

'What makes you think it's The Rising Sun?' Inspector Johnson eyed him thoughtfully. 'You'd better tell me all you know.'

'We don't have time for that, Inspector. Let's assume I've heard a whisper.'

The Inspector let out his breath slowly. 'Lennox, put someone on watch here, they'll need to stay in the bushes out of sight. We need to know when it's collected and by whom.'

'What about the tavern?' Lennox couldn't bring himself to say its name.

'Until we know when it's picked up, we can't put a watch on it, we can't spare that amount of manpower.'

'I have a contact there, if that helps, but I insist they remain anonymous.'

'Very well, I will contact you once we know it's on its way.' He nodded to Finch and Ambrose. Picking up the carpet bag he and Lennox made their way out of the basement to the drive.

Ambrose went upstairs to fetch Mallory and the three of them made their way back to the station, they walked to clear their heads.

'What if they try to add more to their haul?' Mallory frowned. 'They will know they've been discovered.'

Ambrose shook his head. 'Not necessarily. They may well think they've been double crossed by one of their gang.'

'Let's concentrate on the fact that the police now have their haul,' Finch replied, 'and I think we need to hurry as I can hear a distant train whistle.'

The train rumbled into view just as they reached the station. They hurried to a first-class compartment; the whistle blew just as Finch slammed the carriage door; the train chugged away from the platform wafting clouds of steam into the air.

Chapter 30

Young Constable North quietly trudged up the drive and took stock of his surroundings. Spotting a thick, tall shrub on the overgrown lawn, he made his way across the dew ladened grass and parted the stems of the shrub to force his way into it. It was no easy task to find a central position. He snapped several woody stems by standing on them with his heavy boots. Finally, he found a good position. The shrub overlooked the top of the drive of Pinnerton Lodge, Constable North felt it was an ideal spot. Early morning dew clung to its leaves. He risked shaking a few branches to clear the glistening drops. His view was partly obscured, so he bent a few stems to make a wider space so he could clearly see the house. He realised, as he peered out, that this only covered the front of it. Would the barrel come out through the front door? He shook his head; he had observed that the drive forked to the left towards the back of the house. He trod some more woody stems down so he could turn and then made a hole so he could see the side drive.

The sky was beginning to lighten, bringing a grey start to the day. If he thought he was going to see a beautiful sunrise, he would be disappointed. All the sky promised was rain, as dark clouds appeared on the horizon. This was his first undercover duty, he was determined not to mess it up, so a little bit of rain was not going to deter him from doing his job. He felt both elated and nervous at being given the opportunity. If he did well he might get transferred to the detective side. He patted his jacket's right pocket to make sure his notebook and pencil were there. The left pocket held a packet of sandwiches wrapped in paper and muslin cloth. He reckoned he had enough food to last a day. He had no idea how long he would have to spend cooped up in the shrub, although he was expecting someone to relieve him at the end of the day. He focused on the front of the house. There was no movement. He turned and viewed the side, that too was still. He repeated these movements for some time, wondering when the action would start.

He sighed; the excitement was beginning to pall. Would it be like this all day with no action? He heard the church clock strike six times. Surely it was later than six o'clock? As the first drops of rain started to fall, he took a sandwich from his pocket and munched on it. All was quiet except for the soft patter of raindrops as they splattered onto the leaves. His job was clear, he was there to observe not to apprehend. When the job had first been mooted, he wondered why no-one volunteered except him. Now he was beginning to realise, watching duty was boring. He checked his pocket watch, nearly eight o'clock, he had been there nearly four hours!

As the rain eased, the house began to come to life. He saw the curtains being drawn back from an upstairs room, a few minutes later the front curtains had the same treatment. He noted these facts in his book along with the time. Just as he began to think the job might be a waste of time, he heard a distant sound of horse's hooves and the rumbling of wheels. The first promising sound he had heard so far. He kept very still and listened – they were coming closer. This was more like it. He took a quick look at his watch and slid his notebook out of his pocket. He hoped and prayed that the horse was coming up the drive. He waited with bated breath, a few seconds later a cart drawn by a pale horse came into view. He took note of the driver and cart details. He was disappointed not to be able to see what was in the cart. The cart swung down the left-hand fork – it was going to the back of the house.

He gently turned to look through his side viewpoint. The cart pulled up to the side. The driver jumped down, patted the horse's neck and then walked off; he could see his head getting lower so presumably he must be going down some steps. He waited patiently; all boredom forgotten. After a few minutes, the man re-appeared carrying a barrel on his shoulder, followed by a grey-haired lady. He stood the barrel in the cart and secured it in the corner with the aid of some rope, presumably to stop the barrel rolling about. Nodding farewell to the lady, he leaped up into the driver's seat, clicking his fingers to the horse. There was just enough room to turn the horse and cart around. As it clopped down the drive, Constable North noted everything down. He waited for a few more minutes to make sure the horse and cart had gone and then gingerly made his way out of the shrub and marched down the drive, careful to stick to the lawn so that his footsteps couldn't be heard. He needed to make his report as quickly as possible. Time was of the essence as he had an idea where the cart was heading.

******

Inspector Johnson swore when he read the constable's report. He sent Lennox to interview Bob Miller and organised a watch on the Rising Sun as a precaution.

Bob Miller sat in his parlour with Lennox sitting opposite him. He blinked in confusion when Lennox told him why he was being interviewed.

'It's quite simple, Mr Miller, I'm being courteous by not dragging you down to the station, but I need you to start giving me answers – understood?'

Bob nodded. 'All I did was pick up a barrel from Pinnerton Lodge and take it to the station. I do favours for people from time to time.'

'Does that happen frequently?'

'What the favours?'

'No!' Lennox pursed his lips; he glared at Bob unsure whether he was being made a fool of, he narrowed his eyes. 'The fetching and carrying of barrels.'

Bob shook his head. 'No, this was the second time.'

'Go on, I'm listening.'

'The first time, I was asked to collect a barrel from the station and take it to Pinnerton Lodge. This time it was the reverse.'

'Who asked you?'

'I presume the old lady. I was given a note at the station by the porter.'

'What happened next?'

Bob shrugged his shoulders. 'The note just said a barrel would be arriving by train and could I pick it up and take it to Pinnerton Lodge and leave it outside the servants' entrance.'

'I need more information than that. You've told me nothing.'

Bob sighed. 'It was several days before the porter told me the barrel had arrived for collection. Well, I loaded it on the cart, and knocked on the door of the servants' entrance. I wasn't going to just leave it outside, was I? Not when there was a chance of payment on receipt – it takes up a bit of space.' He pulled a face. 'Nobody answered, so I left it there.'

'What about the recent one?'

'Same thing really. The station porter passed me a note. The note said almost the same thing, could I pick up a barrel from the house at around eight o'clock in the morning and take it to the station.'

'Who passed you the barrel?'

'Mrs Thornton.'

'You sure about that?'

'Well, I've never actually met her before, but it was definitely an old, grey-haired lady who answered. She was leaning on a walking stick. I asked about payment, and she assured me that once I'd sent her the bill she would send payment. I haven't done anything wrong, officer.'

'The trouble is, Mr Miller, we only have your word about the notes.'

Bob shook his head. 'No, I still have those notes, and the bill, as I haven't had a chance of putting it through the door.'

Bob fetched the notes. Lennox tucked them in his wallet.

'You're keeping them?'

'Evidence, Mr Miller, they're evidence.'

'I haven't done anything wrong.'

'No, not this time,' he replied as he stood up to go. 'Be careful in future, Mr Miller, what you fetch and carry.' He made his way to the door then stopped.

'Oh, just one more question before I go – was there a delivery label on it?'

Bob nodded. 'I remember seeing one, but I didn't notice the address. My job was just to take it to the station.'

Lennox groaned inwardly. He really needed to know where it was headed. He thanked Mr Miller before striding down to the station. He hoped the station master would be more forthcoming about the barrel's destination.

Lennox reported the results of the interviews to Inspector Johnson.

'Frankly, sir, I don't think we can charge Mr Miller with anything, he hasn't committed a crime. At least we know where the barrel is going.'

'Agreed,' replied the Inspector, 'but I think Mrs Thornton warrants further investigation. Make it your priority, Lennox.'

Chapter 31

The breeze that Mallory had felt the night before had brought rain overnight, it was a relief from the heat of the last few days. She was in the drawing room when she heard the jangle of the front doorbell. It was rather early for visitors, so Mallory and Ambrose were surprised when Finch announced Edward.

'Apologies for the early arrival, but I think I might have some news for you.'

'Did you win your court case?' Mallory asked with a smile.

Edward nodded. 'Yes, and that's how I came across some information regarding one of your cases.' He sat down on a chair.

'As I left court, I was accosted by a member of the public who said he had information that he was prepared to share with me as a thank you for getting justice for one of his friends.'

'Did you know him?'

'No, but I saw him inside the court in the public gallery.'

Ambrose looked at him. 'This information, do you believe it's genuine?

'A good question, Weston. The simple answer is I don't know, but I thought it worth bringing to your attention.'

'What is this information?'

'It's regarding John Kendle.' He paused for a moment before continuing. 'It appears that he was seen near London Bridge.'

'How long ago?'

Edward shrugged. 'I wasn't told. I did ask, but the man just shook his head. It seems he had seen the wanted poster of John and remembered seeing him in the company of two men.'

'So it could be recently, or it could be the night he went missing.' Mallory mused.

'Exactly. That's why I rushed over here at the first opportunity. I did try yesterday evening, but your maid informed me you were out.'

Ambrose told him of the latest event and his idea of going to the Rising Sun and checking whether the barrel arrived there.

Frowning, Edward looked at Mallory. 'I hope that doesn't include you.'

'Why not?' Mallory raised her chin.

'Southwark isn't safe, it's a heaving underbelly of crime, the labyrinths of squalor and violence are breeding grounds for criminals.' Edward informed her. 'I know, I've faced some of them in court. With all due respect it's not a place for a woman – unless you were disreputable.'

'Sanderson has a point.' Ambrose confirmed. 'If I go, it will be with Finch, even the Inspector admitted they hated going there.'

Mallory closed her eyes briefly and let out her breath slowly. 'Very well, I won't go.' She glared at them. 'However, I *am* going to go to London Bridge and try to trace John Kendle.'

'No!' Both Edward and Ambrose shouted.

'Why not?'

'It's the same principle. It's not safe.' Edward was not amused.

'London Bridge is a dangerous place, Lory. I'm not talking about walking across the bridge, I'm talking of the riverside itself, and poking around the wharves, it's full of ne'er-do-wells. Finch and Archie will come with me, Archie may know some of the mudlarks.'

Mallory tapped her foot on the carpet. 'Well, what can I do then? I'm not prepared to sit and do nothing.'

'Newspaper research. Find as much as you can about the Arlingtons, Miss James and robberies. I will ask Finch to bring you all the papers in the archives.'

'What if the information is a trap?' She looked at both in turn.

'I have thought of that, believe me,' Edward replied. 'With your permission, Weston, I will stay the night, otherwise it will leave Mallory vulnerable. I don't know how long it will take you, but information might be better found during the evening, though it would be riskier.'

Ambrose rubbed his chin thoughtfully. 'That is a good point, the house could be a target again.' He looked at Edward.

'How much credence do you give this new information?'

Edward shook his head. 'Impossible to judge. I could have been targeted because of my earlier involvement in the attempted burglary here.'

'Well, you are going to have to go, Rosy. If you ignore it and it's true, we could lose a valuable lead. I shall be fine by myself, although I would rather join you in the search.'

Ambrose came to a decision. 'I will take up your offer, thank you, Sanderson. I will go immediately, the sooner we act the better. I'd prefer to do it in the daytime if possible. But stay the night anyway.'

'I've come prepared.'

Before leaving, Finch brought all the papers to the dining room.

'It will be easier to spread them out on the table, madam.'

Edward used the morning room as his office, he had brought work with him. Mallory found the papers neatly stacked by year and month. How far back should she go? She picked out last year's pile and started with January's papers. She had a notebook and pencil ready, not that she had any hopes of finding anything. She knew it was Ambrose's way of placating her, she also felt that Edward staying was wholly unnecessary. Grudgingly she opened the first newspaper and scanned the pages. One by one, she worked her way through the papers, discarding them neatly in date order. Sighing, she picked up one of the more recent papers. She soon became engrossed with the articles. The first article that caught her eye was an item about stolen items from a burglary, they had been listed in the hope that someone had come across them. Idly she read the list and then frowned. Something sparked a memory, something felt familiar. She read the article again paying particular interest to all the items: silver twisted candlesticks, pearl necklace, serpent ring, gold carriage clock, ruby necklace, emerald drop earrings.

What was it that caused a flicker of remembrance? She rubbed her temples hoping to refresh her memory. It must be the concussion that played havoc with her memory, normally her recollection was excellent.

'Are you alright, Mallory?' Edward eyed her anxiously. He had come to see how she was faring in her research.

'I'm fine, it's just this article. There is something familiar about it, but I can't remember – oh, it's so frustrating!' She slapped the paper down in annoyance. Edward picked it up and gave it a quick look.

'I presume it's the piece about the burglary items?'

She nodded. He briefly glanced at it. 'I haven't got time to study it at the moment.' Tucking the paper under his arm Edward glanced at her. 'Leave this with me, Mallory.'

'Why?'

'So I can look at it in detail.'

He sighed as he looked at her irritated expression.

'Two pairs of eyes are better than one. I might discover why it's familiar to you.'

She nodded resignedly. He left the room, and she settled down to the papers once again.

Flicking through a paper she saw an article about Elowen James. 'Oh no!' She sighed as she put the paper down. Resting her elbows on the table with her hands cupping her chin, she gathered her thoughts together. What should she do about it? Bring it to Ambrose's attention? She wanted to spare him pain, but she needed to handle it in the right way. As she pondered her next move, a fierce knocking on the front door interrupted her soul searching. She looked up and frowned. Who on earth could that be?

She heard Gertrude's quick footsteps on the hall floor as she rushed to answer the insistent knocking.

'Where is that bitch?' a man snarled.

'I think you have the wrong house,' Gertrude replied, trying to close the door in his face, but the man would have none of it.

'I want the bitch that shot me!' He shoved her out of the way and limped into the hall.

'Come out you cowardly bitch!' he yelled.

200

Edward stormed out of the morning room and faced the man, signalling for Gertrude to leave. Joe's name was etched on his memory as the man who tried to knife Mallory.

'So, you're Joe Archer. Shot in the leg with a pistol, I believe. Remove yourself at once from this house or I will summon the police.'

Joe looked at him in amazement, his mouth hanging open.

'You ain't supposed to be 'ere, I watched you all leave and 'ow the 'ell do you know me name?'

Edward smiled mirthlessly. 'You saw the owner and his butler go.'

Joe shook his head. 'No. You arrived this morning and three males left the 'ouse.'

'Then you're either not very observant or very stupid, the third male you counted out was a kitchen boy, not me.' Joe made a sudden movement, Edward, surprised at his turn of speed, found himself grabbed by the throat and pushed against the wall.

Mallory had crept into the hall, seeing Edward pinned by his throat she grabbed Ambrose's beloved potted Aspidistra and smashed it over the assailant's head. He slumped to the floor.

'Are you alright?' she asked Edward.

'Of course,' he replied, massaging his throat, 'although I can't say the same for the plant.' He looked at the debris on the floor. Clumps of earth and broken china were scattered across the black and white tiles, whilst the plant itself seemed to be intact – the Aspidistra appeared indestructible.

'I saved your life Edward, now we are even.'

He shook his head. 'No,' he pointed out, 'my life wasn't in danger, but thank you for your assistance.'

'Neither was mine!'

'Mallory, this is no time to argue the definition of danger! Find me something to bind him with, before he comes round.'

'I'll fetch it, sir.' Gertrude scurried off.

A wail of protest greeted them. Ruby stood in the hall with her mouth open in disbelief.

'Look at my nice clean floor!' she shrieked. 'What a blooming mess! I only washed it this morning!'

'Ruby!' Mallory said sharply. 'Never mind the mess, go and fetch a policeman immediately.'

Ruby brightened up considerably at the thought of being the heroine and fetching a copper. She stepped over the wreckage and into the street.

Getrude came back with a ball of string and scissors. 'Will this do, sir? That's all I could find in a hurry.'

As Edward tied the hands, Joe started to moan as he regained consciousness. When he saw Mallory holding his legs whilst they were being bound, he headbutted her, catching her on her shoulder and knocking her off balance onto the floor. Edward picked her up.

'I'm fine!' she said crossly.

The policeman entered the house and surveyed the scene. He went back outside and blew his whistle.

'Stay outside for my colleagues,' he ordered Ruby. Tingling with excitement, she stood outside watching for the constables.

Inspector Johnson took stock of their prisoner as he stood over the writhing body of Joe Archer.

'Fortunately, I was on my way here to see Mr Weston,' he told Edward as he hauled the prisoner to his feet. 'I heard the whistle; I might have guessed it would be connected to here.'

He thrust Joe at one of the constables. 'Take him to the station and make your report.'

'I'll speak to you later,' he said to Mallory, 'but first I want to hear from Mr Sanderson.' Edward took the Inspector to Ambrose's study, Mallory watched them climb the stairs, her lips pursed in annoyance.

'Shall I fetch tea, ma'am?' Gertrude gave her a sympathetic look.

'Yes please, Gertrude, hot and strong.'

She was interrupted in her newspaper search by Edward and the Inspector entering the room.

'So, Mrs Wynter, do you know which part of the riverside your brother is searching?'

Mallory shook her head. 'I'm afraid not, Inspector, I know no more than it will be in the vicinity of London Bridge – my brother doesn't always confide in me, unfortunately.'

The Inspector blew out his cheeks. 'Well, I'd better go and find them. I'll find my own way out as your manservant isn't here.'

He banged the front door shut, the noise reverberating through the hall.

'What happens now, Edward? Was your information a trap?'

'I have no idea, but it does seem like this thug, Joe, wants revenge.' He eyed her thoughtfully. 'Be careful, Mallory, it seems you have a target on your back.'

'Not anymore, the Inspector has arrested him. I'm going out, Edward, and you're not going to stop me. I need to speak with Miss James.'

Chapter 32

Mallory was perturbed by the newspaper article on Elowen's finances. She knew Ambrose would be furious if he found out about her visit. She felt both guilty and protective – guilty because he would see it as invading his privacy and protective because she couldn't bear to see him hurt. He'd been hurt badly in a past relationship, and she was going to do her level best to stop it happening again. Quite how she was going to do that, she didn't know. Her only hope was to speak frankly with Elowen. It was with a certain trepidation that she stood outside Miss James' house.

Elowen stood up to greet Mallory, her green eyes wide with surprise.
'Thank you for agreeing to see me, Elowen.' Mallory smiled at her.
'I presume you have an update on the barrel of jewellery?'
Mallory shook her head. 'No, it's about a different matter.'
'Oh?' She waved Mallory to a seat. 'Would you like some refreshment?' Without waiting for an answer, she rang for her maid.
'This is a delicate matter regarding my brother, he doesn't know I'm here.'
Elowen frowned at her. 'I'm not sure I follow.'
Mallory took a deep breath. 'Can we be frank with each other? Woman to woman?'
Elowen thought for a few seconds before nodding her consent. 'Why not?'
'I have to say, Elowen, that the police feel your robbery was perpetrated by you, to claim insurance—no let me finish please.' She saw the anger in her face.
'Ambrose is desperately trying to prove your innocence.' The anger was replaced by anxiety.
'He is?' she whispered.

Mallory nodded. 'Yes, so please help him, Elowen. So far, your answers have not been helpful. When asked whether the necklace was insured you refused to tell him, the same when it came to your financial position.'

'Ambrose knows that I made a loss, we discussed it.' She tilted her chin defiantly, her hands clasped in her lap.

'Yes, but not the full amount, only a portion of it. I, on the other hand, do. You owe a great deal of money to someone. You borrowed heavily from a friend to invest in that new opera plus your own money and it failed. I presume your friend now wants his money repaid with interest.'

Elowen gave a deep sigh. 'It seems you are very well informed. Does Ambrose know about the loan from my friend?'

Mallory shook her head. 'I doubt it. That's why I'm here now. If you have any regard for my brother, tell me the truth. It's tearing him apart not knowing if you are guilty or innocent, and it grieves me to see it.'

Elowen remained silent for a few minutes before responding to Mallory's plea.

'The necklace wasn't insured. Oscar insured it whilst he was alive, but I couldn't afford to continue the premiums after his death. The cost was huge – the necklace is so valuable. It's made from a rare Burmese ruby,' she frowned, 'I think Oscar said it was called the Crimson Star, or something similar.'

'So you didn't arrange the burglary,' Mallory mused out loud.

'No. I'm even worse off now; I no longer have a valuable necklace, and an outstanding debt I can't pay.' She looked pleadingly at Mallory.

'Please don't tell your brother, I don't want his pity.'

'Were any documents drawn up over the loan?'

Elowen shook her head. 'No, and as far as I know there was no mention of interest. He was a friend, or rather a friend of Oscar's, he offered to help when he heard I was trying to raise money for my opera.'

'What were the terms?' Mallory was intrigued, why was there no legal paperwork drawn up?

'Well, I had put in some of my own capital, others put in small amounts, he said he would give the rest. As far as I was aware, the loan would be repaid from the takings, over a period – one year I believe was mentioned. I really thought the Opera would be hugely profitable, I did my figures and my research showed it was going to be a hit.'

'Why did it fail?'

Elowen turned a puzzled face towards her. 'That's what's so strange. I had priced and evaluated it, everything was organised, then at the last minute the premises let me down, then the orchestra and it went downwards from there. If I was cynical, I would say it had been deliberately sabotaged.'

Mallory began to see a connection. 'Had this ... friend ... discussed with you what would happen in the case of failure?'

'Not really, he did jokingly suggest the necklace was collateral.' She stopped, her mouth wide open in surprise. 'He wanted the necklace, didn't he?' She thumped the side of the chair with her hand. 'How could I have been so stupid? I should have guessed when things started to go wrong.'

'You couldn't possibly have foreseen it; he was a friend wasn't he? Don't blame yourself, what we need to think about is how to extract you from the mess.'

'You think it's possible?'

'I do. There are no legal documents to prove it was a loan, there is nothing written about the interest. What was he threatening to charge you?'

'Ten percent interest per month, compounded. The debt is growing by the day. Honestly, I had no idea he was going to do that. I would never have agreed had I known.'

'I think that's why he didn't document it.'

'I feel such a fool, I have always prided myself on my common sense.' She bit her lip ruefully.

'You are not a fool, Elowen, you trusted a friend who took advantage of you.'

Elowen took a deep breath. 'I tried hard not to encourage Ambrose, knowing I had this huge debt over me.'

'It would be better to confess all to him. Do not mention my visit. Ambrose will find a way to help you.'

'He will?' A flicker of hope in her eyes.

'There is no better person to defend you than Ambrose. He will fight tooth and nail for you.' She smiled at her, glad that she'd had the courage to visit. The important thing was for Ambrose not to find out.

'We have a friend who is a very good lawyer. I will have a quiet word with him so he is prepared when Ambrose approaches him, but please don't let Ambrose know that you and I have had this conversation.'

Elowen nodded. 'Thank you, Mallory, I wish I could repay your kindness.'

Mallory smiled. 'You can. I need to find a property of my own, Ambrose was very kind to take me in but now it's time to find my own house. Would you be so kind as to tell me how to do this?'

Elowen smiled. 'Start with the newspaper, I can make enquiries for you if you wish?'

'Thank you, I'll start with the paper and see how I go. Please go and see Ambrose as soon as you can.'

Mallory bought a newspaper from the stand before hailing a passing cab. Ambrose, she reflected, needed to think about his future, he couldn't do that whilst she lived there. It was time to move on.

Chapter 33

'Where do we start, I wonder?' Ambrose queried. He eyed the wharf buildings. This side of the river contained many wharves, warehouses and docks. To the right of London Bridge, wharves and warehouses continued all the way down to Tower Bridge. On the left were the docks.

'May I suggest we start with the wharves?' Finch suggested.

'That would be my preference as well.' He whistled quietly to himself while he made his choice.

'I'll start with the first one, you stay here, if I'm not out in fifteen minutes – well, you know what to do.'

Ambrose strolled over the first wharf, containing several warehouses. The building was several stories high, towering over the river. He approached a worker busy loading up a cart, who eyed him warily.

'Watcha want?'

Ambrose smiled. 'Just some information. I'm willing to pay and lend a hand to load the cart.'

'Well, I'll not say no to money, but I can manage the cart, fanks. Watcha wanna know?'

'Firstly, I'm looking for someone who works nights here.'

'That'll be the night watchman but 'e don't start until ten of the clock. We all works 'til then.'

'Then it's possible you can help me.' He produced a card, but the man shook his head at him.

'Can't read, sir. Just tell me what yer wants, and then I'll name the price.'

Ambrose gazed at him, debating whether to trust him.

'That depends on the information you provide,' he replied quietly.

'What's the question?'

'A young man went missing one evening, he was exceedingly drunk and was helped by two friends. It would have been about a fortnight ago, maybe a bit sooner.'

'I know who yer mean. It were about a fortnight ago.'
'Really?' Ambrose replied, a touch sarcastically.
'I knows what yer finking, that I'm lying to get the money.' He glared at Ambrose. 'Well, I ain't one of those, so what I saw, I saw.'
'Carry on.'
'Well, I saw a young man who was up the pole—'
'I'm sorry?' Ambrose frowned, perhaps he wasn't the best choice for information, either the man was slow witted or trying to make a fool of out of him.

The man sighed and gave him a disbelieving look.

'Drunk, unable to stand! It was just before I finished for the night. He were being helped by two mates; I felt sorry for the fella, they were rough with him. Anyway, I had to go inside to fetch somefink and when I got back outside, they'd gone. I did 'ear a splash though, but that ain't unusual, probably someone doing a bit of illegal fishing, the tide is high at night.' He looked at Ambrose. 'I fink that's worth a bob or two.'

Ambrose handed him a shilling. The man raised his eyebrows, gave him a dirty look, put the coin in his pocket and walked off shaking his head.

Ambrose surveyed the scene. What was the splash? He was beginning to fear the worst for John Kendle.

******

It was low tide on the Thames. Finch directed Archie to the riverbank at the docks.

'Go and talk to the mudlarks, they'll respond better to you than me.' Archie wandered down to the muddy bank. Carefully taking off his boots and long socks, he tucked the socks inside a boot and then tied the laces together and slung them round his neck. Mudlarks, the scavengers of the river, were still at work along the bank wading around like birds. Some had gone past the mud into the brackish water, wriggling between the boat chains and anchors searching for anything useful. Mostly they were ragged children, but he could see one or two bedraggled women bent double, searching the stinking mud with their hands for riches that had been either dropped or thrown overboard: silent figures carrying baskets on their backs. They scratched a living by picking up bits of coal, rope, copper, nails, occasionally a clay pipe – anything they could sell for a few pence. It was sheer, hard, physical work but they would rather flounder in the mud than face dying in the workhouse.

Archie rolled up his trousers, as high as they would go, before entering the sludge and mud of the Thames bank with its distinctive sulphurous odour. He sniffed the air and pulled a face as the smell of rotten eggs reached his nostrils. He scanned the shoreline looking for the nearest mudlark, he really didn't fancy going too far into deep mud. He squelched his way to the oldest of the mudlark children, whom he reckoned was about his own age. He hoped he wouldn't encounter shards of glass or sharp nails as the mud sucked and clawed at his feet as he moved.

'This is my patch, mate!' an indignant mudlark told him, as he bunched his fists ready for a scrap. He stood upright, his filthy trousers rolled up to his thighs and a nosebag slung across his slender body ready to hold his pickings. He would defend his patch; he couldn't afford to have it taken away.

'I guessed.' Archie replied. 'Wot I'm after is a bit of information.'

'Oh yeah? 'Ave yer got money, cos I need to earn, see?'

Archie nodded and produced a coin from his pocket which he quickly thrust back into his pocket before it could be grabbed.

'Wot yer wanna know?'

'About a man that was seen 'ere with two friends. 'E was really scammered – couldn't stand up, by all accounts. These mates were 'elping 'im. Did yer see 'im, only 'e's disappeared.'

'Who wants to know? Cos it ain't bleeding you.' He looked him squarely in the eyes.

'Yer right, it's me guvnor.' He nodded his head in the direction of Finch who was standing on the path, watching.

The mudlark remained silent. Archie tried again.

'This man were a friend of the guvnor, the rozzers don't wanna know so it's not good asking them, which I'm pleased about cos I don't trust 'em.'

The expression on the mudlark's face relaxed. 'Well, I'll tell yer what I know, but it'll cost yer two shillings.'

Archie shook his head. 'No, the guvnor won't pay that.'

'A shilling then?'

Still Archie shook his head.

'I ain't talking then.'

'Please yerself, I'll just ask another mudlark.' Archie went to move.

'Not so fast,' the boy said. 'I'll talk for sixpence.'

''Ows about fourpence? It'll take yer most of the day to earn that much and this won't take a minute for yer to tell me, so you'll still 'ave time to work.'

Archie thrust out his hand, the mudlark hesitated for a few seconds before shaking it. Archie felt the slime transfer to his hands.

'Go on then, wot do yer know?' Archie wiped his hands on his thigh.

'Don't know exactly 'ow long ago it was, but it were recent.' He nodded his head. 'Wouldn't remember it otherwise.' He took a breath and continued. 'The man could 'ardly stand upright, 'e were being 'eld by one of 'is mates – though I'd 'ardly call 'em mates as the uvver one were punching 'im. It were night time, that I do remember cos I were in the process of selling me pickings. Up the top there.' He pointed towards the wharf.

'If it's night time, 'ow did yer see it all?'

'Cos it weren't that late, it was only just getting dark but late enough that the workers were leaving, I only just made it in time to sell me wares.'

'What 'appened next?'

The mudlark shook his head. 'Dunno, I got me money and I scarpered before the river police came along. Now, I've told yer all I know, where's them coins?'

Archie handed over four pennies and squelched back towards Finch.

Finch handed him a square of cloth and told him to dry his feet before he put his boots back on. Inspector Johnson came towards them.

'Ah, I heard you were here. I came to tell you that the barrel has been collected.'

'Good news, Inspector, we'll go there soon.'

'What's he doing here?' The Inspector pointed at Archie and glared. 'Mudlarking is an offence, I'll have you know.'

'He was just talking to them, they're a mine of information,' Finch replied.

'Hmm ...' The Inspector was unconvinced.

'What did you learn, Archie?' Ambrose walked towards them, having just left the warehouse. 'Was it worthwhile? I also learned something interesting.'

Archie nodded but before he could repeat the information, a cry arose of a body in the mud. One of the wharf workers was pointing to a woman holding on to an overturned boat.

'Old Meg has found a cadaver,' came the shout, hands waving in the air trying to attract attention.

'The river of lost souls,' murmured Finch as he crossed himself. Archie shivered; he was glad he didn't find it.

The Inspector, unwilling to wade into the mud, called one of the constables who fetched a boathook. When the mudlarks saw the constable, they scarpered as fast they could. Only Meg remained, defiant of the police.

'I ain't doing any 'arm,' she screeched as she saw the constable approaching. 'You leave me be and I'll 'elp yer bring in that body,' she shouted at the constable. 'It were caught underneath this little boat.'

Despite being hampered by the basket on her back, she bent over the body and grabbed the jacket and waited for the constable to grab it with the boat hook. Between them hauled the body across the mud to where the Inspector stood. As quick as a flash, the woman disappeared, they were too busy looking at the body to notice her withdrawal.

The body was bloated, the face bruised and nibbled. 'Did he drown, do you think?'

The Inspector nodded. 'It looks like it, but we will have to do a postmortem to find out. Luckily it snagged on the boat, otherwise it would have fetched up in Limehouse.'

'Could it be John Kendle?'

The Inspector frowned. 'What makes you think it is? I grant you it's a young man.'

Archie piped up. 'I learned from a mudlark that John was beaten by two men, just on that wharf.' He pointed to the nearest building.

All of them turned to him in surprise. 'It cost me fourpence,' he muttered. 'I didn't 'ave a chance to tell you, Mr Finch.'

'That's alright, my lad, you would have done if you had time.'

'He's been in the water for some time, wouldn't you say Inspector?' Ambrose concluded.

The Inspector nodded. 'It's certainly been there longer than a few days. If that information is correct, then that would fit in with John Kendle.'

'I think it is,' agreed Ambrose. 'I heard the same thing from a warehouse worker, only there was a splash after.'

The Inspector sighed. 'We'll have to get it identified.'

Ambrose frowned. 'That will require you asking Mary Gage, she may not be strong enough to face it.'

'I know, but I can't think who else would know.'

Ambrose thought for a few minutes. 'Mrs Fortescue's cook is the aunt of Miss Gage; she may well have seen him enough times to identify him.'

The Inspector raised his eyebrows. 'Then I'd better go to see her, I've already got her address.'

'If it is John, then the likelihood is that it happened the evening he disappeared with those two thugs.'

The Inspector was cautious. 'Possibly.'

'Then he couldn't have murdered the landlady.'

'Let's not get ahead of ourselves,' warned the Inspector. 'We need to make sure that it is John Kendle, and how long he was in the water for. It's not impossible that he killed his landlady first, then met his friends here where an argument developed, and was thrown in the river.'

Ambrose sighed. The Inspector took pity on him.

'You may be right, but I can't afford to jump to conclusions at this stage. I shall head back to interrogate Joe Archer. I might have answers for you after that.'

'You've arrested Joe Archer?' Ambrose was amazed.

The Inspector nodded. 'Of course, you wouldn't have heard. There was an incident at your place today involving Joe Archer.'

'What?' Ambrose was stunned. 'What happened?'

Inspector Johnson merely smiled. 'Don't go to the Rising Sun without me. I'll call as soon as I finish the interrogation.' He tipped his hat and left, striding along the embankment to the police carriage.

Ambrose turned towards Finch.

'So, the house was the target again.'

'Looks like it, sir.'

'Thank God Sanderson was there; I hope Mallory was safe.'

'The Inspector would have mentioned it, sir, if somebody had been hurt. Let's concentrate on the here and now.'

'You're right, Finch.' He sighed, with great difficulty he pushed his concerns over home to one side and turned his attention to the case. 'So why do you think John was beaten by his friends?'

Finch shrugged and looked at Archie. Archie shook his head.

'Didn't say, 'e was too busy trying to sell 'is wares.'

'That kind of behaviour would be common around here, nobody would turn a hair,' Finch advised. 'They may see it, but they wouldn't remark on it. You did well, Archie lad, to get him to talk. They're a close-knit bunch I reckon.'

Archie nodded. 'Reckon you're right. Can we go 'ome now? I want to know what's 'appened.'

Ambrose agreed. 'I think we should. Let's not speculate about home. We will learn soon enough from Mr Sanderson. You've done well today, Archie.'

Archie smiled proudly. 'Thank you, sir.' He frowned. 'It's a shame about the dead body though.'

'Indeed.'

As they made their way back to Kensington, Ambrose contemplated the possibility of John Kendle being dead. It was looking more and more certain.

Chapter 34

They made their way through the cobbled streets and lanes in Southwark. Ambrose ducked under some clothes that were pegged on to a washing line strung across the narrow yard. Finch merely brushed away the flapping garment near his head.

'Was that a well?' Ambrose asked, referring to a small brick-lined pit they had passed before turning into another alley. 'It's rather pungent.' He sniffed the air and took out his handkerchief.

'No, sir, I believe it's a cesspool.'

'How revolting,' remarked Ambrose quietly, holding the linen cloth to his face.

'Sir, I'd advise you to put that away, remember we don't want to stand out.'

A few women lingered in the doorways, chatting with their neighbour whilst they rinsed some clothes in a bucket. Ambrose could feel the curious stares of a couple of men leaning against the wall, their arms folded. Ambrose immediately tucked the handkerchief away in his pocket and they quickened their step, anxious to get away.

'Are we lost, Finch?' he muttered. 'I don't feel very comfortable.'

'Yes, sir. I think we left the main road too early. Thankfully, we haven't strayed too far off the path. If we turn right here, and right again, we should be back on Borough Road.'

Ambrose breathed a sigh of relief as Finch's prediction proved correct. They asked for directions from a passerby. The alley they needed was further along and in a much more notorious place. There would be no room for error.

The sign outside The Rising Sun creaked as it swung, a light breeze having caught it. It was an ironic name for the public house, for the sun would have a hard time appearing in the tiny alley as it was overshadowed by taller buildings. Shady Alley nestled amongst other dark lanes under the shadow of St Alphege Church in Southwark. On leaving the Rising Sun, if you turned in the wrong direction you would soon find yourself in the undesirable lanes and alleys inhabited by the lawless and those in deep poverty – where your throat would be slit, your blood spilled over a mere shilling. Life was cheap, survival was everything.

Ambrose eyed the sign with misgiving. 'Not the most welcoming of places, is it?' At the insistence of Finch, he had dressed down in worn jacket and trousers that Finch had stained to look workworn.

'No, sir, it is not. I doubt it will be inside either.' Finch too was dressed as a labourer. They were joined by the Inspector.

'You're late,' he remarked.

'We got lost.'

The Inspector grunted. 'At least you're in one piece.'

'Just me to go in, Inspector. No offence, but you look like a copper and you, sir,' he turned towards Ambrose, 'the minute they hear your accent we're done for.'

The Inspector agreed. He had positioned his men discreetly around the area. One blast of his whistle and they would come running.

'I'll keep my eye on my men. I don't like the look of that beggar over there.' The beggar in question was sprawled on the cobbles opposite them. Even without the upturned hat in front of him, he looked the epitome of a beggar with his black eye patch and ragged jacket.

It was early evening, far later than any of them would have wanted. Early evening drinkers would be wending their way to the inn. More people meant more danger. By the time Inspector Johnson had finished with Joe and arrived at Ambrose's home he was in a grumpy mood. Ambrose walked across to the beggar, leaving Finch to enter alone. The Inspector positioned himself further away from the inn, he didn't wish to go deeper into that particular alley.

'Ain't seen you around before.' The beggar glanced up at Ambrose.

'No,' replied Ambrose, only briefly glancing at him.

'Ah, you're a toff!' He cackled, showing his black teeth. 'Best not to 'ang around 'ere then.' He looked curiously at him with his good eye. 'You wiv that copper? You after the landlord then?'

Ambrose moved one step away.

'It's alright, guv, your secret is safe wiv me. One-eyed Jack, they call me. Me eye patch is real, by the way, I ain't one of those thieves pretending to be beggars. Look!'

With dirty fingers he lifted the eye patch so Ambrose could see a space where his eye once was, the hole had been stitched up badly leaving a red patchwork scar.

'If you're after the landlord you'd best nab 'im while you can. He's more slippery than an eel, that one.'

'You know him then?'

'Yerse! Biggest criminal around. I go in there when I've earned a few pennies more than I usually do. Billy's a nice kid though, I hope you don't 'urt 'im,'e treats me nicely.'

Ambrose had a sudden thought. 'Do you remember a young man named John Kendle?'

One-eyed Jack nodded. 'The one they beat up?'

'How do you know he was beaten up?'

The beggar cackled. 'Talk of the 'ouse it was.'

'You saw him?'

'Only briefly. I were there that night 'e won a raffle prize. That's what started it, yer know.'

'A raffle prize?'

'Yerse.' One-eyed Jack nodded. ''E won a prize 'e weren't supposed to 'ave I reckon.'

'How do you mean?'

'Well, he was 'oping for a barrel of ale, but that weren't going to 'appen.'

'Why not?'

'Corse the barrel is always won by one of them landlord's friends.' He nodded sagely at Ambrose. 'It weren't ale in that barrel that's for sure.'

Ambrose was beginning to understand how the coins got to the agents.

'Where does John come into this?'

'I'm telling yer, though a coin or two in me 'at would 'elp.'
Ambrose threw some pennies into the hat.

'Ta, guv. Well, that John, as I said, didn't get the ale but got anuvver prize which 'e weren't 'appy about. 'E grabbed the prize and then left the Rising Sun.'

'Wait a minute, you said he wasn't supposed to get a prize, how do you know that?'

'Corse the raffles are fixed, ain't yer been listening to me? The barrel's always the last prize, people 'ad started to drift away when the barman told 'em there was an extra prize.' He shook his head. 'Never been known before, yer see, so I reckon it weren't for 'im.'

'What about John's friends, how did they react to it?'

'Nah, they weren't there at the time, neiver was the landlord, it were the new barman that gave 'im the prize.'

'How do you know John was beaten up if he'd left the pub?'

'Corse 'e came back, a bit later. By that time Joe and 'is mates were there and so's the landlord. I were tucked up in the corner of the bar, so Billy could serve me some free ale, 'e were good like that.' He checked his hat before continuing his story, wondering if he had enough to spare for a drink.

'I 'eard the landlord tell Joe to get that prize off 'im at any cost. So they plied 'im wiv drink and pretended to take 'im 'ome.'

'You didn't see him being beaten though.'

'Nah, true, but I 'eard the next day they'd beaten 'im up for breaking the code of honour.'

Ambrose put some more pennies in his hat and nodded to him and crossed the road to find the Inspector. Things were beginning to make more sense.

******

Finch straightened himself and pushed open the door and entered. Much to his relief there were few people inside; the hum of conversation stopped, they stared at the stranger in their midst. Billy, who had been wiping glasses behind the bar gave the customers an anxious look before coming to serve him.

'Not often we get strangers here,' he remarked loudly, then under his breath he muttered quietly, 'what are you doing here, you'll get me killed.'

'Half a pint of ale, mate. Yeah, I think I got the wrong inn, I'm supposed to be meeting an old army mate in a pub off Borough High Street. This ain't it, is it?' Finch enquired.

Billy shook his head. 'Nah, we're off Borough Road, you've got your roads mixed up, easily done for a stranger. When you've had your drink, I'll show you where to find it.' Billy pulled the handle on the barrel and sloshed some ale into a glass.

Satisfied with the stranger's answer, people returned to their conversations and laughter.

Finch muttered quietly to Billy. 'I need to know if a barrel arrived recently, It's been marked by the police with a red PL on the base. They're waiting outside.'

'There you go. Tuppence please.' Billy put the coins in the till and walked out the back.

Despite the return of the conversation, Finch felt eyes on his back, he couldn't risk turning around, so he drank his ale and waited for Billy.

'You done then? Let me show you the way, it'll be quicker than trying to give directions.'

Finch followed him out, adjusting the cap on his head. He made sure they weren't followed.

Billy turned to face him. 'It's in the landlord's room. It's empty though as it's lying on its side. I do know he's in a foul mood but I'm not sure where he is. He's probably upstairs, or hiding. Look, I'm not stepping back in that pub, they'll kill me, you gotta get me out of here.'

Finch grabbed his arm. 'Wait over there by that beggar.'

Finch waved at the Inspector and Ambrose.

'It's been opened, you'll find it in the landlord's room. Billy thinks the landlord is upstairs or hiding. Can you give us a couple of minutes to get away? All hell will break loose when you go in.'

'One minute only, whilst I call my men together. That's all you're going to get.'

Finch beckoned to Billy and the three of them ran as fast as they could back to the main road. They heard the police whistle as they tried to hail a cab as they turned into Borough Road. Ambrose wasn't surprised at their failure to secure one, their appearance didn't inspire confidence.

'We'll have more luck once we get to St George's Circus. Come on.' They took a quick breath before walking quickly, more police whistles could be heard in the distance. Ambrose risked a quick look over his shoulder.

'There's no-one following us. We can slow down.'

They reached The Circus and managed to get a cab, but only after brandishing a silver coin.

'You'd better come home with us,' Ambrose told Billy, 'the police will want your statement, and I've got some questions to ask you. Finch will give you some supper.'

Chapter 35

A weary Inspector visited Ambrose and Mallory the next day. He was sporting a black eye.

'Things didn't go well then,' Ambrose commented, noting the bruised eye.

'You could say that. It turned into something of a scrap, good job me and my men are good with our fists. It seems the people of The Rising Sun objected to us arresting the landlord and his wife.'

Mallory grimaced. 'Did they talk?'

The Inspector shook his head. 'Not yet, but they will. We have the barrel that held the jewellery, and we uncovered from the premises some packs of counterfeit money, all stored in a barrel. So thanks to you we have broken a counterfeit ring.'

'I'm not sure if you're aware that the inn had regular raffle prizes, each time it was a barrel of ale which was always won by one of the landlord's friends, probably Joe and his mates. I assume it wasn't ale in that barrel but coins.'

Inspector Johnson whistled. 'No, I didn't know that. The evidence is stacking up, thank you.'

'The other thing we found out yesterday was that John wasn't meant to have won a prize.'

Mallory, listening quietly to this exchange, had an idea.

'Then could it be that John wasn't killed for his counterfeit activities but for winning that prize? We could be following the wrong path if we only consider counterfeiting as the motive.'

The Inspector put his head to one side as if considering the point.

'No,' he concluded, 'it has to be the counterfeiting, winning a prize you weren't supposed to is too weak a motive.'

Ambrose gave her a sympathetic look; she took it as a warning not to pursue the point. She sighed but smiled pointedly.

'I came here for two reasons,' the Inspector continued, 'the first is that the postmortem has come through and the second is that I need to take statements from yourself and someone called Billy.'

'He's here, Inspector, we thought you would find it easier if we were all at the same premises. You will find him in the basement with Finch.'

'What was the result of the postmortem?' Mallory was eager to know.

'Well, he wasn't alive when he was thrown in the water, that we do know. You can't inhale water if you have stopped breathing, there wasn't any water in the lungs.'

'So,' mused Ambrose, 'he died, presumably from a blow, and they threw his lifeless body into the water, in the hope it would wash up miles down the river.'

'That about sums it up, yes,' agreed the Inspector.

'When will you take the aunt to identify the body?'

'As soon as I finish here, so if I could make a start with yourself?'

'You won't need me, Inspector,' Mallory informed him, 'so I will be downstairs talking to the staff.'

Mallory found Billy in the basement room that Finch used for the accounts.

'The police will be taking a statement from you shortly, Billy. Why don't you tell me what happened so you can keep it fresh in your mind.'

'There's not much more to tell other than what I told Mr Finch. Although …' he paused, 'I did learn from the new barman that he was in trouble about that raffle prize won by John Kendle. He had been left in charge to draw the raffle; he assumed the parcel near the barrel was another prize but as it didn't have a ticket on it he just drew one out of the hat and stuck it on there and shouted out the winning numbers. He only found out later that it belonged to someone else and was not part of the raffle. He thought he was gonna get the sack over it. It wouldn't surprise me if he did, the landlord was furious.' He added gloomily, 'don't know what I'm gonna do with meself now.'

'If it helps you, I've got temporary work for you here.' Finch informed him. 'Make sure you arrive tomorrow morning at seven o'clock sharp. It's a long day so be warned, you'll get paid at the end of each week, I can't promise how long it will last.'

'I appreciate that, Mr Finch, thank you.'

Billy was called to give his statement and Mallory returned upstairs.

She repeated to Ambrose Billy's extra information.

'Which is it, I wonder, that got John killed?'

'We'll keep an open mind, unlike the Inspector,' agreed Ambrose.

'I think we should pay the cook a visit a little bit later to find out if it's John Kendle. She may need a friendly face.' He looked at her hopefully.

Mallory was amused. 'What you mean is that you want me to go and see her!'

'If you wouldn't mind,' he cleared his throat, 'Miss James is coming to see me later today.'

'Ah, then you will definitely want me out of the way!'

He remained diplomatically quiet. She looked at him and said ruefully, 'on that note, I really do need to search for a house of my own, Rosy. I bought a paper the other day, I thought there might be some advertisements in there.'

Was it her imagination or was there a flicker of relief in his eyes? If so it was gone just as quickly.

'Well, if you insist on looking, maybe I could put some feelers out, Finch is probably the best person to ask.'

Of course he is, she thought, why didn't I think of that?

******

Mallory took a seat in Mrs Fortescue's pleasant drawing room. The pale striped wallpaper complimented the dark blue patterned sofa and chairs with their scrolled arms and intricately carved frames. In front of them on a small table was a tea tray. Mrs Fortescue poured the tea. Mallory waited for the steam to subside before taking a tiny sip of tea. It was very hot, politely she put the cup back on its saucer and waited for it to cool. She was worried about dropping the cup; it looked an expensive set with its white and gold fleur de lys design.

'It's so sad, isn't it my dear, to think Mary's fiancé might be dead. So young with a life ahead of him.' She shook her head sadly before sipping her tea.

'I know, I think Mary is being very brave. It must be hard not knowing whether he was alive or dead.'

They sat in silence for a short while before Mrs Fortescue asked her a question.

'How is Edward?' Mrs Fortescue asked, a glimmer of amusement in her eyes.

'Very well, I believe.'

'Have you not had a chance to visit the Italian Gardens with him?'

'No, I'm far too busy with the cases, Mrs Fortescue. Perhaps when all this is over.'

Mrs Fortescue sighed. 'Life is far too short to procrastinate, Mallory, look at Mary Gage.'

'I know, but when I go I want it to be free of cases otherwise my head will not be concentrating on the gardens. Edward deserves better than that.' She picked up her cup and took a sip, hoping to avoid further conversation on the matter. Mrs Fortescue gave her a keen glance but changed the subject.

'How are you doing on your search for houses?'

'Not very well. My time is tied up in the investigations, but I really need to do it soon.'

'Ah.' Mrs Fortescue replied knowingly, 'you are referring to Miss James and Ambrose.'

Mallory looked at her in amazement. Mrs Fortescue burst out laughing.

'Oh, my dear! It's been obvious for a while that he is very keen on her.'

Mallory smiled back. 'I know, it seems everyone but Ambrose knows.'

'Is it reciprocated?'

Mallory sighed. 'I truly hope so.'

They heard footsteps on the stairs followed by a light knock, Cook shyly entered the room.

'You wanted to see me madam?' It was clear she had been crying.

'Yes. I was going to ask you how it went but I can tell by your face that it was Mary's fiancé.'

A fresh set of sniffles ensued; Cook wiped her tears away with the corner of her apron before nodding.

'How is Mary?' Mallory asked.

'As well as can be expected, madam, thank you.'

'I was rather hoping to have a word with her about John's raffle prize, but this is probably not the best time.'

Seeing her puzzled expression, Mallory explained.

'It could be the reason why he was killed, until we see it we can't rule it out. If it is, then it's possible she might be in danger.'

'Oh!' Cook looked horrified. 'I'll mention that madam, I shall be seeing her later on.'

'Thank you.' Mallory nodded her head.

'Take the rest of the day off, you will need to be with Mary.'

'Thank you, madam, I've left a cold supper in the pantry.' She bobbed and left the room wiping a stray tear from her face with her forearm.

'Do you really think she might be in danger?'

Mallory turned her face towards her, her blue eyes holding Mrs Fortescue's gaze. 'I'm sorry to say this but she might be, it really depends on why he was killed. If she has something the killer wants, it's feasible he may search for her.'

'Oh dear, I didn't think of that. How very astute of you, Mallory.'

They finished their tea in silence.

'It was very good of you to come and see how Cook was bearing up.'

'I'm sorry it's bad news and that Cook had to identify him. It would have been too difficult for Mary.'

Mrs Fortescue nodded. 'Indeed. Do let me know how the house-hunting is going.'

'I will.' She smiled and rose to take her leave.

'Mallory!'
Mallory turned back towards her, her hand on the door handle.
'Do go to the Italian Garden with Edward.'

Chapter 36

It was another hot day, the sun streamed through the drawing room window shining onto the gleaming table with its vase of flowers. Finch showed Edward into the drawing room. Mallory looked surprised to see him.

'Hello Edward! This is a pleasant surprise, is this a social visit or connected with the case?'

'Both.' He smiled as he took a seat. Out of his case he produced the newspaper that he had taken from her a few days ago.

'Do you remember showing me this article on burglary items?'

She nodded. 'It's annoying me why I can't remember.'

'I've done some digging.'

Ambrose walked into the room.

'Ah, Sanderson, the very man I wanted to see.'

Edward raised an eyebrow.

'It's not to do with the case, it's a private matter.'

'Then we'll discuss it in a minute.' He held up the paper to Ambrose.

'I've been looking at this article that Mallory gave me as it puzzled her, she thought there was something familiar about it. I offered to give it some thought, but unfortunately I can't offer an answer.' He turned towards her. 'Apologies Mallory.'

'No need to apologise, Edward. Thank you for looking anyway. Maybe it will come back to me.'

Ambrose briefly read the article. Frowning, he asked what was familiar about it. 'Do you think it was the items in the barrel?'

'I wish I could remember, Rosy.'

'I had a chat with some colleagues,' Edward commented. 'I came across this information, I have no idea if it's helpful to you but it's the only thing I have to offer.' He produced a slip of paper from the inside pocket of his jacket. He passed it to Mallory.

Mallory glanced at it.

18 Boulevard de Mer, Cannes

She looked at him in astonishment. 'South of France?' She passed the paper to Ambrose.

'How does this connect to the case?'

Edward shrugged. ' I don't know, but if you lift your thumb you will see the owner's name.'

'Oh!' Ambrose frowned as he read it.

'I don't know the authenticity of it, it could be out of date information,' Edward warned them.

'Indeed,' Ambrose nodded. 'Nevertheless, thank you.' He picked up the newspaper article. 'I'll file these away for the moment, I need to talk to you on a different subject.'

Ambrose took Edward into his study. Mallory guessed what the conversation was going to be about – Elowen's financial predicament.

She sighed. It was about time she sorted out her own problem, a house of her own. Whenever she had broached the subject, it was waived away airily as though it wasn't important, but it was to her. Now was the ideal time to ask Finch, she could rely on him not to dismiss it offhand.

She unearthed him in the kitchen. Billy was busy polishing the silver with Archie. Gertrude and Ruby were elsewhere with cleaning duties.

'Finch, I think it's time to find a place of my own. Where do I start to look? I've tried the paper.'

'Indeed, madam, I believe you've mentioned it before. I have been keeping a discreet eye on some places, one I think you will like, but it's not available just yet. I was going to mention it to both of you once I knew the actual date. Would you like me to enquire?'

'Yes please, although I don't suppose I can view any premises until these cases are solved.'

A loud jangling of a bell interrupted their conversation. She looked up at the board on the wall containing all the bells, and saw the front door bell moving. Finch hurried to answer it. Mallory followed him, surely it couldn't be the Inspector already.

'Mrs Fortescue, how lovely to see you! Oh, you've brought your cook. I presume this is not a social visit. Shall we go up to the drawing room?'

Mrs Fortescue smiled at her and shook her head. 'I think my cook would feel more at home in a smaller room.'

'Forgive me, let me show you into the morning room.'

Once they were ensconced on chairs, Mrs Fortescue encouraged her cook to talk.

'Do tell Mrs Wynter, she will understand. It's vital she knows.'

Cook nodded and took a deep breath. 'It's like this, madam, I spoke to Mary about that raffle prize of John's. She broke down in tears and told me to get rid of it, she want's nothing more to do with it. She said it was cursed, and if John didn't want it then neither did she.' She swallowed before adding, 'it's never been opened. Can I give it to you?' She held out a small wrapped parcel tied with string, the waxed seal still intact.

'Thank you,' Mallory replied as she took it.

'As soon as Cook mentioned it, I thought you ought to know, so we came straight here.'

She looked at Mallory in concern. 'My dear, I don't believe it's cursed for one minute, but I do hope it doesn't put either of you in danger.'

'Thank you. I really hope it provides some answers. I will update Ambrose and Edward when they have finished their conference.'

Mrs Fortescue looked delighted. 'Edward is here?' She smiled mischievously at her.

'He brought some news regarding the case.' Mallory frowned and her hand flew to her lips. 'Where are my manners! May I offer you both some lemonade? It's another hot day, far too hot for tea I fear.'

'Thank you but no. We really must get back before the heat becomes unbearable.'

As Mallory showed them out, Mrs Fortescue took her arm gently.

'Remember what I said, my dear, about life being too short.'

She patted her arm and then withdrew her gloved hand. Mallory let her breath out slowly once the door closed. Why did everyone want to guide her? It was really infuriating. Clutching the parcel, she went upstairs to the drawing room to discover its contents.

Sitting on a chair, she sniffed the parcel first in case it contained contaminated food. Satisfied, she neatly cut the string and opened the parcel. On seeing the muslin cloth, she frowned. Was it really just a cloth? Why would you give a cloth to someone? She picked it up and prodded it, there was something inside it. Unfurling the cloth she discovered a black velvet bag. Discarding the cloth, she put the bag on her knees and gently pulled open the drawstrings and peeped inside. All she could see was some blue silk. Gingerly, she teased the silk out, it was neatly wrapped around something, delicately unrolling it she caught her breath when she saw its hidden secret. The Crimson Star! There nestling on the blue silk, twinkling in the sunshine, was a beautiful ruby necklace, its large central ruby flashing fire and passion. It was the only way she could describe its colour.

Quickly she rolled it back in its silk cocoon and returned it to the bag. Raising her hand to her lips, she considered the puzzle, there were so many questions. What did this mean? What did John have to do with Elowen James? How did John end up with the necklace? No wait, that wasn't correct. It wasn't how John ended up with the necklace it was more a case of how it ended up at The Rising Sun. She knew how it got into the raffle – Billy explained that. The real question was what did The Rising Sun have to do with Elowen? The Rising Sun, she mused, was part of a counterfeit gang. It was also connected to Pinnerton Lodge. Did Mrs Thornton have a part in any of it, and was she really the sweet old lady she appeared to be? So many questions, her head was spinning in trying to find the answers. Mrs Thornton, maids, Elowen, John and Mary were all whirling around inside her brain.

It was impossible to think straight. She groaned and rubbed her temples with her fingertips. She needed to show Ambrose and Edward the necklace.

Knocking on the door, she waited for the invitation to enter. Normally she wouldn't bother knocking, but as he wanted to discuss a private matter with Edward, she felt obliged to knock for admittance.

Chapter 37

Mallory produced the necklace from the silk. She heard their gasps as the Crimson Star seduced them, its flaming light shining like a beacon. Just as it must have seduced the thief who took it – not by its beauty but its value.

'It's beautiful, isn't it?' She put it quickly back into the silk nest and pouch.

'It raises so many questions.'

'I know,' Ambrose replied, 'and we probably haven't got all the answers.'

'It might help if you list them in order,' Edward advised. 'If you permit, I will tell you if any of your theories hold water – in a legal sense.'

'I am now wondering if John was killed for the necklace – or is that just a coincidence?' Mallory looked at both of them.

'There is certainly a case for both,' Ambrose reflected. 'That begs the question then, was he the thief?'

Edward shook his head. 'That's not logical, if he were the thief, he wouldn't have been upset at getting the necklace as a prize.'

'But Mary said he hadn't opened it, so how would he have known it was the necklace?'

'No.' Edward replied. 'He could have felt the parcel, guessed what it was and simply handed back the prize to the barman– clearly it was at The Rising Sun to be fenced.'

A few minutes of silence followed whilst they thought through the scenario.

'What if John was part of a jewel gang? What if he recognised the parcel, after all he might have been the one to parcel it up. If he thought the gang might believe he intended to steal it, would he pass it to Mary for safety?' Ambrose queried.

Edward shook his head. 'He would still have just handed it back, his friends weren't there.'

'However, if he decided to keep it for himself, isn't it likely he would pass it to Mary as quickly as possible?'

Edward considered it. 'It's possible,' he conceded, 'but unlikely. I'm not convinced by it.'

Mallory could see Ambrose was working through a theory in his mind. 'Although ...' he hesitated before continuing, 'it would also work if he only knew about the necklace through his friends. We know they weren't there at the time, he knew if he tried to give it back to them there was a risk they wouldn't believe him.'

Edward sighed. 'There's too many errors in that theory. Point one: he wouldn't have recognised the parcel if he had only heard about it through his friends. Point two: if that was the case, he would have handed it back over the bar before they arrived, the parcel would be intact and no-one would be the wiser.'

'Both of you have overlooked the one obvious, important fact.' Mallory said firmly.

'Which is?' Puzzled, Ambrose turned towards her. Edward raised an eyebrow.

'He clearly didn't know what the parcel contained, because he would never put his fiancé in danger by handing it to her if he knew its contents.'

'That's a very good point.' Edward confirmed. 'I believe we can rule out his part in the theft.'

'Then how did it end up at The Rising Sun?' Mallory was perplexed. 'There are no known links, yet Elowen's necklace ended up there. We know it wasn't part of the Norwood haul. It was stolen before those burglaries started.'

Mallory thought for a few seconds before continuing. 'I can only think of a tenuous link. Both Elowen and Mrs Thornton had maids that left.'

'Go on.'

'Don't you find that mysterious? Elowen's maid leaves to look after her mother straight after the burglary, Mrs Thornton's maid leaves to look after an ailing sister.'

Edward shook his head. 'It's too tenuous, unless you can prove it.'

'Wait ... I remember the Norwood Junction railway porter mentioning that a woman asked about large houses who might need a maid. He directed her to Pinnerton Lodge.'

'That doesn't mean it's the same maid, it's circumstantial evidence at best.' Edward informed her. 'You will have to do better than that.'

Mallory sighed. 'Do you think the Inspector could be right about the counterfeit connection?'

'It's something we can't rule out at this stage.' Ambrose frowned. He pulled the bell for Finch.

'We need some sustenance if we are to work this thing through.'

They took a break for refreshments in the drawing room. Ambrose brushed away crumbs from his shirt, like Edward, he had taken off his jacket due to the heat. As he flicked the last crumb from his trousers he hazarded a guess.

'We know that the landlord was a fence, and it is likely that he was given the necklace to sell. Mistakenly it was put with the raffle prizes – you can see just by looking at the rubies that it's extremely valuable – so the thief and fence have lost a huge amount of profit. It follows that they would want to recover it as quickly as possible. If it was known John had won it—'

'He would have been attacked to recover it.' Mallory finished the sentence for him. Ambrose nodded. He was used to her interruptions, so it didn't irritate him.

'So,' Edward concluded, 'we can safely assume John was killed by his friends, because that's the likely conclusion the court will draw. The friends didn't find the necklace on him, so they searched his lodgings but were interrupted by the landlady – hence her murder.'

Ambrose agreed. 'That seems to link his friends to the theft or at least the landlord.'

Mallory looked at him thoughtfully. 'If the landlord was supposed to pass on the necklace, does that mean the burglar or burglars were local to the inn, or a regular drinker there? If not, surely they would take it to another fence?'

Edward considered this. 'Yes that's logical. So it still comes down to the link.'

'Wait,' Ambrose frowned. 'Lory, you said burglar or burglars – what makes you think there was more than one person involved?'

'Well, I've been thinking. It must have taken some planning to steal that necklace. I don't believe it was a spur of the moment action. The thief must have had prior knowledge of the necklace, where the safe was hidden, when to strike, and how to gain entrance to Elowen's house.'

Edward glanced at her, impressed with her critical thinking.

'You are right. Inside knowledge had to be gained, which likely means the maid was involved, given that there was no other staff. That maid must be connected to someone in The Rising Sun, otherwise there is no other way it would end up at the inn. Well done, Mallory!'

'So, all we need now is to find Kitty Bunbury. Which reminds me, has Finch had any information back from his friend regarding Kitty?'

Ambrose shook his head. 'Not yet, which means Kitty Bunbury isn't her real name.'

Mallory blew out her cheeks. 'Still no nearer to solving it. At least, Ambrose, you can give Elowen the good news about her necklace.'

Ambrose smiled. 'Indeed.'

Mallory rubbed her temples and closed her eyes; a headache was beginning. Ambrose noted it.

'Let's take a break from trying to puzzle things out. It will do us all a power of good to spend some time away from it. We can come back much more focused.'

'I think that's a good idea,' Edward agreed, concerned that Mallory was showing signs of strain. 'Mallory, I have nothing urgent on, why don't we visit the Italian Gardens today?'

'Good idea, Lory,' Ambrose agreed. 'I will visit Miss James to tell her the good news. The necklace will remain in my safe until the police clear it.'

Edward was waiting for a reply, Mallory knew he didn't deserve excuses. Perhaps a break would be helpful. She smiled back at him. 'That would be nice, Edward, thank you.'

They walked to Kensington Gardens, taking their time due to the heat. Although her parasol shaded her from the sun, they kept to the shadows of overhanging buildings and trees to avoid the glaring sunshine. A question suddenly sprung into Mallory's mind as they walked.

'What do you make of the French address?'

'No, Mallory,' he said gently, 'no more talk of cases. You need a break.' They came to a busy road.

'It will be easier to cross if you take my arm,' he advised, 'I won't have to worry that you are keeping up.'

They made it across safely despite a dray cart driver shouting at them to get out of the way. Edward steered Mallory through the Lancaster Gate entrance and took the path to the ornamental water garden. It was pleasant to hear the birds in full song, the splashing of water from the fountains cooled the air a little.

'Did you know,' Edward said pleasantly, as they strolled towards one of the four water basins, 'that Prince Albert designed the water garden as a gift of love to the Queen in 1860?'

'That's a rather extravagant gift, most people just give flowers or jewellery.'

Edward laughed. 'What a mourning brooch like the maid of Mrs Fortescue's sister?'

Mallory chuckled. 'Oh, yes, I'd forgotten that story. Wait a minute, you got that Prince Albert fact from Mrs Fortescue, didn't you?'

She stopped in her tracks and turned towards him, an amused smile on her face. 'You were too young to know that fact. Admit it, Edward Sanderson, Mrs Fortescue told you!'

'There was me thinking you would be impressed by my knowledge,' he said with a broad grin.

'I probably would have been, if Mrs Fortescue's name hadn't cropped up, I knew you accompanied them here. It's the sort of thing Mrs Fortescue would know.'

'Ah, but I do know some history about this place.' He gently took her arm and pointed to a statue near the far basin. 'Over there is a sculpture of my namesake, Edward Jenner, for his work on smallpox. It was paid for by international subscription. Are you impressed now?'

She laughed. 'Very.'

He was good company; Mallory enjoyed his anecdotes as they strolled around admiring the fountains and the marble rosettes. All too soon they made their way back to Century Square. She felt a weight had been taken off her shoulders.

'Thank you, Edward. I really enjoyed it. You were right, I did need a break.'

'Have I heard you correctly, you are actually agreeing with me?'

'Just this once. Don't get used to it!'

Chapter 38

The following day, the sun was still shining fiercely, no imminent sign of a change in the weather. The air was beginning to feel oppressive.

'When will it end?' Mallory complained to Gertrude as she brought the post on a tray. Putting the tray down, Gertrude drew one of the curtains to block out the sun.

'Is that better, ma'am?' Mallory nodded her thanks.

'I never thought that I would be longing for the rain again.' Gertrude said as she picked up the tray. 'Now we've got sunshine all I want is rain!'

'Any of that post for me?'

Gertrude shook her head. 'It's all for sir.'

'He's in his study, shall I take it for you?'

'If you wouldn't mind, ma'am, I have the laundry to sort.' She put the post on the table and left. Mallory picked up the letters, examined them one by one before taking them into the study.

'Here's the latest post.' She put them on his desk. He glanced at them before putting them in his drawer.

'Aren't you going to open them?'

'Was there anything of interest amongst them?' He asked drily as he closed his newspaper.

'How would I know?'

'Because you've been through them.' He looked up at her, an amused smile on his face. 'You will have to learn to be neater when you inspect them, you've left one upside down.'

Huffing as she sat in a chair, she asked him how Elowen took the news of the necklace.

'Delighted. Although I can't release it yet.'

'So, she's no longer a suspect.'

'No.'

'We need to let Lord Arlington know.'

'Yes, but we have no real address for them. I'm going to delay putting an advertisement in the paper. We need to work on who took the necklace. I still don't think we have strong links to build a case.'

'Then let's start at the beginning again and throw away all our preconceived ideas. I'll fetch my notebook.'

She flicked open a page. 'Why don't you list things, it might help put them into an order.'

He wrote furiously, his pen flying across the paper without pause. She waited patiently for him to finish.

'Has that helped?

'I'm not sure,' he replied. 'It's helped me concentrate on the facts, but it's not providing any immediate answers.'

'As far as I can see,' she said, idly flicking through her book, 'everything ends up at The Rising Sun.' She picked up a pencil from his desk and chose a fresh page and wrote down the links as she saw them.

Ruby necklace ends up at THE RISING SUN
John won a prize at THE RISING SUN
John was killed by his friends who worked for the landlord of THE RISING SUN
Proceeds of the Norwood burglaries were taken to THE RISING SUN

She tore the page out and handed it to him.
'See? The Rising Sun is the common denominator.'
'Agreed, but it's not proof.'
'We need to work out the people involved.'
She chose another sheet.

Norwood burglaries are connected to Pinnerton Lodge by way of a barrel.

Tapping the end of the pencil on her teeth, she pondered what to write next.

Therefore, somebody in the house must be involved – the maid Ellen Ward, or Mrs Thornton. The barrel is sent to THE RISING SUN, so that person must have a connection to the inn.

She showed her page to Ambrose. He grunted.

'I thought I'd uncovered Pinnerton Lodge's secret.' She shook her head. 'Clearly not, it still has a secret to tell – who is involved with the inn?'

'Let me look at those pages again.' She passed them to him.

'One thing stands out. There have been two burglaries, the proceeds of which both end up at the inn, there must be a connection between them.'

Mallory frowned. 'Two maids as well. One at Elowen's house, one at Pinnerton Lodge. Coincidence?'

Ambrose considered it. 'Possibly. We do seem to be getting somewhere at long last. I think John having the necklace confused the issue, leaving him out of the equation is making things clearer.' He smiled. 'The short break away from the case must have been beneficial to both of us.'

Mallory nodded. 'I do feel refreshed, which is why I think we are able to view the whole thing differently.'

They sat there for some time in silence, both trying to fathom the puzzle.

Mallory broke the spell. 'What if Elowen's ex maid *is* the maid at Pinnerton Lodge?'

'Can we prove it though?'

'Let's test it out.'

He sat back in his chair and stared at his sister.

'I'm listening.'

She flicked over a few pages in her book.

'Elowen said the maid left a day or so after the theft, due to her mother being ill. Could that be Mrs Thornton?' She shook her head at her brother. 'I know you're going to say that's wild speculation but that's all we have for now.'

He rubbed his chin. 'Actually, that does make sense. It's entirely possible the same person or persons were responsible for both burglaries.'

'We never saw the maid at Pinnerton Lodge. The one and only time she arrived when I was there, she locked herself in a bedroom. She clearly didn't want to be seen. As we don't know when she started work at Pinnerton, it's feasible she could have been working at Elowen's at the same time because she was only part time at both properties. It's entirely possible that once she left Elowen's she could have been eyeing up potential targets on those days.'

Ambrose nodded to himself. Mallory remained quiet whilst he marshalled his thoughts.

'If they are one and the same, that puts Mrs Thornton as a possible suspect. Finch hasn't come back with any information on – what's the maid called?'

'Ellen Ward.'

'So Ellen Ward could also be an alias, which is why nothing has turned up. Yes, it's starting to look like a theory, Lory.'

Mallory nodded. 'Good. I've just remembered something.' She looked at him.

'Have you still got the newspaper that Edward gave you with the French address?'

He reached across to a shelf and produced them. 'What's troubling you?'

'A vague idea, let me read the article again.'

She began nodding her head. 'Yes, I see … I knew there was something but couldn't remember because of the concussion.' She handed the paper back to her brother. A seed of an idea had been planted in Mallory's mind; she would leave it to germinate fully before sharing it with her brother.

'What is it?'

She shook her head. 'It's only an idea, I'm not ready to share it yet, I need to think it through properly.'

He read the article hoping to gain an insight.

'I can't deduce anything from this.'

'I'm not telling you until I'm sure it works. How old is that paper?'

He glanced at the paper to check. 'About three months ago.'

He gave her a keen glance. 'What does it mean?'

'It means we have been lied to.'

Chapter 39

'Are you going to tell Inspector Johnson about our findings?' Mallory queried as the chilled soup was served.

'I think we must tell him about the recovered necklace at the very least,' he replied, thanking Finch with a nod of his head.

'I'll write to him once we've finished supper. Are you ready to share your theory?'

'Possibly.' She sipped her soup as her mind worked out the finer details of her idea.

'Is it water-tight? You always did have father's legal brain. I, on the other hand, have his financial acumen.'

She shook her head. 'I'm not sure. I think it's really going to need a confession to seal it, and the Inspector will need to hear that first hand.'

'Tell me about your idea over coffee, I'll be able to concentrate fully then.'

In the event, Ambrose didn't have to write. The Inspector called as they were drinking coffee. Billy brought up another cup and saucer as Finch showed the Inspector into the drawing room.

'Could you bring the brandy please as well. I'm sure the Inspector could do with a stiff drink.' Finch nodded at Billy.

The Inspector frowned. 'You've given Billy a job?'

Ambrose shook his head. 'No. Finch is training him in the hope it will help him to find employment.'

'I called to update you on a couple of things. Bob Miller, the carter at Norwood was the one who picked up the barrel.'

'Really?' Mallory stared at him, open mouthed.

'Does that mean …?'

The Inspector nodded. 'Yes. We are investigating Mrs Thornton.'

Mallory pulled a face. 'I confess I didn't think about Bob Miller. That complicates things.'

'The good news is that finally we have a confession from Joe Archer over the two murders. It seems Joe was responsible for the landlady and Arthur for John. We now have Arthur Cripps in custody, not to mention the landlord and his wife.'

Ambrose smiled. 'That's definitely something to celebrate.' He poured two large balloon glasses of brandy.

'There's another reason for you to celebrate. I need to show you something. Drink your coffee whilst I fetch it.'

He returned carrying the black drawstring bag.
The Inspector gave him a questioning look as took the bag.
'What am I supposed to be looking at?'
'Open it and see.'
He put down his cup and peeked inside the bag. He looked at Ambrose in amazement.
'Is it what I think it is?'
Ambrose nodded. 'Indeed.'
The Inspector gently pulled the necklace from its nest of blue silk. He stayed silent as the rubies winked and glowed at him.
'How did you get this?' He put the necklace back in its bag and went to put it in his pocket.
'No Inspector, that necklace doesn't leave this house. It will remain in my safe until such time as you release it.' He held out his hand for it. The Inspector glared at him.
'It's safer here than in your station. No-one knows it's here except you, however, if you took it to your station …'
'Yes, I see your point.' He grumpily conceded and handed the bag back. 'It can't go anywhere without my permission though,' he added, a touch testily.
'I will sign a receipt for you if you like,' Ambrose offered.
The Inspector shook his head. 'Not necessary, hopefully it won't be long until we get to the bottom of the theft.'
'Ah, we can help with that,' Ambrose smiled. 'Mallory has a plan.'

'I see,' he replied, after Mallory explained her thoughts. He rubbed his chin with his hand and nodded. 'Yes, it could work. Let me know when you need me.' He swallowed the last of his brandy and stood to leave.

'Much obliged to you for the brandy and the plan.' He nodded at them before leaving the room.

'Oh, that was easier than I thought, I was expecting an outright rejection.' Mallory said as they heard the front door closing with its customary bang.

'Yes, I expected more of a fight. I'm glad John and his landlady's murders have been resolved. At least we have completed one case.'

'Are you going to send Mrs Fortescue a note of our fees?'

Ambrose tilted his head to one side as he considered the question.

'I'm not sure. We have a few expenses but we didn't do very much.'

'Perhaps just include a small amount of expenses to keep her pride intact. I think she will be offended if we don't send her an invoice.'

'Talking of invoices – it's time to contact Lord Arlington.'

He took some paper and a pencil from the writing bureau in the corner of the room. Hastily scribbling out a message he rang the bell for Finch.

'This is for The Times.'

Finch nodded and glanced at the paper.

If both A's would like to make contact they will hear some good news – by appointment only, please advise by letter.

Finch raised an eyebrow.

'I'd prefer to be prepared for their visit, I don't think they're going to like the outcome.'

'Indeed, sir.'

'I think it's time to retire for the night. Tomorrow I will prepare invoices.'

******

Ambrose slit open the letter. He recognised Lord Arlington's slanting writing. Mallory waited patiently while he scanned the sheet of notepaper.

'What does he say?'

'Nothing much. He's coming tomorrow at four o'clock. I need to sort out Mrs Fortescue's invoice, though I would rather not charge her.'

'I know, but if we don't we will risk upsetting her. She's a proud lady, she would feel she'd be taking advantage of us if we didn't charge. Why not compromise?'

He frowned. 'What do you mean?'

'Give her the fee note but tell her it's such a small amount that you would rather a charity receive it.'

He chewed his lip as he thought about it. 'Actually, that's not a bad idea.'

'Do you want me to take it to her?'

Ambrose nodded. 'I have some business to take care of.'

'Then you might as well write notes to Elowen and Edward inviting them to dinner tomorrow, I can deliver those as well.'

Ambrose hesitated for a few seconds, then saw the steely glint of his sister's eyes and nodded.

'Good, I'll collect them in a few minutes.'

Mrs Fortescue was delighted to see Mallory. She frowned when she saw the amount of the invoice.

'My dear, this only covers your expenses, not your time.'

'I know but given the sad results we feel it should be expenses only.'

'But it's such a small amount.'

Mallory nodded. 'May I suggest you pay that sum to Mary; it might help with his burial costs? As far as I know there was no family and I'm sure Mary would want to do right by John.'

Mrs Fortescue smiled. 'That's an excellent suggestion, I have a sum in mind. My cook tells me that Mary is deeply unhappy at the millinery shop and wants to get away from it all.'

'I can understand that, there are too many reminders for her here. I do hope she finds something else.' She smiled sadly at her. 'I must go now; I have several errands to run for my brother.'

'I do hope you will find time for the Gardens,' Mrs Fortescue remarked artfully.

Mallory sighed. 'The Italian Garden was beautiful, Mrs Fortescue.'

'You've been with Edward?' Mrs Fortescue smiled. 'I'm so pleased.'

Mallory smiled. 'I really must get on with my errands.'

The Hansom cab drew up outside Elowen's mews house. As she stepped down from the cab she could smell the fresh dung the horse had made. The horse steamed in the sunshine as it stood patiently waiting, after snorting several times it was rewarded by a bag of hay. The driver nodded his consent to wait for her as he wiped the horse's back with a cloth.

'Yerse, he could do with a bit of a rest. You'll likely find us sheltering under the trees, down there.' He nodded towards the end of the mews where the overhanging branches of trees provided the road with partial shade.

She rang the bell. She was greeted by the young maid and invited inside where it was cooler.

'I'm very sorry but madam isn't at home to visitors at the moment.'

'Really?' Mallory replied as she heard laughter, and in an instant recognised the laugh – Edward's. What was he doing here?

'I was told she was not to be disturbed, as she is in a business meeting.'

More laughter followed.

'It sounds as though their ... business ... has concluded.' The maid gave her a sympathetic smile. 'Sorry, miss, they're my orders.'

Mallory took a deep breath. 'Of course, may I confirm whether Mr Sanderson is her visitor?' The maid nodded.

'Very well, can I leave these notes for Miss James and Mr Sanderson?'

She passed the maid two envelopes.

'May I take your name please?'

Mallory handed her a calling card and nodded her thanks, she heard the drawing room open and Elowen calling for her maid. She had no wish to be seen so she strode through the door quickly, biting her lip to hide the disappointment she felt.

Out in the sunshine she took a deep breath. She recalled that Ambrose was going to ask Edward to help Elowen over her debt. She frowned as she made her way to the end of the Mews for her cab. She doubted Edward mixed pleasure with business, he always seemed to take his legal cases with the utmost seriousness. Debt didn't seem to be a laughing matter. She was still puzzling over the visit as the cab reached her house.

'Everything alright?' Ambrose asked her as he noted her puzzled face.

'Of course.'

'Then why the frown?'

'It's nothing really, just something odd.'

'Odd?'

'It's not important.' She smiled brightly at him, but he wasn't fooled.

'It clearly is, so tell me.'

She sighed. 'It's just … no – it really doesn't matter.'

He folded his arms. 'Out with it, Lory!'

She sighed again. 'I dropped off Edward's note at Elowen's.'

'Why?' he frowned.

'Because he was with her. The maid said she wasn't at home to visitors, yet I heard Edward's voice. A business meeting, I think it was described as.'

'But you're not convinced?'

She put her head to one side as she considered it. 'That is what I find puzzling, I could hear them both laughing.'

'Hmm …' Ambrose was thoughtful. 'I asked him if he would help her with the legalities of a debt.'

'It struck me that Edward is not the type to treat his legal cases with such frivolity.'

'I too would not have expected laughter.' Ambrose frowned.

Mallory sighed. She recalled Edward's warning that he wouldn't wait forever, his definition seemed to be remarkably short term. Making a decision she thrust out her chin and looked at her brother.

'Let's put it aside for now, we have other matters to think about such as the plan. Have you informed the Inspector?'

He nodded. 'It's all in hand, now we simply wait.'

Chapter 40

The following afternoon, the weather changed. Thunder could be heard, at first it was distant then the rumblings turned into an overhead crash just as Edward and Elowen arrived together the following afternoon. Ambrose raised an eyebrow as they were shown into the drawing room.

'Sanderson and Miss James, how convenient both of you arriving at the same time,' he said pleasantly as he stood to greet them. He waved them to two empty chairs; however, they chose to sit next to each on the sofa. Mallory forced herself to smile sweetly at them from her chair.

Edward gave her a curious glance, before turning towards Elowen. Elowen smiled happily at him.

'I'm so glad that we arrived in time to avoid the storm.' She turned to smile at Ambrose and Mallory. 'I don't like thunder, but I'm sure it will be easier to bear with Edward by my side.'

A muscle twitched in Ambrose's jaw.

'Has Finch spoken to you?' he asked, his eyes narrowing as he watched them sitting side by side. 'Lord and Lady Arlington are due here shortly, would you mind waiting in my study when they arrive, Finch will bring you refreshment. I'm sure it won't take long.'

The first sheet of lightning lit the room just as the doorbell jangled.

'I'll show Elowen the way,' Edward insisted loftily, 'you can't keep your visitors waiting.' He offered Elowen his arm. She smiled happily at him. Ambrose gave them a tight smile, frowning, he watched them leave.

'I see what you mean, Lory.' He pursed his lips, before he could say more, however, Finch showed in Lord and Lady Arlington.

'This had better be the good news that you promised, Weston.' Lord Arlington demanded as he stood by the fireplace, an arm resting on the mantelpiece just as another sheet of lightning lit the sky. 'Otherwise I shall be extremely annoyed that you have commanded our presence in such haste and in such inclement weather.'

Mallory rose from her chair and offered it to Lady Arlington as it was the nearest chair to the fireplace. She moved towards the window and fiddled with a flower arrangement, moving it from a table to the centre of the windowsill.

'I thought you would like to know that we have recovered the necklace.'

'What?' spluttered Lord Arlington.

'You have? That's wonderful!' Lady Arlington clapped her hands together in joy.

'So where is it?' he demanded.

'All in good time. First there is the matter of the invoice to be settled.'

Mallory glanced out of the window into the street. Smiling, she turned around to face the Arlingtons.

'Would you like some tea?' she enquired as she walked across the room and gave the bellpull a firm tug.

'No thank you!' Her husband replied brusquely.

'I'm sorry, my husband is a touch impatient to see the necklace.' She smiled at them.

'About the invoice,' Ambrose continued smoothly as he heard the front door open and close.

'Yes, yes, let us see the necklace first,' Lord Arlington said testily. 'I'm not paying for a glass necklace; I want to make sure it's the real thing. You can then furnish me with the invoice, I will settle by post, I don't have my cheque book with me.'

'Of course!' Ambrose fished the velvet bag from his pocket and reverently withdrew the necklace. Sparkles of brilliant red flashed in the ray of sunlight as he dangled the necklace from his hand. Lady Arlington gasped in delight.

'That is indeed our necklace,' she said joyfully. 'May I hold it please?' She held out her hand.

'Alas no. As I explained, it was stolen, so the police need it as evidence.'

'We'll keep it safe for the police,' Lady Arlington assured him, 'until they need it for court.'
Ambrose shook his head. 'I'm afraid not, your Ladyship.'
'Now look here!' Lord Arlington blustered. 'We've promised to keep it safe; you have no right to refuse. I shall raise your impertinence with the Commissioner of Scotland Yard!'
'Please do, your Lordship.'

Finch entered carrying the tea tray. Taking advantage of the distraction Lord Arlington moved quickly, snatching the necklace from Ambrose's hand before returning to his place by the mantelpiece. Unperturbed, Finch set the tray upon a side table, picked up the table and placed it where Mallory stood by the fireplace. After pouring two cups of tea he nodded at Ambrose and left the room, leaving the door ajar.
'It doesn't belong to you,' Ambrose commented. 'The police will require it back.'
Lord Arlington shook his head. 'This necklace belongs to us, and we intend to keep it.' Lady Arlington moved to his side.
'Indeed,' she confirmed, grinning. 'It's travelling back with us, right now.'
'To France?' Mallory asked with a smile.
Lord Arlington frowned. 'What on earth are you talking about you stupid woman!'
'My sister isn't stupid,' Ambrose calmly replied. 'Lord and Lady Arlington live in Cannes, not in England.'
There was a stunned silence then Lord Arlington produced a gun aiming it at Ambrose.
'We are leaving with this necklace and there is nothing you can do about it.'
'I wouldn't be too sure about that,' the Inspector grinned as he entered the room along with two constables.
'Well, well, I might have known – Charlie Spinks and Betty Briggs, the jewel thieves,' he added, moving to the centre of the room with the constables.
'Oh gawd! We've been rumbled, Charlie.'
'Put the gun down, Charlie, you're outnumbered.'

'No, we're not – as long as I have this gun in my hand.' He swung the gun suddenly, pointing it at the Inspector's head. 'Now Inspector, you and your men are going to do exactly as you are told.'

Out of the corner of his eye, Ambrose saw Mallory stealthily reaching for a cup of tea. He leaned forward ready. With all the attention on the Inspector, she flung the cup at Charlie. Hot tea suddenly hit him in the face. He yelled as the hot amber liquid touched his skin. Ambrose leapt out of his seat and grabbed the gun. The Inspector and constables rushed to help.

'You bitch!' yelled Betty, her face contorting with fury. She launched herself at Mallory, a small dagger in her hand. Edward, entering the room, grabbed Mallory in the nick of time.

'That's Kitty Bunbury, my maid!' Elowen confirmed, as the Inspector grabbed hold of Betty and forcefully removed the dagger. Betty subjected him to a stream of verbal abuse as another thunderclap rendered the air.

'Are you hurt, Mallory?' Edward gazed at her anxiously as he held her gently by the shoulders.

'No, Edward, I'm fine.' She twisted herself from his grip, and picked up the cup, staring at the stain on the hearth rug.

'Oh, that's going to take some scrubbing.'

Once the couple had been handcuffed and taken away by the constables, the Inspector turned towards Ambrose.

'We've been wanting for some time to get hold of this pair. Betty's speciality is working as a maid in wealthy houses to gain information on jewels which Charlie then steals. She started life as an actress,' he added, 'before turning to crime.'

'I think you'll find, Inspector, that Betty is also Mrs Thornton's maid – the elusive Ellen Ward. Mrs Thornton will be able to confirm that for you.'

The Inspector shook his head. 'No. There is reason to believe she is working with them. Bob Miller identified her when he collected the barrel.'

'We did wonder about Mrs Thornton, Lory.'

'I know, but I can't believe ... wait a minute ... how did he describe her?'

The Inspector sighed. 'Grey-haired old lady, bending over a walking stick.'

Mallory laughed. 'Mrs Thornton is quite sprightly, she certainly doesn't need a stick. You said Betty Briggs used to be an actress, didn't you?'

The Inspector groaned. 'I should have guessed!' He frowned before adding, 'that would explain all those Norwood burglaries. It links them to the landlord at The Rising Sun, he was their fence.'

'It also explains how the ruby necklace ended up there,' Ambrose explained, 'and why John was killed. The landlord's cut for the fencing of the necklace must have been worth a small fortune to him.'

'He got his bully boys, John's friends, to get it back for him, at any cost.' Edward replied quietly.

Ambrose nodded. 'Indeed. It was John's misfortune to win a prize in the raffle which was almost certainly fixed to offload their criminal activities under the cover of a beer barrel.'

'That purchase of a raffle ticket cost him his life, all he wanted was a barrel of beer for his wedding.' Mallory sighed. 'It's so sad.'

The Inspector nodded. 'Well, thanks to you two we have rounded up a counterfeit gang and nabbed two prolific jewel thieves. No doubt we will get a few names from them and rid the criminal underworld of a few more thugs. I'm much obliged to you.' He doffed his hat and made his way downstairs.

'I think you are going to have to tell me the whole story from the beginning over dinner, Edward.' Elowen took his arm, 'as you seem to be involved in solving the case, you should be the one to tell me.' She gave him a quick grin with a sidelong glance at Ambrose. So that's their game, thought Mallory, noticing her brother's stony face.

'Ambrose, I think you and I should check with Finch about dinner, I think it calls for something celebratory to drink.' She took his arm and motioned with her head towards the door.

'What is it?' he hissed as they made their way towards the basement. 'Why are we leaving them alone together?' He clenched his jaw.

'Because brother dear, they are playing a silly game. Elowen and Edward are trying to make you jealous, in the hope they will force your hand. She is hoping you will be mad with jealousy, declare your love and offer her marriage. Waiting is not her style.'

'I presume Edward is playing the same game, forcing you to admit you love him.'

'What?'

'Oh come on, Lory, be brave enough to admit it. You are too young to remain a widow.'

She ignored him and changed the subject. 'So how are you going to play them at their own game?

'I'll think about it as I choose the wine.'

Chapter 41

Ambrose was in a jovial mood over dinner, and a genial host.

He raised his glass. 'Here's to a successful closure of cases!'

'Here, here!' Mallory clinked glasses with everyone and dinner was served. It was while they ate their dessert of lemon tart that the conversation turned to the case.

'So, Edward, do tell us how you solved the case.' Mallory smirked.

'Elowen's dying to hear it from your own lips.' She took a sip of her wine, an amused smile hovering on her lips when she saw Edward's startled expression.

He stared at her, considering his next move; it was like playing a game of chess with her, except she seemed to have the advantage. One wrong move could result in defeat, he wasn't going to accept defeat without a fight. Giving her his best piercing stare, perfected in courtrooms, he took his time in examining his options.

He opted for a tactical manoeuvre, in the hope of forcing an error. 'I'm quite sure you are capable of telling the story.'

The error came.

'Oh, I'm sure it would be much more fun if you told it. Elowen would enjoy it far better.' Her eyes glinted with mischief.

'How very perceptive of you.' He smiled sardonically. 'Perhaps it *would* be better if I told it, less fantasy, more logic.' He raised his glass to her and took a sip, acknowledging his advantage. Victory was in his grasp, and it tasted sweet.

'Perhaps Mallory, we should retire to the drawing room and let Elowen and Edward have some privacy.' Ambrose gave an amused smile.

'What an excellent idea, Rosy, let's do that.' She picked up her wine glass ready to leave the table.

Any idea of snatching an early victory was gone. The best he could hope for would be a stalemate, a draw.

'Let Finch know when you are ready for coffee, and we'll return.' Ambrose grinned.

Elowen and Edward looked at each other in horror, their plan in tatters.

'No, no, I'm sure Ambrose will do an equally good job,' Elowen said quickly.

'Oh no, we wouldn't want to spoil Edward's moment of glory. He deserves it.' Mallory smiled sweetly at him. Checkmate.

Edward looked at her lovely face, her blue eyes brimming with laughter and accepted his defeat graciously.

'The glory is yours, Mallory. Why don't you both tell the story, I'm sure I've missed some of the finer details.' He raised a glass to her.

******

'So, it was the serpent shaped ring that set the alarm bells ringing,' Elowen said as she sipped her coffee, sitting on the sofa with Ambrose next to her.

'Yes, I saw an article in a newspaper about a burglary and one of the stolen items was the serpent ring. Unfortunately, I couldn't recall the exact item that alarmed me, my bout of concussion affected my memory. That's where Edward came to the rescue and did some digging.'

'All I did was to provide some information. I came across an address for the Arlingtons in France. I had no idea how old the information was, so the French address could easily be explained away as a previous home.'

'It was the date of the paper that gave it away.' Mallory confirmed. 'The burglary happened before I saw him with the serpent ring. There were other little pointers too, such as Lord Arlington getting a relative's name wrong. The biggest clue though, came from you.'

'Me? What did I say?' Elowen looked amazed.

'You said your maid was an ex-actress and she left just after the robbery.' Mallory took a sip of her coffee before continuing.

'She left because if she had stayed the police would almost certainly want to question her further, especially as they thought it was an inside job. There was a high risk that they might have recognised her as Betty Briggs.'

'It would have been too risky for her and Charlie to stay in the same area, so they had to move. Betty had already established herself at Pinnerton Lodge, so they decamped there.' Ambrose added. 'Norwood was far enough away but close enough to send the spoils to The Rising Sun.'

'The rest we know.' Edward confirmed.

'Well done to you, Lory, for working it all out.'

'It was down to Pinnerton Lodge. I felt, rather than knew, that it had a secret. Once I discovered its secret it led to solving the cases.'

She raised her coffee cup. 'Here's to Mrs Thornton and her house of secrets.'

They all remained silent while they finished their coffee. It was Elowen who broke the silence with her question.

'What will happen to Mary now?'

'Ah well. I do happen to know something about her possible future.' Two pairs of eyes turned towards her; Ambrose of course knew.

'Mrs Thornton no longer has a maid, so I'm hoping to visit Mary and persuade her to become the housekeeper. She will be able to hire staff to help her. It will give her the new start she needs, away from all the memories her current home and job hold, and I would imagine Mrs Thornton is a delight to work for.'

'Now all you need is a place of your own.' Ambrose reflected. 'Could you pull the bell for Finch please, Mallory.'

Finch came in, followed by Billy.

'Finch, could you give Mallory the good news?'

'Certainly sir.' He turned towards her.

'Do you remember I said I thought there might be a suitable house available in the near future?'

She nodded. 'Yes, and I said it would be better to wait until the cases were resolved before visiting any premises.'

'Indeed, madam. The house in question is 7 Century Square.'

Mallory opened her mouth in surprise. 'The house next door?'

Ambrose laughed. 'Yes, Lory, the one next door. Finch believes we can put in an adjoining door in the basement without too much trouble.'

'Oh! But what about servants? We can't expect our current ones to run two houses at once.'

'I thought Billy here might make you a good butler, once I've trained him properly.' Finch smiled and turned towards him.

Billy smiled shyly. 'I would be honoured, ma'am to be your butler – if you'll have me.'

'And as for an extra servant to help Gertrude,' Ambrose added, 'I believe Elowen's maid might need to seek another position.'

Mallory looked confused.

'I don't think 5 Century Square will be to her liking.'

The End

Printed in Great Britain
by Amazon